Impelled

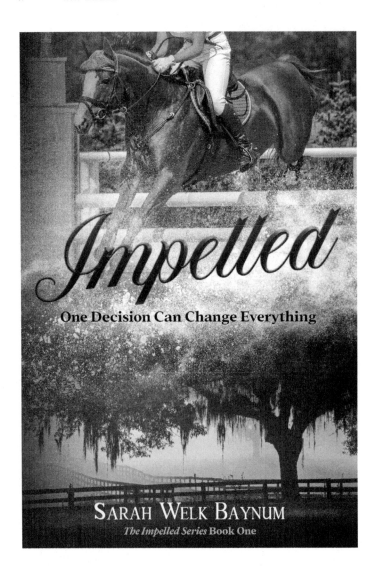

Impelled

One Decision Can Change Everything

SARAH WELK BAYNUM

The Impelled Series Book One

Impelled

A Novel by Sarah Welk Baynum

Copyright © 2022 by Sarah Welk Baynum

Editor: Laurie Berglie

Cover Designer: GermanCreative on Fiverr

ISBN: 979-8-9863339-0-8

Website:

https://sarahwelkbaynumauthor.com/

Contents

To my first horse and my heart horse:

Lexington – you taught me more about myself and life than I realized in my younger years. You put up with my silly teenage antics, let me jump bareback without letting me fall, and showed me what true love is all about.

Valentine – you were my heart horse and the inspiration for the horse in this book. You loved to jump, and you gave me wings. The connection we shared was so special, and I will always love you and cherish every course we conquered together.

To my husband: Thank you for believing in me on my author journey, and especially while writing my debut novel. I love you, and I couldn't do this without your support.

To my sister: You are my person, my best friend, and your love for horses has always mirrored mine. I could not have done this without you! This book is in part dedicated to you and the horses we have loved throughout the years.

To my parents: Thank you for putting up with the horse crazy kid I was and helping me in any way you could. Every lesson and trip to the barn you drove me to, every penny you gave me that you could barely spare, led me to where I am and who I am today. Thank you for everything you gave me and for supporting my dreams.

To my long term-friends: Many of you inspired characters in this book. Your friendship made writing about these characters so easy, and I am so thankful for the friendships we have built over the years. Maleisha, Kerry and Kendall – We practically grew up together and I wouldn't be the person I am today without you. Thank you for all your love, support and encouragement during the process of writing this book!

Sarah– thank you for putting up with me for hours (trapped in a car) while I looked through a billion pictures for this book's cover. I am so thankful for all the years of memories we have together. Mandy how could I not put you in my book? You are my best friend and we learned how to be real adults in the world together. Thank you all for your love and support over a decade later!

To my "horse friends": The bond we share over horses is one that cannot be replicated in any other friendship. You will always be the ones who truly understood the endless days, evenings and weekends spent at the barn or at horse shows. We devoured horse books, played horse in our backyards or on our bikes, rode our own horses together and talked for hours about the one thing we couldn't get enough of. As adults, you are the ones that "get" why we spend so much of our previous time and money on these incredible animals. Thank you for all the years of horse girl friendship I have shared with you.

—elle

Chapter One

Emma Walker stared at a chestnut mare huddled in the furthest corner of a large auction pen.

Despite the mud and filth she was covered in, Emma could make out a wide blaze that ran from under the mare's forelock and white markings on all four legs. The auction pen was cramped, and the other horses shifted nervously around the mare. She never moved and only glanced Emma's way once, but if looks could melt a soul, hers would have been a puddle on the ground.

"She looks too sweet to be here," Maggie, Emma's riding instructor and friend of ten years said in a hushed tone, as if reading Emma's mind. The air was hot, humid, and the cracks in the roof above the pen were shining beams of light around the dusty old pole barn.

This was far from their first trip to this auction; Maggie had a soft spot for rescuing horses from this place. If it didn't come from an auction, it came off the track. Joining Maggie on this venture was something Emma did at least several times a year. After Maggie spent some time getting the rescues healthy and well-schooled in the show jumping or eventing disciples, she sold them to good people and started the process all over again.

The sound of the announcer broke Emma's train of thought as his voice echoed from the speaker above; the auction was about to begin. Maggie and Emma had spent almost an hour scouring different round pens for her next project horse, but this was the first horse today that truly caught their eye.

When the mare was led into the sales ring, Emma resisted the emotions that flooded her when she came into view. The horse hung her head low, and she ignored the rumblings of the crowd when asked to halt in the center of the ring. The announcer informed the crowd that there was very little history on her, only that she was probably around ten years old and broke to ride. This was not uncommon; most of the horses Maggie had purchased from this auction in the past came with little to no history.

Out of the corner of her eye, Emma saw Maggie's white sign fly up as she placed the first bid. Two others across the room lifted their signs up as well. The auctioneer called out fifty dollars, then another one hundred dollars, then two hundred dollars as the bidders continued to challenge each other. The man across the room shook his head and put his sign down after the price reached two hundred. Emma remained nervous for the little chestnut's future, as the other bidder made it clear he was not ready to back down. Maggie had lost to other bidders in the past when the price was pushed too high and simply moved on to her second-choice horse.

This, however, was the first time that Emma felt such a strong pull towards one of these auction horses; she wanted the mare to go home with Maggie. Feeling the tension in the room between bidders, Emma heard the auctioneer call out two hundred and fifty dollars. Maggie's white sign flew up once more, this time without being met with a challenging bid.

The auctioneer yelled, "Sold for two hundred and fifty dollars," and Emma thought her heart may have skipped a beat knowing they had won.

Maggie led the skinny, dirty horse from the pen towards the trailers, and the mare all but loaded herself. Emma watched the horse stare out the window of the trailer, her eyes looking softer now; she seemed happy to be away from the overly crowded pen she came from.

The tires on Maggie's truck crunched along when they pulled into the driveway of her farm, and the horses that had been grazing lazily on lush summer grass in the pasture near the drive flung their heads up and called out to the new arrival. Maggie looked over at Emma with an all-knowing smirk.

"You know it's your turn for the first ride this time, right?" Maggie said.

The riders at her barn who helped with Maggie's project horses would take turns with the 'first ride' whenever a new auction horse or off the track Thoroughbred was ready to be ridden for the first time. This usually went one of two ways: surprisingly well, or with someone almost or actually falling off. It was somewhat of an event at Maggie's, and Emma found herself laughing, crying, or crying with laughter at her friends or herself during these infamous first rides.

A memory of Emma's most epic 'first ride' flooded her mind as the truck continued to bounce down the long drive. It was years back on a young sorrel Quarter Horse gelding who had come from the same auction they had just attended.

"Now, just walk him around for a while, get a feel for him and let him check out everything in the ring before you trot him," Maggie had warned. Emma walked in a figure 8 pattern around the arena, enjoying a perfect summer day on the back of Maggie's newly acquired horse that she had affectionately named Beau.

Back then, Maggie had not yet purchased the farm they were currently at, and the arena of this smaller farm directly bordered the backyards of some neighborhood homes. Aside from children's screams as they played outside, it usually didn't bother Emma or the other riders that they were in such close proximity to the neighboring yards while riding.

Until that fateful day, of course.

"Ok, Em, gently ask him for the trot."

Emma responded to Maggie's instruction by gingerly asking the gelding into an upward transition, and he moved forward into an energetic trot.

"That's fine Emma, just post slower, find a nice rhythm," Maggie called out.

Emma trotted around the far-right side of the ring and rounded the corner, making her way along the fence line bordering the neighboring yards. The next few moments Emma only remembers parts of; the sound of sprinklers popping up out of the ground and the blasting of high-pressured water into the fence railing and Beau's haunches.

The moment the sprinkler water blasted onto the surprised horse's back end, he bolted down the long side of the arena and headed straight towards the metal gate at the end of the ring. In what felt like the blink of an eye, Beau stopped dead in his tracks when he reached the end of the arena and spun to the left, consequently, flinging Emma into the metal gate.

She remembered hitting the gate full force, bouncing off of it, and onto the hard, unforgiving ground. Beau cantered away from her seemingly lifeless body, nostrils flaring and eyes wide, almost as surprised as Emma at the sprinkler-induced dismount.

Emma chuckled to herself at the memory, now much funnier years later than it was the day that she was left sitting in the dust. Snapping back to the present as the truck jolted to a stop, she knew Maggie well enough to know that the first ride on this new mare would not be anytime soon. It would weeks, maybe a month, before the mare would be ready. This horse needed time to decompress, gain weight, and do some groundwork first.

The chestnut mare unloaded uneventfully, and Emma led her to the empty stall at the end of the barn aisle. Maggie tossed her hay, fed her grain, and the little mare gobbled up her dinner thankfully. Maggie's barn-mate and friend Hailey rounded the corner and watched the mare as she munched casually on her hay.

"So, what are we calling this one?" Hailey said, turning to Maggie. Maggie smiled, and Emma had a hunch Maggie had already been thinking of a name for this sweet horse since the moment they left the auction.

"Valentine," Maggie stated assuredly.

Emma slid under the stall guard and put one hand on the mare's warm, soft back. "Val for short; I like it," she whispered softly so as not to disturb Valentine's happy hay crunching.

"There is just something special about you, isn't there?" Emma said to the mare.

She stood there, contemplating why this horse had already seemed to steal her heart faster than any other horse Maggie had brought home. Maybe it was her sad expression or the way she looked in the corner of that auction pen.

Either way, her pull to the little chestnut was irrevocable.

Chapter Two

For Emma, the days passed slowly, but pass they did.

Emma rested her head on the top rail and hung her arms lazily over the fence line at Maggie's barn as she watched the group of mares in this large green pasture gallop wildly around. Valentine was among the horses in the pasture, and she was shaking her head as she galloped full speed towards the gate at the far side. It was a beautiful day in Ohio, perfect riding weather in Emma's opinion.

It had been a little over one month since Valentine was rescued from the auction, and she was already looking healthier and enjoying the life of a horse who was loved and properly cared for. Emma was always amazed what time in their new home and good food could do for a horse who had come from less-than-ideal situations. Maggie and Hailey walked up behind Emma, halters and lead ropes in hand, interrupting her train of thought. Hailey giggled as she watched Emma staring longingly out at Valentine galloping around the pasture.

"I see someone is excited about first ride day!" Hailey exclaimed.

Emma tried to hide the smile that broke over her face; she was excited, of course she was. Everything about her relationship with Valentine had been special thus far, and she imagined her first ride on the mare would be no different. Her excitement was quickly washed away by a wave of guilt. A few years back, she lost her first horse, Lexington. Since then, she had not been ready to entertain the idea of owning another horse. The heartbreak of losing her first horse was something that still haunted her, even now.

Emma unlatched the gate and walked over to where Valentine had finally stopped to eat grass. The horse lifted her head and gave a low, friendly nicker to the young woman as she approached her. Leaning into the horse's warm body, she scratched her neck before slipping the halter and lead rope around her head, leading her out of the pasture. The smell of horse and warm air filled her nose and she breathed deeply, taking in the moment and her favorite smell as she walked the horse towards the barn.

Emma's heart raced slightly as she put her saddle on Valentine's back. The mare stood quietly with one leg cocked, still savoring the treat Emma had offered a few moments ago. Calming her mind and racing heart as she stepped up to the mounting block, she swung her leg over the mare for the first time. Maggie and Hailey were in the center of the large outdoor arena, leaning against a jump standard as they watched Emma take several laps around the arena at the walk.

"She looks pretty relaxed Emma, go ahead and trot," Maggie called from the other side of the ring.

Emma asked the mare forward into the trot, and Val happily began trotting off in a nice rhythm. As the ride progressed, Emma couldn't help but notice how smooth all four of Valentine's gaits were, especially her canter.

"It's like riding a lazy boy," she shouted to the other girls across the ring, laughing.

"Why don't you try seeing how she does over a small fence? Take her over that little jump on the diagonal," Maggie said as she pointed to the cross rail.

Emma pointed the mare toward the small jump, encouraging her with her leg as she posted confidently along. Valentine marched towards the cross rail and jumped it with enthusiasm, shaking her head as she landed.

"Well, she seems to like that! If I had to guess, she probably has jumped before since she seems comfortable enough over it. That, or she's just a straight up natural," Maggie said with a chuckle. Beaming as she slowed the horse to a walk, Emma patted the mare on her neck. She had tried to fight it, but there was no denying that the thought of buying Valentine from Maggie had crossed her mind more than once during this ride.

Her mind was buzzing with the thought that maybe this horse could be the one, the horse that would help heal the heartbreak of losing her first horse.

"Emma, you have another table that's ready to order in section five!"

Shoveling three more bites of food into her mouth before tying her apron back around her slim waist, Emma headed out of the break room and towards the voice of her co-worker, Mandy.

"Coming!" She yelled back, power walking through the kitchen. Emma was in the middle of a typical double shift at the local Italian restaurant where she worked, which meant she ate whenever she had a free moment. Emma and Mandy were not only co-workers, but also roommates and best friends. Some days, she was pretty sure Mandy was the only thing that made this job bearable.

After quickly getting her table's order and entering it into the computer, Emma pushed the door to the kitchen open and beelined back towards the break room.

"When I graduate and no longer have to work in a restaurant ever again..." Emma mumbled, cutting herself off by taking another bite of her now cold food, although, she was too hungry to notice.

"I know, me too. I take it you're still not happy with me for taking that big girl job?" Mandy said, frowning.

"You know I'm happy for you; I just can't imagine working here without you, Mandy. You will be so much happier at that marketing firm though; I know you will," Emma said, trying to convince Mandy as much as herself that this was part of growing up and becoming a real adult.

"So, I guess you're not mad enough to not attend my birthday get together?" She said, playfully elbowing Emma in the side as she gulped down her last bite of food.

"Never! It's not every day you turn twenty-three now, is it?" Emma chimed back.

The girls finished what seemed like an endless shift at the restaurant and headed back to their apartment a few miles away to prepare for Mandy's party that evening.

Emma showered and looked through her closet, unsure of what to wear. Her mind wandered as she stared at her clothes; so many things seemed to be changing in her life right now. Mandy would be starting her new job soon, which involved a lot of travel.

That meant she would be missing her friend not only at work but at home too. Emma did not have a boyfriend either, and honestly, had no interest in one; she was not ready to even think about dating again. Her last relationship had ended not so long ago, and it hadn't ended well. The only bright spot in her life was the time she spent at Maggie's barn, and specifically, with a certain chestnut mare.

Emma smoothed the wrinkles out of a mid-length, timeless looking black dress and pinned one side of her wavy dark brown hair back behind her ear. The image of her slim hourglass figure, light olive colored skin and hazel green-brown eyes were mirrored back to her as she reviewed her overall appearance once more in the bathroom mirror.

"I suppose it's not so bad getting dressed up once and awhile," she thought. Although, she still preferred a pair of jeans and a t-shirt most days.

Ten minutes later, Emma walked through the doors of the pub down the road. Most of her and Mandy's friends were already there when she arrived.

"Emma! Over here!" Ashlynn, a mutual friend of Emma and Mandy's, yelled over the loud music that thumped in a speaker nearby. Sliding onto the bar stool beside Ashlynn, Emma spotted Mandy talking to a tall and well-built guy across the room.

"Who is *that?*" Emma asked Ashlynn.

"Not sure, but it looks like that flashy birthday sash you bought Mandy is paying off," Ashlynn said, winking.

Mandy laughed at something that she apparently thought this gentleman said was funny. It was not all that surprising to her though.

"Paul Bunyan is her type," Emma thought, chuckling a little out loud.

Leaning over the smooth wood bar, she prepared to make eye contact with the next bartender who looked her way because suddenly, she really needed a margarita. Two drinks later, Emma was feeling a little less sorry for herself and a little more ready to celebrate Mandy's birthday.

Mandy and several of their friends were now sitting side by side at the bar, while Mandy's short lived love interest had wandered back to his friends, apparently too interested in whatever sports game was on to continue talking to her. Emma consciously tried to be engaged in the conversation with her friends. It wasn't that she didn't love her friends or that she didn't enjoy their company, because she did, but her mind was elsewhere tonight. Glancing back toward Mandy's momentary love interest, Emma let her mind wander to her own previously failed relationship.

She continued to stare, as her thoughts floated back to the day her ex said goodbye...

"Emma, can we talk a minute?" Jordan had said, without letting emotion creep into his words. The sound of loud, live country music filled the thick, humid summer air, and despite being in nothing but a tank top and jean shorts, Emma remembered being hot. She had already kicked her shoes off to cool down, with little relief. Country music festivals were the highlight of Emma's summer every year, and this one was no exception.

Her eyebrows raised slightly in surprise, and she replied casually with, "Sure."

They walked uncomfortably behind the long row of food trucks lining the outskirts of the festival, the grass soft and spongy under her bare feet. Each step she took, she felt the weight of unexpected and impending dread; she did not like how cold his words were or how far away from their group of friends they were with each footfall.

Suddenly he turned, as if he couldn't take not speaking the words any longer. "Emma, we can't be together anymore."

Emma stood frozen in her tracks, stunned.

"What...? Why?" She stammered.

"You're great Em, you're sweet and caring but I... I want a life like my parents. I want the big house and to be able to travel and..."

"...You want someone who's going to make a lot more money than you think I will," she said, cutting him off. He paused, unsure how to respond.

"I don't know, I guess so. I've just been thinking about it lately, and I can't get past it."

"Well, how do you even know how much I will make, Jordan?! I'm twenty-two you know; I'm not planning to be a waitress forever. In less than two semesters I will be graduating college for Pete's sake!"

"Em, you're an Equine Business major and you don't even have a plan for what you want to do with that when you graduate...do you?"

Emma bit her lip hard, hoping the pain of biting her lip would distract her from the tightness in her chest as she willed the tears to stay in her eyes. She didn't have a plan, and she knew going into her major that she wasn't doing it because it made loads of money. She loved working with horses, and the rest she would figure out later. He wasn't wrong, and she knew it.

Without thinking she spun around and walked quickly towards a quiet tree lined area that appeared to be free of people who would judge her. She couldn't hold back the tears any longer as she sank to her knees while a slow country song filled the air around her, as if on cue.

Emma shook her head, bringing herself back to the present. She excused herself and stepped outside. Staring up the clear, star-filled sky, Emma let the tears fall before quickly brushing them away, mad at herself for letting a memory spoil a perfectly good night out with friends.

"Em?"

She heard Mandy's tentative voice behind her.

"I'm so sorry, Mandy, I swear I'm not trying to ruin your birthday."

Mandy followed Emma's eyes up to the star lit sky and sighed, wrapping an arm around Emma's shoulders.

"This is about Jordan again, isn't it?"

Emma nodded, afraid speaking would cause another wave of emotions to trigger more tears she didn't want to cry. She didn't want to still feel this way; after all, it had been more than six months since the breakup. She couldn't explain why this break up still haunted her, but it did.

"Your adult life is just beginning, you know? You can do anything you want! You just have to figure out what that is and chase down your dreams."

"Like you did. I hope you know how proud I am of you, even though I'm terrified to face life without you."

"I know, Emma; I am too."

The bond between these two young ladies ran years and many memories deep.

They didn't need to say anything else to one another; they simply stood there, side by side staring at the stars, thinking about what their respective futures might hold.

Chapter Three

The sun was shining, instantly lightening her mood as Emma rounded the corner of Maggie's barn.

Opening the large barn door, she was hit with the smell of fresh hay, sawdust, and horses; a few of her favorite scents. It was almost impossible for Emma to feel anything but happy when she was here.

"Emma, just in time!" Hailey exclaimed, peeping out of the stall she was cleaning to greet Emma as she came in the door. "I'm almost done cleaning this stall, and then Maggie is ready to load the horses on the trailer. Are you excited about taking Valentine out for her first trail ride?!"

Emma felt her body physically relax as she walked through the aisles of the barn, peering into each stall to catch a glimpse of horses as they napped or chewed lazily at their hay on the ground.

"Hailey, you have no idea," she said, feeling the weight of the world beginning to lift from her mind and body the deeper into the barn she walked. Further down the aisleway, she spotted Valentine. The mare was hanging her head out of the stall door, leaning gently on her stall guard, and was staring right at Emma as she approached.

"Hey Val," she cooed, wrapping her arms around the horse's neck and burying her face into her mane. "Are you ready to hit the trails?"

"I am!" Hailey said answering for the horse as she all but skipped down the aisle, her small bay Thoroughbred mare walking quickly behind her, trying to keep up.

"Alright ladies, let's load these horses up!" Maggie's voice drifted down the long barn aisle, coming from somewhere near the tack room.

A few minutes later, Valentine, Hailey's horse, Charlie, and one of Maggie's favorite horses, Jet, were loaded into her spacious three horse gooseneck trailer. After sliding into the passenger side of the truck, Emma rolled her window down, taking in the beautiful day as she enjoyed this weather while it lasted. It was always at the end of summer she felt she needed to soak in every ray of sunshine before the frigid mid-western winter took away all green and warmth from her world.

She rested her head against the side of the truck's interior, letting the wind whip her hair around as they gained speed. After fifteen-minutes of driving, the girls were unloading the horses from the trailer and tacking up with saddles and bridles. Emma attempted to sooth the excited Valentine, who was jigging next to the trailer while she waited for her rider to finish putting on her helmet and gloves. Emma spent a few moments calming the excited mare the best she could before swinging her leg into the saddle and heading down the path towards a wooded trail behind Hailey and Maggie.

Tall pines and thick oak trees surrounded them and shaded the wide trail path as they plodded along at the walk. The horses' hooves padded softly on the dry, pine needle filled terrain. Emma breathed deeply; there was nowhere else she would rather be. Trail rides always held a certain kind of magical power for her, as if the rest of the world didn't exist while she was out in the middle of nowhere. They approached a large open field after a long stretch of cool, wooded pathways.

"Can we go a little faster?" Hailey asked with a whine.

"Em, how is Val doing, is she relaxed now?" Maggie said turning around in her saddle trying to catch a glimpse at the rider behind her.

Emma smiled down at the mare, whose ears were pricked forward attentively.

"She seems to be having a great time. I think she would be up for some cantering!"

Needing no further encouragement, Hailey made a kissing sound to her horse who cantered off into the open field. The other two horses followed suit without hesitation. Emma sat up in her saddle, getting into a soft two-point position and allowing the horse to stretch out underneath of her. Valentine's muscles powered her forward, gaining speed with each stride.

All Emma could hear was the sound of pounding hooves and wind whipping across her ears as they ate up the ground towards the end of the clearing. Closing her eyes for a moment, she felt the stress and pressures of her young adult life fly away as the steady hoofbeats continued underneath of her. She was flying, and Valentine had given her wings. The horses broke into a trot, then down to a walk a few minutes later at the edge of where the open field met the woods. Breathing heavily, the horses and their riders casually walked back to the trail head leading into the forest.

Emma's mind was clear now, much clearer than it had been in weeks, actually. Or perhaps even longer than that.

"Maggie, I want to buy Valentine."

Maggie stopped Jet in his tracks and spun him around, with an all-knowing smile.

"Well Emma, it's about time," she said laughing. Hailey's laugh joined hers, resounding through the otherwise quiet forest.

"We all saw that coming, Em," Hailey chimed in.

The rest of the trail ride was spent at a much slower pace, as the girls' excited chatter continued. Emma didn't even try to wipe the smile from her face as she dreamed about what Valentine could become; with a horse this special, she suspected a bright future in the jumper ring and even eventing was not out of the question.

Closing her eyes, she thought of her first horse; she would always love him and cherish every minute they had spent together, but it was time to allow herself to move on and love another horse again.

Back at Maggie's barn after the short trailer ride home, the girls unloaded their horses and began hosing them off to cool them down. Emma and Maggie come up with a plan to allow Emma to pay Valentine off in monthly installments, since she was still in college full time and could only work so many shifts at the restaurant. Emma relished in the feeling that things were finally looking up for her. Emily and Hailey slumped exhausted against the barn's old, worn, dark stained wood walls, chugging what was left of their water bottles.

"What are your plans tonight?" Hailey inquired.

"I'm having this get together at my apartment with my room-mates and a bunch of our college friends are coming over. You should come!"

Emma took another long drink of water, hoping to buy herself enough time to think about if she was interested in having any kind of social interaction this evening. It had been a while since her breakdown at Mandy's party and since then, she had used every excuse in the book not to go back out into the real world. The longer she avoided going out, the harder it became to do so. Her life the past few weeks consisted of college, work, and riding, of course, because the barn was still her happy place.

While she knew she was well overdue to spend time with her friends, she had not expected to be confronted with it here.

Hailey was great, and one of her roommates, Lily, also rode and had a horse named Annie at Maggie's Barn. So maybe stopping by a small friendly get together wouldn't be so bad after all? However, if she was honest with herself, she would still much rather spend time with horses than people. Emma lowered the water bottle from her mouth and sighed slightly, regretting the words almost as soon as they left her mouth.

"Sure Hails, what time does it start? I'll be there."

"Oh, this will be so much fun, Em! The party starts at 7:30 pm sharp," she exclaimed in her typical sweet, bubbly manner.

"Well then, I guess I had better go home and get ready because I'm pretty sure the rest of your friends won't appreciate me showing up covered in horsehair, sweat, and dirt," she added, trying to match Hailey's enthusiastic tone.

A few hours later, Emma was pulling into Hailey's apartment complex while giving herself a pep talk in the car.

"You are going to have a good time tonight," she told herself aloud. Hailey's apartment complex was all townhomes and set in an area surrounded by forest. Hailey and her roommates had been lucky enough to snag a great end unit spot on the edge of the courtyard and wooded area. Before Emma had reached the door, Hailey was opening it for her, smiling from ear to ear.

"Em, you made it! I almost wondered if you were going to cancel on me again," she teased lightly.

Emma forced the most genuine smile she could, reminding herself of her in-car pep talk.

"Wouldn't miss it Hailey, thanks for inviting me!" She added, with perhaps a little too much enthusiasm. Hailey did not seem to notice though, and ushered Emma in.

"We've got beer in the fridge and in the cooler out back, oh and there's pizza on the way. It's really nice out, so almost everyone is outside on the deck or in the courtyard!"

"Thanks Hailey. Is Lily outside too? I heard she just took an internship in Florida for the winter, and I wanted to congratulate her," she added.

"Yeah, I think she's just outside on the deck. I'm sure she would love to tell you all about it," Hailey replied. Emma thanked Hailey one more time and headed through the sliding glass door to the string-light lit deck.

Unfortunately for Emma's anti-social mood lately, the 'roommates plus a couple college friends' description Hailey had given her was inaccurate. There had to be at least twenty-five people lingering around the decking area alone. She weaved through the small clusters of chatting people in search of Lily, hoping a nice horse-centered conversation would help her get her social groove back. The sky was clouded, blocking the light from the moon, which made it darker than she anticipated as she moved further away from the well-lit deck.

Emma breathed in the cool late summer night air, enjoying this evening walk through the courtyard as she continued searching for her friend. She finally found Lily by the fire pit with one of her roommates and a couple other people she didn't recognize.

"Hey Lil!" She said, happy to have finally located her.

"Emma?" Lily said, sounding surprised. "I'm glad you made it! We weren't sure you were going to come." Emma's face flushed red, but she hoped it was dark enough for no one to notice.

"Ok, so, everyone thinks I'm as anti-social as I've been feeling. I should probably work on that," she thought.

"I hear congratulations are in order and that you are interning at a very well-known eventing farm down in Ocala this winter," Emma said trying to change the subject quickly. Lily's face lit up at the mention of her internship.

"Em, I can't tell you how excited I am," she gushed. Emma felt her body relax, excited to be talking about something she was interested in. She moved further into the circle around the fire pit, sliding into an unused chair.

"Tell me everything!"

"Ok, so you know how I am graduating college this semester? Well, I wanted to spend some time really being in the thick of one of the biggest winter horse show locations in the country. You know, get some real hands-on experience with top notch horse and rider athletes of that caliber, before going to veterinary school next year. What better way to do so than to work for Ben David, world class rider and trainer?" She babbled excitedly.

"I hear Ben's horses are always placing well at eventing trials and the show jumping competitions in Ocala," Emma added, genuinely enthusiastic. "So, what will your day to day look like working for him?"

"Since I was an Equine pre-vet major, I'll be handling a lot of the medical and health care of his horses. You know, wrapping the horses' legs after competitions, monitoring medication and supplements, prepping the horses' food, that kind of thing. But the best part is he's also allowing me to help exercise some of his horses before the shows," Lily said beaming. "Plus, I'm allowed to bring my horse down with me, and he can stay at Ben's barn."

"Lil, that's incredible," Emma said, genuinely happy for her friend, while simultaneously fighting the pang of jealousy that tried to creep into her mind. Lily was incredibly smart; she took extra courses over the summers so she could finish college early and maintained an all but perfect grade point average. She had also been smart enough to go the route of pre-vet, which was going to be much more lucrative than Emma's chosen major once Lily was done with Veterinary School. No doubt, her shining school records and genuinely sweet personality had won her this incredible opportunity working for the best of the best rider and trainer in Florida.

"I heard you have some good news of your own! Although, I can't say I'm surprised, you had a special connection with Valentine right from the beginning."

Lily and Emma spent the next thirty minutes talking about Valentine, how Lily's horse, Annie, was doing, and her future internship.

"I better go mingle; if Hailey catches me, she will be sure to remind me that it's rude for the host to stay in one place too long. Enjoy the party, Em!"

Lily headed back toward the twinkling deck lights. There were a couple people sitting across from her lost in their own conversations, leaving her alone with her thoughts once again.

"I've probably been here an acceptable amount of time," she thought, reasoning with herself as she began walking towards the darkness that lay between the fire and the deck. Halfway to the deck, her body thudded against someone else's in the dark as they collided.

"I am *so* sorry, I can hardly see a thing out here. I should have been paying better attention. Did I hurt you?"

Emma strained her eyes to see the person she had crashed into in the dim light. From what she could make out, he was tall with dark hair and had a very impressive jaw line. The kind Emma would have fallen for once, before she was burned by his type, of course.

"I think it would take a little more than a little lady like you to take me out," a charming male voice responded, flashing a smile at her. Emma paused awkwardly, unsure how to respond.

"Well, um, anyway, sorry about that," she stammered, as she began to walk away. She felt a hand gently catch her wrist before she had completely passed the stranger.

"You're not leaving now, are you?" his voice was smooth and confident.

"Actually, I was just on my way out. I have to work early tomorrow and I'm pretty tired from my ride this morning so..."

"...Ride?" He said, cutting her off.

"Yes, a couple friends went on trail ride with our horses for five miles or so; it was pretty tiring, believe it or not."

"So, you don't just sit there and let the horse do all the work then?" he teased. Emma felt her cheeks flush with discontent. He was probably innocently flirting, but for some reason it rubbed her wrong way.

"No, actually that's not how it works. You use every muscle in your body when you ride; you're essentially holding your own body weight up above a thousand-pound animal that constantly moves underneath of you. You know what, never mind," Emma pulled her hand free of his grasp and walked quickly towards the back door of the house.

"I was just teasing!" He called after her. Emma powered through the small clusters of chatting people and into the townhouse, bumping shoulders with at least one other person as she fled.

Hailey was pulling a fresh beer out of the fridge when she caught a glimpse of Emma's rage-filled expression.

"Emma? Are you alright?"

"Hey Hails, yeah I'm pretty beat actually. I think I'm going to head home," she said, trying to sound casual.

"Ok, but your face is all red and..."

"I'm fine Hailey, thanks for inviting me," her voice was not as casual that time.

"I'll see you at the barn later this week I guess," Hailey offered, sounding a little hurt. Emma forced a smile at Hailey and walked back to her car.

Slamming the car door behind her, she sat in silence for a minute trying to clear her head. She probably shouldn't have been so sensitive; she knew she had overreacted. But the last thing she needed was some cocky, good-looking guy ready to break her heart.

Chapter Four

Emma opened her eyes, awakened by a pounding migraine as she fumbled to find her phone and shut off the alarm ringing in her ears.

Perhaps that extra glass of wine she poured when she came home last night was not the best idea. Making no additional effort than what was necessary to be presentable for public, she showered quickly and let her hair air dry as she changed into her work clothes.

"We're going to be late!" Mandy called from downstairs. Emma popped a few ibuprofens into her mouth, thudded down the stairs, and hopped in Mandy's car. It was an incredibly slow Saturday morning at the restaurant. While Emma knew she needed the money to finish paying off Valentine and her other bills, she also had a killer hangover that created zero desire to work that day.

"Can you believe we've been in our apartment almost another year now? I was looking over that letter the landlord put on our door yesterday; you know we have to give notice or renew our lease in about two months or so, right?" Mandy said to Emma, who was laying her head on the cool break room table in hopes it would ease the pounding.

"I don't think I have the brain capacity to think about whether or not we should move right now," Emma groaned.

"Well, we should probably talk about it soon. Em, I know you're not going to want to hear this, but I won't really be home much when I start my new job. I love our apartment and living with you; you know I do, but honestly, I don't know that I want to pay this much for an apartment if I'm never home."

Emma's head shot up from the table as she said, "You want to move out?!"

Mandy backpedaled a little at Emma's reaction. "I mean we can talk about it, but maybe I should just live at my parents' house or in a hotel when I'm not traveling for work. They said I may be home a total of one week a month on average," Mandy said as she gave her friend an empathetic look.

Emma stared at Mandy, speechless. It wasn't that Emma was mad at her best friend; she wasn't. She was happy for her and for her new job. Mandy had always wanted to travel full time and now she had her chance.

Mandy added quickly, "Let's just talk about this later. We still have some time before we need to give notice to the landlord." Mandy was trying to make her feel better, but the fact of the matter was, she was moving on with her life – without her.

"Emma, you're sat again!" The hostess called through the break room doors, interrupting what was now a dead-end conversation anyway.

"It's ok Manders, we can talk later," Emma said trying to leave her friend feeling less guilty as she scooted her chair out and left the break room. Emma slapped a smile back on her face as she walked over to her table.

Business picked up a little, and the girls only had a chance to say a few words to each other in passing as they waited their tables. Normally, Emma hated when her and Mandy were too busy to chat during work, but she knew anything she had to say to her friend right now would only make her feel guiltier. Emma felt a buzzing in her apron pocket for the third time in a row and stepped into the bathroom to check her phone. Three missed call notifications from Maggie were on her screen.

"Hey, Maggie I'm at work, can I call you back..."

"It's Valentine; we need to call the veterinarian."

After de-briefing the restaurant manager and Mandy about the situation, Emma left work and sped down the highway towards the barn. As if the weather sensed she had somewhere to be, it began pouring rain. The veterinarian's decaled truck was already parked next to Maggie's barn when Emma pulled in. All but running down the barn aisle, she caught a glimpse of the little chestnut mare in the crossties. Her back left leg was cocked, and Valentine made it clear she was not comfortable enough to bear any weigh on it.

"How is she?!"

"You must be Emma? I'm Doctor Reece. Well, it looks like she had a bad abscess in that hoof. I was able to find and drain it," the vet said with a slight southern draw, noticing the distress in Emma's eyes.

"But don't worry, we will be giving her some pain medication and you will just need to keep the foot clean and wrapped for a while."

"How long do you think she will be lame?"

"Just depends on the horse; could be a week or it could be several weeks," he added.

"There goes our training schedule for awhile," she thought. Emma ran her hand up Valentine's forelock and affectionately scratched her ears behind her halter, and the horse leaned into her owner's hand. "Thank you, Dr Reece, I appreciate you coming out."

The vet nodded to Emma, taking her credit card as he walked back to his truck to run her payment.

"And there goes my extra money," her inner monologue added.

Spending the better part of an hour grooming her mare and spending some much-needed quality time with her softened the blow the sticker shock of the vet bill had left. Emma convinced herself that it could have been worse; it was just a temporary setback. Valentine would get better, and she would continue training. Eventually, she would reach her goals of taking her to her first show jumping competition.

Sighing audibly, she leaned gently into the horse's neck. The mare closed her eyes too, and they stood silently next to one another for several minutes.

ell

Leaves crunched under Emma's boots as she trekked across her college campus towards her first class of the day.

She had spent every day at the barn before or after class for over a week straight now. All the things she had been putting off while caring for her horse flooded her mind as she walked down the tree lined sidewalk past the dorms.

"Emma!"

Rachel, her best college friend flagged her down as she ran out of her dormitory's front door.

"Rachel!" She called back. Emma had been so busy lately that she hadn't walked to class with her favorite classmate in some time now. Most of the time, she was lucky if she slid into the classrooms on time.

"It's about time you walk me to class," she teased. "How is your sick horse?"

"She's doing so much better, finally able to walk around normally and without pain. Thank you for asking, Rach."

"You didn't forget about that test tomorrow in Economics, right? Because I could really use a study buddy later to make sure I know the material. You know how I loathe Econ!"

Emma had most certainly forgot. She felt the blood drain from her face in panic as her friend babbled on. Rachel turned to the unresponsive Emma, whose face was now pale as they continued walking in silence.

"So, you did forget."

Emma nodded sheepishly.

"It's ok, we have all night to study. We can turn it into a study party at the school library; it could be fun!"

Emma added trying not to fail Econ to the running list of things she needed to catch up on. It was all she could do to keep focused during her psychology class, which normally she enjoyed.

"This patient was diagnosed with dissociative identity disorder or 'D.I.D' which was discussed in last week's reading assignment. Can anyone tell me what symptoms this patient may be experiencing?" The professor scanned the crowed, noticing a distracted student looking out the window.

"Emma?"

Snapping out of her daydreams, she racked her brain for the definition from the chapter she had merely skim read.

"Umm... it's when you think you're more than one person?"

"Close. A person with D.I.D has multiple and distinct personalities that, yes, can sometimes manifest in some patients as believing they are different people at times."

Rachel raised her hand, shooting a wink at Emma who clearly had nothing else to add.

"Yes, Rachel?"

"Some symptoms of D.I.D are memory loss, delusions, identity confusion, and this mental disease is usually caused by trauma, more commonly, childhood trauma."

"Excellent answer! That is correct. Let's continue by discussing what some possible treatment options are for patients with more severe forms of D.I.D..."

Emma mouthed a, "thank you," to Rachel, who had always been much more studious than she was. After classes, the girls met up at the library for what Emma knew would be a very long evening of studying. She was thankful her friend had kept excellent notes and used them to study when she could in between classes so she would be at least mildly prepared for their study session.

"Ok Em, what does 'scarcity' mean?"

Emma chewed her lip as she pondered the answer.

"Consumers have limited financial resources and limitless demands?"

"Correct!"

Maybe she wouldn't fail Econ after all. Another hour passed by slowly, and eventually the girls called it a night and packed up their things. Emma stepped out into the dark evening, glad to be outside of that stuffy library. Walking along the path towards her car, she felt hopeful that she would, at least, pass tomorrow's test.

"Hey horse girl," a smooth familiar voice chided behind her. Emma spun around and faintly recognized the jaw line of the man she collided with at Hailey's party.

"Oh, it's *you*. You go here?"

"Best private college in the state, right? Go Cardinals!" He teased. Emma decided she should probably apologize for her melodrama that night.

"Hey, I'm sorry for how rude I was the night we met," she said meeting his gaze this time.

"It's ok, I'm guessing my teasing about your horse probably hit a nerve. So, riding horses is important to you, huh?" He said flashing her a goofy, charming grin. Emma reminded herself not to let his charm fool her.

"It's my favorite thing in the world."

"Well why don't you tell me about it while I walk you to your car or your dorm? I'm guessing that's where you're going right? It is almost 10:00 pm after all."

Emma was all too aware how late the study session had lasted. She paused a moment staring at his goofy grin, ready to tell him she was perfectly capable of walking herself to her car.

"Sure, I live off campus. My car is in the back lot," she replied. She had stared at him too long apparently, and the words managed to fall out of her mouth without her realizing it. Turning towards the direction of the parking lot, Emma set a rather quick walking pace. It would be rude to tell him never mind now, so if she was going to be escorted to her car, she may as well make it clear she was in a hurry to get there.

"Are you going to ask me my name or just let an anonymous stranger walk you to your car?" He said, gently elbowing her in the arm.

"Sorry, you're right. What is your name?"

"I'm Liam Anderson. And you are...?"

"Emma Walker."

"Emma. I like it."

"Well, it's my name you whether you like it or not," she added, teasing him back, but smiling his way this time.

Liam let out a deep laugh. "How long have you been riding horses?"

"Since I was twelve. I've been riding with the same trainer, Maggie, ever since."

"Do you own your own a horse? My aunt in Florida owns a few."

"I do. Her name is Valentine. I just bought her actually; I'm working on training her to do some show jumping competitions soon, hopefully. Although, she's coming along quite nicely so far."

Emma had no trouble talking about her horse, or her riding, or anything to do with horses for that matter. She was now rambling on non-stop, and Liam was politely chiming in with additional questions when he could get a word in. Despite her attempt to keep him at arm's length, she found herself enjoying their conversation.

"What's your major, by the way?" She asked, feeling a little bad about the conversation centering around her.

"Construction management. It was what my dad did, so I decided to follow in his footsteps."

"That sounds like it would be a pretty cool job. What kind of job do you think you will take after you graduate?"

It came out as a reflex, and she regretted asking it the moment it left her lips. She always hated when people asked her that, mostly because she never knew exactly what route she wanted to take with her own career after college.

"I'm not entirely sure yet, although my dad owned his own company, so maybe after I get some experience of my own, I'll do the same."

"I get it, I still feel like I'm figuring out what I want to do after college too."

They walked in silence for another minute through the parking lot, meeting each other's gaze on occasion.

"Oh sorry, this is me," she said, fumbling to find her keys. "Thanks for walking me to my car and for not calling horse riding easy again," she said with a playful grin.

"You're welcome. So, I'll see you around campus?"

"Yeah, I'll see you around."

Before she made any poor judgment decisions, she pulled open her car door and quickly pulled it shut behind her, pulling out of the parking space as fast as safety allowed. Liam stood where she left him with the same handsome, goofy grin.

"The last thing I need is a charming guy trying to sweep me off my feet," she reminded herself.

Emma brushed out Valentine's soft, freshly bathed and dried coat. Rays of sun that peeked through the cracks in the barn were gleaming off her back.

"You might be more ready for today than I am," she told the mare. Emma heard the trailer hitch connecting to the truck outside the barn. *"Here goes nothing,"* she thought.

Although Emma had much less time for the intensive training she had planned due to Valentine's healing abscess, Maggie had still suggested they come to the schooling show with her and a few of the other girls. Valentine had been sound and willing to work for three weeks now, so Emma agreed to go. Leading her horse out of the barn and into the crisp morning air, Emma was still trying to shake off her pre-horse show jitters. Valentine loaded into to the trailer like an old pro, unaware of the importance today held for her owner.

The show grounds were already bustling with activity, despite how early it was, as the trailer pulled through the gates of the show grounds. Emma felt good about how easygoing the mare seemed as she nibbled on the flake of hay she had just thrown into her show barn stall. Walking towards the ring to memorize her jump course, she took in the atmosphere of the small schooling show. Horses stood around lazily waiting for their turns, and the three arenas were busy with riders on course and those waiting anxiously at the gate.

Emma watched the first few rounds of the class before hers since they were riding the same course she would be. Hanging over the fence, she traced the path her horse would take with her eyes over and over, hoping it would be committed to her memory when her nerves found her. She watched as horse after horse completed the course; some successfully, others taking down poles.

"Two foot three jumpers, please make your way to the schooling ring."

It was time. Emma's heart hammered as she power walked back to the show stables to tack up her horse. Fully tacked and ready to go now, she swung her leg over Valentine's side as she headed towards the crowded warm up area. Horses were going in every direction; some trotting, some cantering, others walking, sometimes getting in the way of the horses at higher gaits.

Emma rubbed Val's neck as she walked into the ring. The first horse was already on course in her class, which meant she had about six riders in front of her. She gave a soft cluck to her horse who trotted off at an eager pace. Emma focused on relaxing her mind and body, while keeping her weight centered on her horse. Emma sat down into the saddle, putting her leg on, and Valentine broke into her typical comfortable rocking horse style canter.

"So far, so good," she thought.

Maggie and Hailey were standing next to the warmup jump in the middle of the arena, and Maggie waved to get her attention before pointing towards the jump. Emma nodded at her trainer, knowing she meant it was time to start warming up over fences. Cantering down the center line, they jumped over the cross rail, turning around to jump it the other direction after they landed. Maggie raised one side of the jump and Hailey raised the other side, matching the jump to their competition height.

"Let's take this a couple times and head to the ring," she called out.

Emma took a deep breath and asked for Valentine to canter again, this time pointed at the much larger warm up fence. She felt the mare pick up speed the last few strides in anticipation and cleared it with ease. Smiling, she circled around and took it the other direction, clearing it again.

"That's good enough Em, we don't want to fire her up any more than she is already; let's head to the ring."

Emma brought her horse back to a walk and patted her neck.

"We got this," she whispered, maybe more to herself than the horse. They watched a few rounds once they reached their ring. Now, there was only one rider left before it was her turn. Focusing her breathing, she tried to calm her nerves. Why was she so nervous? Maybe she felt she had something to prove; Valentine was so special to her, and she had come so far from the hopeless looking horse she once was. This mare had blossomed into the talented little jumper she knew she could be. Emma wanted to show everyone what this horse could do, even if it was just a schooling show.

"Do you know your course?" Maggie's words interrupted her thoughts, and she noticed the gate was opening for the rider in the ring to come out and for her to enter. She swallowed hard before answering.

"Got it," she said as she nudged Valentine forward towards the gate. The mare hesitated slightly at the gate, staring at the daunting empty ring behind it, but walked through with a little more encouragement.

Now they were alone in the ring with all eyes on them. Emma tried to keep the now prancing mare quiet for what seemed like an eternity before the whistle blew, signaling that the timers were set and that they could begin the course.

Emma fixed her eyes on the first fence and asked Valentine to canter. Valentine's canter was forward and eager as she approached jump number one. Fences one, two, and three blurred by as they managed to continue to keep the jumps up. Feeling herself relax the further they were into the course, she turned her head and body to the left over fence four to be sure her horse knew it was time for a tight turn. Valentine tossed her head; sharp turns were not her favorite, and she made it clear she would much rather canter openly down a long line. Fence five, despite a slightly unbalanced turn, was also a clear fence. That left the in and out combination fence and one single oxer before they crossed the timeline.

Emma knew she needed a slightly deeper take off to the in and out if she wanted to make the striding. Valentine fought her, wanting to take her usual long spot, and ended up chipping in a stride at the last minute. Her front leg grazed the top rail as they sailed over the jump. Emma heard the rail hit the ground as she began setting her up for the next fence. She was hoping to make up the striding so they could clear the second jump of the combination, but Valentine took a long spot anyway and consequently took another rail down. Landing off the in and out combination, Emma turned her head and pointed the mare towards the last jump.

Taking off at a much better distance this time, they cleared the final fence of the course. Emma sat deep in the saddle, asking Valentine to walk as they headed towards the exit gate. She tried not to let her own emotions affect the mare, who was now jigging as if she had just jumped an Olympic sized course clear. She forced a smile instead and rubbed the mare's neck. For her first time out on course in a new place, her horse had given it her all. Maggie and Hailey were waiting for them at the gate, smiling as if they had just completed a clear jumping round.

"Emma, she did great out there! She was very brave; she jumped everything nicely for you, and now we know what we need to work on at home. If you aren't winning, you're learning, right? You should be proud of her."

Maggie was right, she had every reason to be proud; just a few months ago they had pulled this once-sad-looking mare from an auction, and now here she was, holding her own in a competition setting. Emma slid off Valentine and put her forehead against the bridge of her horse's nose.

"This is only the beginning for us," she said, looking into her horse's eyes.

Chapter Five

"That's all for today's class, have a great weekend," the professor said, dismissing them.

Emma sighed in relief as she gathered her things and walked out of her last class of the week. Looking down at her phone for the first time since class began, she noticed she had missed a call and voicemail from a number she didn't recognize. Clicking the phone's voicemail button, she raised her phone to her ear.

"Hello, Miss Walker, this is Cheryl Louden in the financial aid office. If you could please stop by sometime during business hours, we just have a few things to discuss with you regarding next semester. Have a great day."

Checking her watch, Emma decided she may as well take care of this today while she was still on campus; she still had about an hour before they closed. Emma stepped out of the brick building, shoving her hands further into her pockets. The cold weather was officially here, and she was not thrilled about it. As if to taunt her, light flurries began falling from the sky. She grimaced at the sky spitefully and continued her long walk across campus towards the financial aid and administrative buildings.

Shaking off the cold that lingered in her bones as she walked into the admin building, she scanned the map for Cheryl's office location and headed down the appropriate hallway. As she walked through the office door, the woman smiled warmly to Emma and gestured toward the empty chair in front of her desk. "Please, come in. May I have your name please?"

"I'm Emma Walker. I received a voicemail a couple hours ago about speaking with you regarding next semester. Is there a problem?"

Cheryl smiled at her again, but this time a little less enthusiastically and said nothing as she turned back to her computer to pull up her student account.

"Well dear, I'm not quite sure how to tell you this, but your financial aid is being dropped."

Emma stared at her, stunned.

"You see honey, your father was unemployed when you started college, is that correct?"

Emma nodded, still unable to find words.

"So, because he was unemployed at the time of your college application and throughout most of your time here, you have been receiving quite a bit of financial aid due to his lack of employment. It appears he has since found a good job, so essentially, he now makes too much for you to qualify for this funding," she continued.

Emma still made no effort to speak, so Cheryl continued.

"In addition to this, much of the other funding you were receiving has simply run out. You have a few loans in place, but they are not nearly enough to cover your last semester of college."

Silence hung heavily in the room as Emma continued to stare blankly at the woman on the other side of the desk.

"So, um, essentially you have to come up with the funding on your own in order to sign up for classes for your final semester."

"How much money will I need to finish college and graduate?" She finally asked. Cheryl smiled again, awkwardly this time, and clicked a few buttons until Emma heard her printer kick on.

"Here you go dear, this is what you will need to come up with. Now, you could certainly start looking into other grants and loans, although you should know it may be a little harder to get those this time around..." Cheryl was still talking but Emma didn't hear a thing she said. Instead, she stared at the number on the page that had far too many zeros.

The financial aid employee might still have been talking, but Emma was already on her feet heading towards the door. She just needed out of this office, immediately.

"Thanks," she muttered as she pushed the office door open as quickly as it would allow.

"If you have any questions, please let me know!" She heard the voice behind her say as she all but ran down the hallway towards the exterior door. She didn't notice the cold this time as air rushed through the open exterior door, smacking her in the face. Since the moment she read that astronomical number that she couldn't possibly afford, she had gone numb.

Head spinning, Emma walked mindlessly towards what normally was her favorite spot in milder weather to read or study. A thickly tree lined courtyard behind the library, now lacking other students studying due to the changing seasons, came into view as she rounded the corner of the building.

Emma let her backpack drop beside her without attempting to set it down gently. She slid down the stoned wall of the courtyard and sat on the cold concrete patio ground. It took her almost two full minutes before her emotions caught up with her. Maybe it was shock, or maybe it was that her head still spun with the realization that she may not be able to finish college after three and a half years of hard work. Either way, she spent those two minutes staring off at the almost leafless trees before allowing the emotions to overwhelm her.

Thick snowflakes started to fall around her, melting when they hit the ground as she wept there alone. Never had she been thankful for the cold, but in this moment, it made campus all but silent with only the occasional student walking past quickly on the sidewalk nearby as they headed to the next warm building.

She thought. Some of what Cheryl said rang in her mind "...you can try and get another loan, but it may be a little harder to get one this time around."

In financial aid terminology, she was pretty sure that meant she was out of luck. Her dad may make too much on paper, but the debt they were already in due to years of unemployment and contract work meant they couldn't help her even if they wanted to. He had far too much credit card and IRS debt, and his credit score was sure to be shot. Wiping the tears from her eyes angrily, and for fear they would freeze to her face, her mind began turning over the viable options she had left.

Option one: she could do an internet deep dive into what loan options she did have left and what kind of other funding she could get. After that, she would still have to work to pay for the rest and this option more than likely included picking up a second job.

Emma pushed aside the option to sell her horse; that wasn't an option to her. Even so, it would hardly put a dent in what she owed next semester.

Option two: drop out of college and hopefully find a full-time job with what college experience she did gain. She could start somewhere that offered an entry level position and work her way up to a better, and hopefully better paying, position. Sure, she could also work for one of the barns in her hometown but most of them were western disciplines which she was completely unfamiliar with.

She really didn't love either of those ideas. All she wanted was to get her college degree and move on. If she was honest with herself, she also had no interest in proving her ex-boyfriend, Jordan, right.

Her hands were beginning to lose feeling now. How long had she been sitting here? She pulled her phone from her pocket; an hour had passed.

"This pity party is far from over, but I'm going to lose my hands to frostbite on top of everything else if I don't get inside," she thought.

Begrudgingly, she pulled her stiff body up off the stone-cold ground. Gathering her backpack still slumped against the wall, she headed back toward her parked car on the other end of campus.

"It's not like I have to make a decision today," she thought. Doing some research and taking a few days to think about it might be a better idea than rushing into any life-altering decisions.

Emma stared up at the snowy sky a moment, as if the answer would fall from above, as she trekked down the abandoned campus path.

ele

Emma put her palms on her forehead in frustration; another dead end. She was starting to lose count of how many loan facilitators she had called, applied for, and been rejected by.

It had been a week since she had received the news that had thrown her whole life off course. Rubbing her temples, she felt the start of what would be yet another stress headache. Pushing away from her desk, she headed down the hall, and stepped outside on her back deck.

"Time for a break," she thought, pulling out her phone.

"Hey Hailey! I know I've been in isolation trying to figure out what to do with my life, but does that offer to get dinner and drinks from four days ago still stand?"

"Of course, Em," her friend on the other line said. "I get it, I can't imagine what you're going through. I actually had plans with Lily tonight, but I bet she would be fine if you joined us!"

Before hanging up, they made plans to meet at their favorite local Mexican restaurant, Las Margaritas. Some chips, guacamole, and drinks would do her some good. An hour later, Emma spotted Lily and Hailey outside the Mexican restaurant as she pulled into the parking lot.

"Thanks for inviting me, guys," she said after hugging each of her friends. "I just couldn't take another endless evening of research after working at the restaurant all day. I haven't seen Valentine in days, and I feel awful about not spending any time with her, but I feel like I can't focus on anything else until I know what to do next."

The girls were seated in a corner booth and ordered drinks and appetizers immediately. For once, sweet bubbly Hailey didn't seem to have anything to say to her sad friend. Lily gave her an empathic look before asking the question on both her friends' minds. "How has the process been going? Have you found any loans?"

"I think I've contacted about a hundred student loan companies at this point. I had one loan company accept me so far, but it's not much. The problem is, I won't have enough time outside of class to make the money I need to pay for the rest of my last semester, even with that loan. I'm really regretting going to an expensive private college now."

Lily and Hailey exchanged worried looks. What were they supposed to say to that? Saying it out loud, Emma could only assume her friends were thinking that going back to college may not be a viable option anymore. It was the same realization Emma was also starting to have herself.

"Enough about me, I'd rather not talk about it anymore anyway. Lily, how's the packing going? I can't believe you are a few weeks away from leaving us and heading down to your internship in Florida."

Lily and Hailey's body language relaxed a little as the topic shifted to something a bit more uplifting.

"I don't even know where to start," she gushed. "I'm realizing just how much winter gear I own, and that is clearly not going to work for Florida!"

The mood continued to brighten and Emma watched her friend's face light up as she went on about her packing and travel plans for the upcoming weeks. She felt the burden of her hopeless situation lift away from her, if only for a few hours. Too soon, the girls were saying their goodbyes and Emma was left alone with her thoughts once again as she drove home. Trying not to be jealous, she thought about how excited Lily was about her internship. Her friend deserved it though; there was no doubt about it. She had worked hard for this.

"But here she is with this incredible opportunity and a college degree and here I am with...," her mind trailed off as tears welled in her eyes.

There was no avoiding the reality she had been avoiding for days now; she wasn't going to finish college. At least not now, and certainly not anytime soon. She didn't have the money, the time, or the loan funding. If she was completely honest with herself, she hardly had a plan after college even if she did graduate. When she had started college, all she thought about was her love for horses and that she wanted a career with them. Things like how much she made afterward or what type of job she would pursue when she finished never crossed her mind.

Passing the exit to her apartment without hesitation, she knew she wasn't ready to go home and face Mandy. Her best friend would want to know why she was upset, and Emma wasn't ready to say out loud what her mind had finally concluded. In fact, she already knew where she was headed, even if it was almost 9:00 pm. Pulling into the gravel driveway of Maggie's barn, she parked off to the side of the fence line and headed towards the pasture the mares were always turned-out in. Slipping through the cracks of the fence, Emma walked through the pasture as her eyes adjusted to the darkness.

She watched as surprised horse heads popped up briefly as they looked at her, only to continue eating grass moments later once they realized she was not a threat. One horse head continued to hold her gaze as she approached: Valentine's. Jogging through the uneven grass, she quickly reached her horse and flung her arms around her neck. Letting pent up tears fall, her mare's warm neck soaked them up as she nuzzled Emma's shoulder. The horse stood perfectly still otherwise, sensing her owner's sadness, proving to Emma once again how perceptive horses really are.

Emma released the mare's neck and allowed her to continue grazing. She leaned face first against the barrel of her horse's side, her arms wrapped partially over the mare's back as far as they would go, resting her chin on her back. There was no other place she wanted to think about what to do with her future than right here, beneath the dark sky next to her favorite horse.

"Work at the restaurant full time? No way, that job would be miserable long-term. What about a new career entirely? One that was accepting of her lack of college degree where she could work her way up to a higher paying managerial type position?" She thought.

However, working with horses was the career her whole being longed for. Her passion for them impelled her, and there was no denying it. College degree or not, nothing was changing the fact that there was nothing else she wanted to do.

Other than waitressing, all the skills she had right now involved horses. So why not just get a job working with horses without a degree? Why waste what college experience she had gained and years of working at Maggie's barn prior to that? The conversation she had with Lily that evening about her upcoming internship suddenly sprang to her mind.

"An internship," she said aloud, gasping a little. She almost couldn't believe the thought hadn't crossed her mind sooner. She had plenty of experience and would only gain more as a working student. Experience that would build her resume and make her desirable to future employers, even if she couldn't finish her college degree.

While Lily's internship had a focus on the veterinary medicine skills she had from school, Emma could easily find a working student position with a focus on equine barn management or she could even become a professional groom for the higher end show jumping or eventing farms that flocked to Ocala and Wellington, Florida, in the winter. A cold gust of wind ruffled Valentine's mane as she lazily grazed on.

"Skipping winter certainly would be an added benefit," she thought.

Her mind wandered on to some of the possible cons of this idea. She would have to leave her home, family, friends, and Maggie's barn – literally everything good and familiar in her life. There just weren't that many internship opportunities near her hometown and what few might be out there would never compare to the caliber of opportunities Florida held for her. What about Valentine? She knew it was possible to bring her horse; Lily was doing it after all. That was going to be a deal breaker for any farm she decided to intern with.

For the first time since the financial office employee had given her the news that has crashed her world to the ground, she had a glimmer of hope. An internship in Florida would be an incredible opportunity, and it was honestly the best option she had right now that didn't involve doing a job she hated. She pulled away from Valentine's side, and the horse lifted her head to look at her. Kissing her mare's muzzle sweetly, she now felt a ping of excitement to begin what she knew would be another internet deep dive search into every possible opportunity.

"It's going to be just me and you soon, kid," she whispered to the mare as she jogged back towards the fence line and her parked car.

Chapter Six

Emma hung up the phone for the third time that morning, writing notes frantically in her notepad about some of the important information from the call that she did not want to forget.

"I think that went well," she said to herself aloud, pushing her chair away from her desk at her apartment to stretch. It had only been a few days since her decision to find an out of state internship, but so far it was going better than she expected. Crossing Bend Side Farms off her list of phone interviews, she reviewed the remaining farms to email and to set up phone interviews with.

She had already spoken with close to ten farms this week alone and had several more she planned to reach out to. Two of which had tentatively offered her a position. All she had left to do now was narrow down which she liked the best after she heard back from the remaining farms. But first, she promised herself a little closure at college, and more importantly, with her friend Rachel who had always had her back at school. Today was her last day of classes for this semester, and, at least for the time being, it was her goodbye to college and consequently her best college buddy.

"It's certainly going to be a bittersweet day," she thought, pulling her backpack from the ground. Still though, she felt hope that even though college wasn't turning out how she dreamed, she still had a plan to make her life into what she wanted.

Arriving at her college campus, Emma shut her car door and took a moment to look around. This was it, the beginning of the end. In that moment, standing next to her car, she remembered the boy with the goofy grin that had walked her to her car what felt like another lifetime ago now. A small inkling to walk around campus a little longer and find him washed over her, which she quickly dismissed. She was leaving; what good would hunting down some guy she had brief a moment with do for her? It would only make it that much harder to leave if she did.

Shaking her head, she tried to physically clear her mind before heading across campus to her last few classes ever.

Emma spent most of the time in her last class daydreaming about what her life would be like as working student; hard work of course, she wasn't stupid. She had done enough research to know internships meant little to no pay, hard work, and very little personal time. But the payoff was on the job experience that would look excellent on her resume, and, of course, being around some of the most amazing horses, riders, and show grounds in the country. In her mind, that was priceless.

"Have a great winter break!" The professor said. Class must be over, although she hadn't exactly been paying much attention. Out of the corner of her eye she saw Rachel waving from across the room. Her lengthy call this morning resulted in her running late to class, so she couldn't sit near her friend like she usually did. Emma waved back and stood just outside the classroom, waiting for Rachel to make her way through the crowd and out of the room as well.

"I am so ready for winter break," Rachel said exhaling as she spoke. Rachel paused, catching the strange look on Emma's face.

"Rach, there's something I should probably tell you. Can we sit in the library coffee shop area or something?"

"Sure Em, I hope everything is ok?"

"I'll tell you everything once we get there," Emma said, politely smiling at her friend's chatter as they walked. The girls had their coffees in hand and sat down at the booth by the largest window in the coffee shop.

"So, I had some issues with financial aid and the short version is that there isn't enough to cover next semester, and I can't get funding on my own that covers school." Rachel stared, only blinking for a moment. Emma understood her reaction; she had the same one not so long ago.

"What are you going to do now?" She finally asked.

"Well, I'll be honest, it's been a lot to consider and process. I've decided the best thing I can do right now is take an intern-ship out of state with a large competition farm so I can gain experience and improve my resume since it won't say 'college graduate,' you know?"

"I can't believe you are leaving! I'm so sorry that this happened to you, but I get it. If I was in your position, I don't even know if I would have bounced back and figured out a plan as fast as you have."

Emma smiled at her friend; she was starting to realize just how much she would miss her friends when she left Ohio. Certainly, she was already regretting her anti-social behavior a few months back.

Emma and Rachel talked for a while about some of the farms she had been in contact with, and some of the memories they had of the last few years of college. Giving her friend a long hug, Emma said, "This is not goodbye," while fighting back tears.

"It had better not be!" Rachel replied. Emma waved to her friend and pushed the library doors.

"This was only the first of the long list of goodbyes," she thought. Emma began her trek across her now former college campus for the last time.

Yes, this was the beginning of the end.

ele

Dishes clamored as she tossed them into the dirty dish water in the kitchen of the Italian restaurant. It was days like this she was already missing her friend Mandy who was now officially working at her new job at the marketing firm.

They both were well on their way to better things, and that was really the only reason she was surviving what felt like an endless shift today. Emma's phone buzzed in her pocket, and she pulled it out and glanced at the out of state number on the screen. She hadn't been expecting a call, but odds were good it was one of the many farms she had inquired with about an internship. Emma ran to the breakroom and answered just in time.

"Hello! This is Emma Walker."

"Hi Emma, this is Jenn, the barn manager and trainer at Twin Oaks Farm. How are you?"

Emma felt that butterflies in her stomach feeling; this was one of her top choices and she had been hoping for several days that she would receive a follow up call.

"I'm great, thanks for following up with me."

"I hope this is a good time, but after speaking with you the other day, we have you as our top candidate for the working student position. Would you be interested in a video call with the property owners before we make our final decision?"

Emma did not really need to consider this for long. "I would love to! When are you thinking would be a good day for the call?"

"Well, I know it's a little soon, but this weekend? Day after tomorrow?"

Getting her restaurant shift covered on a weekend should be easy; people were always wanting to work on the busy days.

"I can be free anytime that day."

"Wonderful! We will be sending you a link to the video call and will speak to you in a few days."

Emma thanked the barn manager and hung up the phone.

"This is really happening," she thought, trying to convince herself of that reality.

———*ele*———

The next few days passed quickly in a blur of research about the farm she would hopefully be interning with. Fixing her hair nervously, she clicked the link they had sent her for the video call and logged in.

"Hi Emma! This is Jennifer Meyers, we spoke on the phone a few days ago, and beside me are the property owners, Liza and David Williams. "

Emma smiled warmly at the couple and barn manager. "It's so nice to finally speak with you," she said.

"We have heard so many good things about you! We would love to go over some of the details of what your position would look like. So, of course, this position will not be paid; however, you will have housing at our Ocala farm and when we travel to Wellington for the part of the winter. You would be with us at least until the winter show season is over, and at that time we can discuss extending your working student position with us, or potentially offering you a full-time position should things go well. In addition to this, we will also provide you with a stall if you choose to bring your horse with you."

"Perfect," she thought.

"Your responsibilities will include cleaning stalls, turning out horses, feeding, that kind of thing. But we also wanted someone with the ability to warm up our show horses and exercise them during the week. Essentially, you will be learning both the job of a professional groom and a barn manager. The experience you gain here will open doors for you for permanent positions. Does this sound like what you were looking for?"

"Sold," Emma thought.

"This sounds exactly like what I have been looking for," she told them.

"In that case, we would love to officially offer the position to you. We would like to have you down here within a few weeks so we can incorporate you into our regimen with the horses before the shows down here start up. Things tend to get pretty busy at that point."

"A few weeks? Well, why not, right? I'm done with school, the lease on our apartment is up in a month, and we already gave notice to vacate. If I'm going to do this, I may as well dive right in," she thought.

"I would like to accept the position. This sounds like an incredible opportunity, thank you!"

"That's great news, we will be in touch with shipping arrangements for your horse and other information you will need."

The call ended shortly, and just like that, Emma's life was changing forever.

—— *ele* ——

Of all the goodbyes she would need to say, this one was sure to be one of the hardest. Emma walked through the cool barn aisle as she headed towards the cross ties where Maggie was untacking her dappled grey gelding.

"Maggie, do you have a minute to talk?"

Maggie draped a fleece cooler over her horse's back and glanced over at Emma with a quizzical expression. Knowing Emma for over a decade, she caught the sadness in her voice immediately.

"You ok, Em?"

Like a dam of words had broken from her mouth, everything that happened in the past few weeks tumbled out in one long run on sentence. Emma watched as a little shock, sadness, and then a bittersweet smile broke out on her long-time trainer and friend's face. A look she had seen several times now on her friends' faces when she told them the news. Maybe they all thought she was crazy for uprooting her life; maybe she was.

"I get it," she said. Maggie looked away momentarily, as if she needed a moment to think through what she would say next. She picked up a soft brush out of her grooming box and began brushing the drying sweat off her horse's neck.

"You know you and Valentine will always have a home here if you ever need to come back. I'm proud of you, Em, and I think what you're doing is very brave. I'm proud to see that you are taking control of your own destiny despite what life has thrown at you."

Emma fought tears back. Yes, this one was certainly going to be her hardest goodbyes. This barn, the other riders here, and Maggie had been her safe and happy place for most of her life. This is where she came when things hit the fan. So many memories were all but etched into every inch of this place. How was she going to leave this barn and these people after so many years?

"Because I have to," she thought.

She had to do this internship for her future. Emma took a few steps forward to hug Maggie. She stood embracing her for a long moment, still fighting back the fear and tears that were threatening to overwhelm her.

"I can't thank you enough for everything you've given me. This internship would never have been possible without all the knowledge you have shared with me over the years. I'm not leaving for a couple weeks, and of course I will update you on Valentine's hauling date."

Emma peeled herself away, and after exchanging one last bittersweet glance with Maggie, she spun on her heels and headed back down the barn aisle towards Valentine's stall, wiping her eyes as she walked away. She was still trying very hard to shake the feeling that this was a huge mistake.

Right now, she wasn't sure how she could possibly load her horse up and say goodbye to Maggie's barn indefinitely.

—*ele*—

Emma and Mandy sat in the rental office of their apartment complex's leasing office, waiting for the property manager to return with the printed form. There was something about signing this move out form that made this move feel real.

"Here you go ladies. Just fill in your forwarding addresses, sign, and date at the bottom, and you're good to go until you turn your keys in. We will send any other pertinent move out information to your door in the next few days."

Mandy took the form from the manager and scribbled her forwarding address and initials on the line at the bottom of the page, and then passed it off to Emma. Emma hesitated for a moment but began signing anyway. Although she knew this was only a formality and would change nothing about the fact that she was merely a week away from moving across the country, leaving everything she knew behind her, it felt like she was sealing her fate somehow.

Emma still vividly remembered the day she moved in like it was yesterday. This apartment was her first ever; she and Mandy had met at the Italian restaurant when it opened a few years ago and became fast friends shortly after they started working together. When Mandy's lease had ended at her previous apartment only six months after they met, it was a no brainer for the girls; they were going to be roommates. They were inseparable anyway, so why not be roomies as well? Emma let her mind drift to the many moments that made up their friendship over the years.

Being college students and working part-time only made so much money, and sometimes they would have to get creative with their nights out. Sharing a beer, going line dancing, and singing karaoke were their go-to girls' nights out. They had made so many friends together over the years, people Emma would be missing soon.

"Are you all finished, hon?"

The manager had her hand extended out waiting for Emma to hand over the now signed paperwork.

"I'm sorry, yes, here you go."

"Best of luck, ladies!"

The girls thanked the manager and walked back over to their half-packed apartment. Mandy glanced at her friend, with a similar look on her face; it felt like the end of an era.

"Remember that one time we decided to go hiking in the forest behind the apartment complex?"

Emma couldn't help but smile at the memory.

"You mean the time we got super lost and almost didn't make it out before dark?"

Not so funny then, super funny now.

"I'm going to miss this too, Em. This apartment, hanging out with you...our lives are completely changing. I'm scared too you know."

Looking over at her friend, she realized they were both making drastic life-altering changes. In a way, she was glad that while they wouldn't be together like they were now, they would still be able to support each other. Emma saw a lot of phone calls and video chats in their future.

"Don't think I won't end up in Florida at some point. I will be traveling all over the country, you know."

Emma took a deep breath as she opened the door to their apartment. Half-filled boxes scattered around the living and dining room greeted them, a reminder they had much to do still.

"Want to have a packing party?"

"With wine?"

"Obviously."

The girls smiled at one another as they headed to the kitchen.

"The more things change, the more they stay the same," she thought.

ele

With only two days until the hauler was scheduled to pick up Valentine and ship her down to Ocala, Emma felt an immense pressure build as each day ticked by until moving day. Her plan was to follow the horse trailer in her car so she could have the peace of mind her horse was safe, and so she could simply focus on the road and not worry about how to get there.

But there was much to do and so many more goodbyes between then and now.

She had already given notice to the Italian restaurant she worked at, letting them know she was leaving.

"I might actually miss this place a little," she had thought after notifying the general manager. After all, this place had been her second home the last three years she had worked here. Not to mention, it's where she met Mandy and her other close friend, Ashlynn. Hailey, needing no excuse to throw a get together, had already planned out the ultimate farewell party for Emma. The only person they would be missing was Lily who was already headed down to her own internship as of late yesterday evening. It gave her mind a little peace knowing she would be just down the road from a close friend.

Contrary to her anti-social behavior a couple months ago, she was enthusiastic about this particular party because it would make saying goodbye to most of her friends all at once easy. If she was honest with herself, she was starting to feel a little remorseful for all the social events she had put off when she was dealing with her breakup with Jordan. Not so long ago, that was the worst thing happening in her life.

And now here she was, her life turned upside down and starting on a new adventure so many miles from the only home she had ever known. In fact, her college and apartment were not more than twenty-five minutes from her hometown.

Emma shoved the last of her heavy winter clothes into a box labeled storage. Thankfully, her parents' garage had enough free space to store what didn't fit in her car, which was a lot more than she originally thought. She didn't need her furniture either, since the housing provided by her internship included it. Now her whole life was packed into about three boxes, two suitcases filled with clothes, and some other miscellaneous soft sided bags with items she would need to be sure she could find easily, like toiletries.

The room felt empty; the same emptiness it held when she first moved in a few years back. Of course, she had not expected to live here forever, but she certainly wouldn't have predicted this would be the ending to her story. Emma looked at her watch. *"Shoot, I need to get to Hailey's, or she will have my head for being late to my own party."*

Pulling the pre-planned outfit from her closet, she changed quickly before pulling her fingers through her still damp, air dying, wavy hair. Gathering it into a half up loose bun, she applied a little mascara and called it good. *"They are my friends; they know what I look like,"* she thought. She was a horse girl after all, through and through.

When Emma pulled into the parking lot of Hailey's apartment complex, her jaw dropped a little. Typical social butterfly Hailey had outdone herself this time. Twinkle lights were all over the front porch and could be seen glowing behind her apartment. There were also far too many cars parked nearby for this to be a small intimate gathering. Emma shook her head; it looked like she would be going out with a bang. She was now, however, regretting the minimum effort she had put into her appearance.

Emma walked through the front door and was greeted by a large handmade 'Farewell Emma' banner. Hailey, Mandy, Ashlynn, and a few other friends were gathered just under the banner waiting for her.

"Our fashionably late guest of honor has arrived!" Hailey shouted above the music and murmuring conversations. A small cheer broke out for those who were in earshot and then most people resumed their conversations. Some of her close friends met her at the door and hugged her while pressing for details about her trip and if she was packed yet.

Emma made her way to the fridge to get a drink after the conversations died down. Deciding to step outside to get some fresh air, she couldn't wait to see what over-the-top exterior decorating Hailey had done. She was not disappointed; string lights stretched over the trees all the way to the fire pit this time. Coolers lined the decking area, and balloons were attached to over half of the deck railing.

"What am I going to do without you Hailey?" she thought. Emma would miss her bubbly friend. Who was going to pull her out of her shell when her friend and her elaborate parties weren't a short drive away? Emma walked down the deck stairs and through the crowded grassy area where she waved to and made small talk with a few mutual friends and acquaintances. Excusing herself after several conversations, she walked further out into the well-lit courtyard and sat down by the fire. Fortunately, she did not recognize anyone out here; she needed a moment to soak everything in.

Closing her eyes, she felt the warm flames dance near her face and the cold air on her back. It was a little unseasonably warm, but still a cold forty-five degrees tonight. Perfect bonfire weather, in her opinion. Emma opened her eyes and blinked twice to make sure she was seeing this correctly. Where a stranger was sitting just a minute ago, now sat Liam.

"Word on the street is you're moving to Florida, horse girl," he said in his usual smooth, lightly teasing tone. It felt like a twist of fate, because just a few feet from where they now sat is where she had collided with him the night they met.

"Liam?" she said, surprise creeping into her voice.

"What, you think I would miss one of Hailey's famous backyard parties?" He said, grinning the same way she remembered.

His charm clearly had some sort of strange power over her that her independent will was no match for. She could lie to herself like she had before, but she thought he was charming and handsome; there was really no way around that attraction. But what did she even know about him anyway? Hadn't he made jokes about riding and horses when they first met? Also, what was even the point? Talk all night, get to know him better, grow to like who he was as a person, and say goodbye a few days later? Emma closed her eyes again for another moment to clear her mind. He was no one to her, and he would stay that way.

"It's kind of a long story actually. I lost all my financial aid, so I can't finish college, but, yes, I'm moving to Florida for an internship opportunity."

Liam cocked his head a little the left, still smiling at her.

"With horses, I assume?" He said. Emma visibly rolled her eyes, latching on the glimmer of distaste she felt about his commentary.

"I'm kidding, really," he added quickly, perhaps noticing her expression change. "I think it's cool that you are so passionate about something. It seems like you really enjoy it if you are moving so far away for an opportunity to work with them. And Florida is great."

"See, this is exactly what I didn't want," she thought. She didn't want a reason to like him and the affirmation that his prior teasing held no value towards how he felt about the whole horse thing wasn't helping. It felt like he was taking down one of the many walls she had built up since the day her ex-boyfriend, Jordan, said goodbye.

"I didn't really have a lot of options, to be honest. The only thing I kept coming back to was that I want a career with horses, and I wasn't ready to give that up just because I was forced to drop out of college," she said. Yet, here she was still, spilling her guts to some guy she hardly knew while sitting in an extremely romantic setting. Really, this was a recipe for disaster.

"Not just anyone could up and move across the country chasing a dream you know. I take it your horse is coming with you?" He asked.

"I wouldn't have gone without her."

Liam chuckled a little at that before adding, "I thought so."

They sat quietly for a moment, staring into the flames.

"So, what part of Florida are you going to be in?" He said, breaking the silence.

"Ocala and Wellington. The owners I'm working for show at both and have a farm in Ocala and board at the horse show grounds in Wellington for the last half of the winter," Emma said as she stood up, making it clear she was going to be moving on to another part of the yard and that the conversation was over. It wasn't that she wasn't interested in spending more time talking to Liam. In fact, that was precisely the problem. She needed no other reason to miss home when she left in a few days. Emma smiled politely at him, trying not to seem rude anyway.

"Guess I better not monopolize the guest of honor, huh?" He asked.

"I should probably make my rounds; I have a lot of goodbyes to say. It was nice talking to you though."

That last part, she meant.

Liam smiled, this time with a strange look in his eyes she couldn't place. "Maybe I'll see you around, then."

Emma thought it was a little odd; see her around where? She was leaving and odds are she wasn't coming back anytime soon. If things went well, in Florida, maybe never.

"Take care, Liam," she said before she could change her mind. She quickly turned and began walking towards where Mandy and Ashlynn now stood on the deck outside. Emma fought the urge to look over her shoulder but lost. Liam was still standing where she left him, same goofy smile on his face, a glimmer in his eye.

She turned her head back around quickly, hoping he hadn't noticed, as she joined her friends on the deck.

Chapter Seven

With a grunt, Emma pulled the last heavy box from her car and set it down on the floor of her parents' garage. Her brother and dad were behind her in the driveway, unloading the last of her furniture from his pickup truck.

"Well, honey, I think we got it all," her dad said. Emma put her hands on her hips and glanced around at the heap of things they had just finished unloading. There was something strange about leaving most of her earthly possessions behind and starting a new life somewhere she'd never been. But the day had come, and she had only hours before she needed to be at the barn to load Valentine into the hauler's trailer and hit the road behind them. Emma's mother began crying when she saw it was time for her to go.

"She'll be fine, Chrissy," her dad said.

"Call us every hour," her mother said between sobs.

"EVERY hour," her brother repeated, sarcasm dripping from each word.

Emma punched her brother's arm before hugging her mom. Her mother probably wouldn't have let go if her father hadn't peeled her away to get a hug of his own. Emma's brother slapped her back playfully as he hugged her, promising to plan a trip to visit her soon.

This was harder than she'd imagined. This was her family, who she hadn't really left to go to college since she lived so close; she had even commuted from her parents' home her first two years of school.

But now here she was, leaving them indefinitely. She hugged them all one more time.

"I love you all! I will call you the minute I get there."

Emma honked her horn twice, pulled out of her parents' drive-way, and drove down the street she grew up on. In her rearview mirror, she watched as her mother waved as she wiped tears from her eyes.

"Goodbye, home," she murmured to herself. Emma pulled back into her apartment parking lot, backing her car into the space to make it easier to load her hatchback up with the things she was taking to Florida. Mandy met her at the door, box in hand, ready to help Emma pack up her car.

"It looks so empty," Emma said, staring at the now barren apartment.

"So, I guess this is it then."

The two best friends turned to look at each other. This *was* it. Emma wrapped her arms tightly around her closest friend.

"We're going to plan a meet up in Florida, and we are going to talk every day." She said it more as a statement than a question.

"Of *course,* we are! Emma, I'm going to miss you so much."

They stood there a moment in the parking lot of their now former apartment, embracing.

"I'll turn the keys in so you can get on the road."

"Thanks Mandy."

Emma knew if she didn't leave now, she wouldn't have the time she needed to get Valentine's things ready before the hauler arrived. Heading toward her car, she glanced back at her friend one last time before sliding into the driver's seat. Emma put her car in gear and headed for the exit.

"Goodbye apartment," she thought, leaving her apartment complex for the last time.

Emma pulled onto the long gravel driveway; it seemed odd to her that this familiar scene would soon be a distant memory.

Hailey and her horse, Charlie, were landing off a small vertical jump in the outdoor arena; she pulled him up to a halt when she saw Emma's car pull in the driveway. Emma caught her friend's bittersweet expression as she waved to her. The barn was quiet otherwise; Maggie was cleaning stalls, and greeted her politely, but there was a sadness in her voice Emma couldn't deny.

Emma tried to dismiss the guilt it triggered; she felt in some way she was betraying her trainer. On her way to the tack room to pack her riding gear and Valentine's things, she briefly paused at her horse's stall. The mare had her head hanging lazily out over the stall guard with her bottom lip dropped.

"You have a big day ahead of you lady," she said, running her hand up her mare's face and her fingers through her thick fore-lock. Valentine was oblivious to the fact that her life, too, was about to change forever. Emma rested her forehead against her mare's. Saying goodbye to her life here had been so much harder than she'd anticipated, but this horse was going to give her the strength to venture into the unknown. Kissing her velvety nose, she walked down the barn aisle towards the tack room. Time was going to run out soon; the hauler was less than twenty minutes away.

Thankful she had pre-packed most of the things she didn't use very often, Emma stuffed the remaining items that fit in her tack box and the rest in her show tote. She dragged them down the aisle towards the barn door, panting when she finally made it. It was incredibly likely she had more horse stuff coming on this journey than her own personal items.

Valentine's purple plaid fleece cooler lay draped over the blanket bar on her door, and Emma pulled it off the rack, slipping it over her mare before layering it with the matching sheet. Pulling two calming treats out of her pocket, she fed them to her horse, who gobbled them up without a second thought; she never turned down a treat.

Emma hoped they would help; she wanted to do anything she could to keep her horse as comfortable as possible on the fourteen-hour drive. Emma heard truck tires followed by the clanging of an empty trailer coming up the drive. It was then that she realized she had forgotten a hay net. Emma headed to the far side of the barn where the hay and hay nets were stored. There, Maggie stood filling a hay net and a bag of grain lay at her feet, clearly intended for her and Valentine to take with them. Emma wasn't expecting to cry again, but here she was holding back tears.

"Thank you, Maggie; you are one step ahead of me as usual."

Maggie handed her the hay net and picked up the bag of grain.

"I'll be right behind you. Hurry up, your hauler is here!"

Emma jogged out of the barn and greeted the hauler before hanging the hay net up in the horse trailer and placing her tack and tack boxes into the side of the trailer. Now all that was left was to load up her horse and say goodbye one last time.

Emma walked back towards Valentine's stall, slipped the halter over her ears, and snapped the chin strap to the other side.

"I promise, I will be right behind you. It's going to be so much warmer when we get where we are going; that'll be nice, right?" She cooed to the mare as she walked her out of her stall and down the barn aisle. The hauler had the ramp down, ready for her to lead the mare up onto the trailer. Valentine loaded up quietly, snatching a mouthful of hay from her large hay net the minute she was in reach of it. Emma closed the trailer divider and the heavy trailer doors behind her.

Turning around, she saw Maggie and Hailey waiting by the barn doors. Emma jogged over to them and wrapped her arms around Hailey first, then Maggie.

"I don't even know what to say," she said, her voice breaking.

"Say you'll have an amazing time soaking up the Florida sun and riding lots of expensive ponies," Hailey said, hugging her again.

Emma turned to Maggie. "Thank you for everything, and I promise I won't be a stranger."

"You'd better not be! Come visit next time you're in town, ok?"

Emma nodded, her bottom lip quivering. The diesel engine of the truck attached to the trailer turned over behind her.

"Ok, I better get in my car before the hauler leaves me!"

Maggie squeezed her hand, and Emma walked quickly towards her car, leaving the last bit of her world behind her. The truck and trailer rattled down the long driveway with Emma's car right behind it. Horses in the pastures lining the driveway called out to the horse in trailer; it was almost like they knew she was leaving, and perhaps, never coming back.

Emma glanced in the rearview mirror one last time. The barn and everyone in it she loved slowly faded behind her.

ell

Eight hours on the road passed slowly. It was dark now, and with each hour passing, Emma was getting more exhausted. She reached over to the passenger side of her car where a small cooler contained some energy drinks and sandwiches her mom had packed her for the trip.

"Thanks mom," she thought, pulling out a drink. Still six hours away from Ocala, Emma was pretty sure she wasn't going to make it. The packing, the goodbyes, and the sitting endlessly in this car with nothing but headlights and dark blurs passing only added to the draining feeling that overwhelmed her.

Emma pulled up her favorite podcast about horses, called 'Horses in the Morning.' If anyone was going to make her laugh and give her the second wind she needed, it was going to be the hilarious rantings of podcast hosts, Jamie and Glenn. Numerous episodes later, she was crossing the Florida border and in the homestretch to her new home at Twin Oaks Farm. Before long, she was winding down the quiet Ocala back roads, pulling over as the hauler approached the gated front entrance.

Emma hopped out of her car and jogged towards the gated area to punch in the code she had been given in advance. She stared briefly at the grand looking entrance where four palm trees lit by ground lights lined either side of the black metal gate. It was too dark to see much else, but she felt excitement and a little bit of nerves as the reality that she had finally made it hit her. The hauler waved to Emma and began pulling through the gate opening before them. Emma skipped back to her still-running vehicle and sped behind him so she could reach the gates without them closing before she made it through.

It was still too dark to see much when the truck and trailer finally stopped next to the barn. The white wood barn had two small lantern-like lights attached to the siding in the front part of the barn, right beside the sliding doors. She could see the inside of the barn was still lit up as well since light streamed from the windows that lined the top part of the siding, just below the roof.

She pulled her car around to the other side of the barn and parked it there, eager to get Valentine off the trailer and comfortable in her new home. The hauler was lowering the heavy, squeaky ramp down and it landed with a muffled thud on the soft ground below, which appeared to be a mix of dark gray sand and grass from what she could see in trailer's low running lights. Valentine neighed anxiously; it had been a long drive and she clearly wanted to know where she was.

Emma hopped into the trailer and said her horse's name softly, hoping to reassure the mare that she was safe. Backing her out slowly, the mare whipped her head to either side, still calling out to the horses in the barn who were responding to her now. The barn doors slid open before she reached them, and a tall blonde woman in her mid-thirties stepped out; she greeted Emma with a smile.

"You must be Emma. Welcome to Twin Oaks! I hope the drive was not too bad for you."

"The drive was endless," she thought.

"Thank you, and I assume you are Jenn?"

The barn manager reached her hand out, and Emma shook it with the hand that wasn't holding Valentine's lead rope.

"This must be Valentine!" She said, patting the mare's neck. Valentine paid no attention to the stranger's touch; her ears were hyper focused, neck stiff staring intently at the opening of the barn and the horses calling to her inside. Both girls laughed at the mare's expression.

"I'll show you where her stall is."

Emma waved and shouted a quick a thank you to the hauler, who was already unloading her tack and setting it next to the barn entrance as she led her mare into the brightly lit barn. The twenty-stall barn was open and had large light wood stalls with black metal framing and hardware. All the doors allowed the horses to hang their heads out at their leisure and a rubber mat ran the length of the barn aisle. Emma could see a wash rack and two cross tie bays at the end of the barn; both were very clean and everything in the barn was neat and tidy.

"I already love it here," she thought.

The hauler was walking up behind her, hay net in hand.

"That's the last of it, ma'am," he said handing Emma the hay net. Jenn turned around and pulled a pre-written check out of her pocket, handing it to the hauler and thanking him. He nodded, touched his ball cap, and lowered his head slightly before turning to head back to his rig. Jenn turned back toward Emma with a friendly smile.

"Let me show you where the tack and feed rooms are so you can settle in. After that, I can show you where you will be staying. I'm sure you are exhausted from your drive."

Emma was exhausted but arriving at her new home had given her an extra boost of nervous energy that she had not anticipated. Leading the way back towards the entrance of the barn, Jenn opened the first door to their right. Emma grabbed the grain Maggie has sent with her that was slumped near the entrance and followed her into the room. A large feed room with metal bins labeled with different grain lined the walls, and three shelves held an array of supplements and medications. The smell of sweet feed filled the air, one of Emma's favorite familiar smells.

Jenn pointed to a bin in the far corner as she said, "You can put your horse's grain over here, and feel free to toss her a couple flakes of hay as well; the hay room is the sliding door right next to the feed room." Emma nodded and Jenn led her out of the room and back down the barn aisle to a door next to the cross ties and wash rack.

Trying to hide the look on her face when Jenn opened the tack room door, she saw saddles with brand names that she recognized as high end lining almost an entire wall of the large room. Another wall was nothing but bridles with more types of bits than she could easily identify, and the remaining walls were lined with tack boxes engraved with initials. Shelving with other miscellaneous items and a washer and dryer were in the corner. No doubt, it was probably the nicest tack room she had ever seen.

"Feel free to put your tack box and other tack anywhere there is a free spot. The guest house you will be staying in is across from the barn, so we can head out this way," she said leading the way out of the sliding barn doors on the opposite end of the barn.

It was completely dark once they left the barn with just the light of the guest house's front porch the only thing visible. As they got closer, she saw the small guest house sat against what appeared to be scattered trees lining a fence pasture.

Jenn unlocked the small house and opened the door to a one room studio-apartment style layout. A full-sized bed to the far-right, and the lamp on the nightstand next to it was already lit. A little dresser with a tv on top sat on one wall near the foot of the bed, and a small opened closet door was on the other side of the bed. The kitchen was small as well but had everything she needed. A bar height table with two chairs was near the wall across from the kitchen area and a love seat couch sat in the center of the room against the wall.

"This place is perfect, thank you!"

"Of course! Take your time settling yourself and your horse in. Normally your day will begin around 7:00 am, earlier on horse show days, but since you arrived so late this evening, feel free to meet us out at the barn around 9:00 am tomorrow instead. Don't worry, I will make sure your horse is fed," she said, addressing the concern written all over Emma's face. Emma thanked her again and Jenn excused herself to the main house where she stayed with the owners.

Now here she was, alone in her new home. A slight buzz of excitement ran through her as she closed the door to the guest house and headed back to the barn. Valentine nickered at her when she entered, happy to see her owner's familiar face so soon, and more importantly, with a handful of hay. Emma tossed the hay into her stall and dumped the grain into her bucket which Val took a huge bite of before Emma had even finished pouring. Emma snort-laughed a little to herself; clearly her mare was settling right in.

Emma then began dragging her tack box and other tack down the aisle and stood in the doorway deciding where to put everything. She couldn't help but notice how different the tack box her dad had hand crafted out of cheap wood looked against the fancy, expensively-made engraved ones. It didn't matter to her though; she loved the one her father made her, and it felt like she had brought a piece of home down here with her.

After finding a place for her saddle and bridle, she jogged back down the aisle to plant a quick kiss on her mare's nose who was still only interested in finishing her dinner. Emma laughed again and turned off the lights to the barn, shutting the sliding doors and heading to her car to grab a few essential boxes.

Despite her plan to only unpack a few necessities, she had managed to unload her entire car instead; she was still riding the buzz of arriving, and, at this point, she figured she may as well unpack all the way. Almost two hours flew by, and by the time Emma was putting the last of her things away it was well past midnight.

"*I am going to be exhausted tomorrow,*" she thought. Slightly regretting her decision to unpack her whole life in one night, Emma changed, climbed into her new bed and turned off the bedside lamp. While it was comfortable, it felt unfamiliar. Laying there in the darkness in a strange new place, her mind raced.

Sitting up in bed after twenty minutes of trying to sleep without any success, she flipped on the tv and found a familiar show.

She closed her eyes and listened to the familiarity of the dia-
logue and began drifting off to sleep shortly after.

The bright Florida sun was already pouring into the windows
when Emma's alarm went off. Fumbling to locate the alarm in
unfamiliar territory, she accidentally knocked it to the ground
where it continued to chirp at her.

Groaning, she rolled over and opened her eyes, letting them
adjust to the bright light before sliding out of bed. Her first
thought was that she had not closed the blinds or the curtains
last night and that she would be sure to do that tonight. Dragging, she made her way to the kitchen and tossed some coffee
grounds she had brought from her apartment into the small
coffee maker on the counter. Pausing, she added two more
scoops.

"I'm not sure there is enough coffee in the world for this day," she
thought.

Glancing at the clock on the nightstand, she saw there was still
about half an hour until she needed to be out at the barn.
Opening the fridge, she realized she had nothing to eat for
breakfast. In fact, she had not had much of anything to eat
since her early dinner on the road. Taking a sip of her freshly
brewed coffee that was strong enough to put hair on her chest,
she opened the drawer and pulled out her favorite pair of light-
weight riding breeches and a t-shirt.

"Wearing summer outfits in the winter? I could get use to this," she thought.

"Thank you, Florida," she murmured aloud, slipping into her outfit for the day and pulling her thick hair into a ponytail. Pulling on her tall rubber boots before opening the door to the guest house, she caught her breath a little as she got her first real glimpse of Twin Oaks Farm.

About a quarter acre away was the barn and further out past the barn was a wooden fence line that ran the perimeter of the large property. Closer to the entrance of the property was the main house, and it was expansive. If Emma had to guess, it was probably 3,000 square feet, at least, and had a small pool and large stone patio area behind it surrounded by tropical foliage and a couple strategically placed palm trees.

The outdoor arena was not far behind the barn and was much larger than Maggie's back home. Behind the arena and on the back side of the property were acres and acres of rolling hilled pastures. The pastures were dotted with large oak trees, Spanish moss hanging off them that moved a little in the warm wind. Still standing there, frozen, staring at the most beautiful horse farm she had ever seen, she thought, *"do I really live here now?"*

Jenn was leading a fully tacked tall and stocky dark bay Warmblood-looking horse out of the back side of the barn and waved to Emma when she noticed her. Shaking off the star struck feeling, Emma waved back and headed towards her.

"Good morning, Emma! I hope you slept well."

She hadn't, but she wasn't about to start her first day off by complaining.

"Everything has been wonderful, thank you!"

"Liza and David are at the main house; they prepared a huge breakfast this morning and invited you to stop by when you woke up."

Emma's stomach growled a little at the thought of eating what she could only imagine was a delicious homecooked meal. "That sounds amazing! And who is this handsome guy?" She asked, reaching her hand out gently towards the gelding's large regal looking head, letting him sniff her before petting him.

"This is Freaky Fast, or Jimmy John, as we call him around the barn. He's one of the horses me and the farm co-own as a syndicate; he's an extremely talented show jumper and we hope to move him into the Grand Prix ring later this show season."

Emma was like a kid on Christmas morning. She secretly hoped for a chance to exercise a horse of this caliber while she was here.

"I'm going to work this guy for a bit, but please feel free to head up to the house and get something to eat. Once you're done, you can meet me in the barn, and I can start showing you around a bit more."

Emma thanked the trainer and headed towards the main house. Ringing the doorbell, she was greeted by an open door and a woman in her late fifties with short, light brown hair.

"Well, you must be Emma! I'm Liza and this is my husband, David," she said gesturing Emma in. David waved from the large dining room table just inside the doorway where he was reading a newspaper. "Welcome Emma; I hope you're settling in ok."

"I am, thank you. This place is absolutely beautiful."

Liza smiled warmly at her before saying, "Thank you, we are very fortunate."

David pushed his chair out from the table and made his way to the oven where he pulled a large glass dish filled with what looked like a breakfast casserole out of the oven. Cutting a few slices and putting them on three plates, he set them down at the table and motioned to an empty chair.

"Please have a seat," he said.

Emma smiled at the farm owner and sat across from Liza. David sat back at his original spot at the head of the table, and Emma took a quick bite of the casserole as she was downright starving now. Liza and David took a few bites as well, allowing the clearly hungry girl to have a moment to eat.

"So, Emma," Liza began. "We would love to discuss a little bit about how the show season will work and just a little more about us. We will be here at our Ocala farm for about a month and a half or so to compete, then we take about half the horses to Wellington to show, and then we head back here to finish the season. We attend the Million Dollar Grand Prix together at the end of the season and host a party at our farm afterwards."

Emma remembered from her intensive research that this was a big season finale for the Ocala winter circuit.

"We are at the horse show here in Ocala usually Wednesday or Thursday through Sunday with a similar schedule when we are in Wellington. Horse shows are a lot of work, but our previous working students always said it was the part of the position they enjoyed most, in addition to exercise riding, of course," he added with a wink. The Williams chatted with her for another twenty minutes or so, mostly asking Emma questions about her horse and life back home.

"Thank you for the delicious casserole. I should probably get back out to the barn and see what I can help Jenn with," she said.

"I'm sure she would appreciate it. We will see you later this evening. Have a good first day!" David said. Emma pulled the large dark wood doors of the house open and walked across the spongy ground. The warm, humid air smelled like salt and horses, and in that moment, she felt like she may have been born to live in sunny Florida. By the time she reached the barn, Jenn was already wrapping up her ride and cold hosing Jimmy John. Two other men were in the barn now as well that she had not yet met.

"Ah, there she is! Emma, I would like you to meet two people you will be working closely with." Jenn gestured towards the man closest to her, a shorter medium-skinned forty-something with dark features who appeared to be on his way out of the barn with a full wheelbarrow before he was interrupted. The man dropped the wheelbarrow and walked toward Emma to shake her hand.

"I'm Mateo, it's nice to meet you," he said with a slight Spanish accent.

"Mateo handles most of the stall cleaning, turnout, and basic care. You will be assisting him with anything he needs when you are not in the middle of riding, feeding, or at the show grounds with us. Mateo does stay here to hold things down for us when we are in Wellington, so you will oversee those basic tasks while we are there. I am sure he will be happy to show you how things are done so you are well-prepared by the time we head further south," Jenn added.

The other man, who appeared much younger, perhaps late twenties, stepped forward after Mateo's introduction to shake Emma's hand as well.

"Nice to meet you Emma, I'm Michael Hale."

Michael was much taller than Mateo and Emma, but close in height with Jenn who Emma thought was a little over six feet tall or so. He had light skin, green eyes, short dark brown hair that was mostly hidden by a ball cap and had a rugged, muscular 'working man' look. Emma held back a chuckle that threatened to escape when she thought how this guy was exactly her best friend Mandy's 'Paul Bunyan' type. Although, she and Mandy had always had a similar type.

Not that she had any interest in pursuing a co-worker; friendship was the only thing she was interested in at this point in her life anyway. Jenn jumped in again to help with introductions.

"Michael is our resident handy-man, and usually is the one driving the tractors, horse or golf cart trailers, or fixing pretty much whatever we end up breaking," she said with a wink to him.

"It's so nice to meet you both," Emma replied.

"Hopefully Michael can teach you to drive the golf cart trailer before the show season starts in a couple weeks so that he doesn't have to take as many trips to the grounds with the truck."

Emma had *always* wanted to learn how to drive a truck and trailer but had not had the opportunity until now. Maggie had been great about teaching her so many things over the years, but she was extremely possessive about her truck and trailer, so Emma was afraid to even ask.

"I would love to learn," she said eagerly.

"Ok guys, sorry for interrupting your work. I can show Emma around a bit more from here," Jenn said. Mateo smiled warmly at Emma and welcomed her aboard once more before picking his wheelbarrow back up. Emma turned to where Michael had just been, but he was already turning the corning of the barn and out of sight before she had a chance to say anything else to him.

"I'm sure you are pretty familiar with the barn by now, so we can head outside, and I'll point out a few important things," Jenn said.

Emma followed Jenn outside into the bright mid-day sun as she showed her around the rest of the farm. Jenn pointed out the different pastures and how they handled turnout, the jaw dropping outdoor arena with brightly colored jumps scattered around the deep sand, and the barn office which doubled as a break area since it was air conditioned. She spent a little extra time with Emma showing her all the horses' grain, supplements, and medication and left her a cheat sheet to follow.

"So that's pretty much it! Oh, for reference in case you have any emergency issues with the guest house or anywhere else on the farm, Michael does live on property. He has an RV trailer on the edge of the farm, behind the pastures that way," she said, pointing past the edge of the pastures. Emma had not noticed it before, but she could almost see it at the edge of the property, nestled behind two large oak trees.

"Mateo and his family live up the road a bit, maybe ten minutes away. But if you have any issues with the horses that you are not comfortable handling, I live on property as well in the main house's basement apartment." Emma felt confident she would not have to bug Jenn with anything after hours.

"Most of the work for today is done, and we didn't want to overwhelm you too much your first day. If you would like, you are welcome to get your horse out and ride before you feed the horses in about two hours or so. Just don't forget to do night check before you turn in for the night. I have a chart here of what sheets the horses need, if any, based on what the low temperature is at night. This may be Florida, but it can still get cold at night in the winter!"

"I would love that and will be sure to check on the horses before I leave for the night."

Emma felt a rush of excitement at the thought of riding her horse around this gorgeous farm. Jenn made sure Emma had everything she needed and then headed back up to the main house. The farm was quiet now; Mateo had flagged them down a little while ago to let them know he was headed out, and she had not seen Michael for almost half an hour.

Emma assumed Michael was back at his trailer by now. The sun was just beginning to set; it would be the perfect time for her first ride here. Emma all but skipped down the barn aisle, snagging Valentine's halter off the stall door. In the cross ties, her horse craned her neck to see outside of the open barn doors not far from where she stood.

Emma smiled at her horse and rubbed her soft neck before gently tossing the saddle on her back. Valentine was alert, but calm, as Emma led her out into the unfamiliar territory. Emma swung her leg over the horse and walked her towards the large, open fence-less arena. She let the mare walk on a nice loose rein, letting her relax and take in the scenery. After she felt her muscles were stretched and warmed up, she picked up a trot for another ten minutes and then a canter, enjoying the soft thudding sound her hooves made against in the deep sand.

"Alright, that's enough for one day. We can jump next time, ok?"

Patting the mare, she nudged her on and stepped out of the sandy ring and headed towards the perimeter of the farm. Valentine stretched long and low, snorting softly at the unfamiliar cool evening grass; it was like a whole new world for them both. The pink and orange water-color painted sky was breathtaking above them as they continued to stroll under live oaks and across the soft grass with patches of sand peeking out in areas that were heavily trafficked by the other horses.

Rounding the bend that was not easily seen when standing back by the barn and house, Emma approached the spot where Michael's trailer was tucked amongst a small cluster of trees. The lights were on inside and tv light flickered behind drapes pulled shut. So far, Mateo had gone out of his way to make Emma feel welcome and it wasn't that Michael hadn't, but he seemed much more reserved to the newcomer at the farm.

Emma hoped she could befriend him in time; she was all but alone down here, other than Lily, but both girls were busy at their respective internships, and she knew time spent with her friend from home would more than likely be few and far between.

The last thing she wanted was to appear to be spying on her co-worker, so she nudged her horse forward and pointed her back the other way, heading towards the barn. Once she was far enough away from the trailer, she let the mare walk at a relaxed pace, taking in what was left of the stunning sunset above her. After settling Valentine back into her stall, Emma felt the weight of a long first day catching up with her as she walked back to her guest house. She let her body flop onto her bed without making any effort to break her own fall.

Thinking over her day, she had learned two important things:

One: this farm was probably the prettiest place she had ever seen. Horses, rolling pastures, warm Florida sun, gorgeous palm trees and live oaks and that Spanish moss! To some, it held no comparison to the parts of Florida people typically thought of, such as oceans and beaches, but to her it was a magical horsey wonderland.

Two: this working student position was going to be hard work; possibly the hardest she had ever worked. Which, she somewhat expected going in, of course. But the amount of physical labor it involved was certainly more than she anticipated. However, Emma was a horse girl; she had worked hard her entire life just to be part of this world. Closing her eyes now, her mind drifted back to how it all began for her, even before Maggie bought her barn, when she worked as a riding instructor for a small local barn...

"Emma, do not turn around! And close your eyes!" She could hear Maggie's voice in her head clearly still, even over a decade later. Thirteen-year-old Emma kept her eyes shut but spun around anyway to face the direction Maggie's voice came from.

"Why are my eyes closed?"

"Because I have a surprise for you. Now, before you open your eyes there's something I want to you to know first. You will have to work really hard, but the barn owners have agreed to let you feed horses, turn out and clean stalls on weekends, and in exchange..."

Young Emma's eyes flew open before Maggie was finished with her speech. She gasped audibly and stared wide-eyed at the seventeen hand, dark bay Thoroughbred gelding in front of her. She recognized him; he had arrived at the barn as a sale horse but was older, so she remembered Maggie saying they were being extra picky about buyers because of his age. They wanted to find him the right home, and it dawned on her in that moment that that right home was her.

"Is he mine? No way, my parents can't afford him..."

"Well, Miss Emma, if you had let me finish!" Maggie said, scolding young Emma with a laugh. "Yes, he is yours, and, yes, your parents are able to pay the difference. As I was saying, you will have to be here every weekend to care for your horse and the other horses here too, but that will significantly reduce the board costs. Of course, you can still help me out in exchange for weekly lessons like you have been doing."

Still wide-eyed, she approached her first horse slowly, almost in awe. "Hi Lexington," she whispered to him. Taking his lead rope from Maggie, knowing he was hers, that was all the motivation she needed.

Emma exhaled deeply, remembering the feeling of being handed her first horse. He had been worth every single weekend of hard work, even when all her friends were at the mall or going to movies. For her, horses had always been worth it.

"And this will be worth it too," she said aloud to herself.

Chapter Eight

Emma stood in front of the tall pile of manure, wheelbarrow upturned, wiping the sweat from her brow before it made its way into her eyes.

Sucking in the thick, humid air as she pulled the wheelbarrow toward the ground, Emma shook the last of the shavings into the pile before turning it 180 degrees back towards the barn and her next stall to clean. Her first three weeks as a working student at Twin Oaks had been a whirlwind of manual labor, exercise rides, and lots of sweating. *So* much sweating.

"I may never get used to this Florida humidity," Emma thought, as she angled the wheelbarrow in front of the stall so the horse inside couldn't escape while she cleaned. Ocala was expected to get hit with a potentially severe storm, and it was making the humidity climb with each passing day.

Emma stood, pitchfork in hand, catching her breath a moment before starting on her fifteenth stall of the day. While she and Mateo typically did stalls together in the mornings, he was busy today with some last-minute preparations for the beginning of the winter show season and some tasks the Williams' wanted done so the farm looked perfect. This left Emma on stall duty alone on this abnormally humid day.

Emma felt a nudge on her shoulder and turned around to see Jimmy John clearly interested in either affection or treats. Smiling pleasantly at the tall dark bay, she pulled a treat from the pocket of her breeches that was half smashed, probably one she put in there this morning to give to her horse.

"Shh don't tell Valentine," she said with a laugh as the gelding gobbled up the treat acting like she pulled it fresh out of the bag. She scratched his neck a moment, fine with this kind of interruption in her workday. Gently shifting the horse to the corner of the stall, she began picking it out as she thought about the horses she needed to exercise this afternoon. Jimmy John would be the first of about six she needed to work. It had quickly become her favorite part of every day, and she felt a confidence in her work lately. It was a good thing too, because the first classes of Ocala's Winter Circuit were in five short days and that meant more work and changes in her daily tasks.

Some of the horses she had been exercising for the farm were owned by riders who lived up north and stabled with Twin Oaks seasonally so they could show down south for the winter. Typically, they came in for a long weekend or a week to show, went home, and then came back again a few weeks later to compete again. Emma had tried to hide her jealousy when Jenn had told her this; what life must be like for horse people with money like that?

Perhaps this information could have been a little depressing, and at first, it was. However, Emma felt she had already matured so much in a matter of weeks since she arrived here; perhaps it had to do with leaving her "normal life" back home. More motivated now than she had ever been, she had made it her goal to manage a high-end barn like this, or maybe larger than Twin Oaks, and she was going to work as hard as she had to in order achieve her goals. Especially since she didn't have a college degree to fall back on anymore.

Several of these northern riders were due to fly in tomorrow, weather permitting, and she had been tasked with driving the Twin Oaks company truck to retrieve them from the Orlando International Airport which was a little over an hour away. Emma felt a small sense of pride that they trusted her with this task, and a little bit of excitement; she had hardly left the farm since arriving with the exception being a few quick runs to the grocery store and twice to get dinner with Lily.

Two hours of barn tasks later, Emma was swinging a leg over Jimmy John, glad to be moving on to the exercise riding portion of her day. The big bay warmed up quietly, his walk and trot big and floaty thanks to his large Warmblood-like stride. It was cantering, however, that always fired up the gelding.

Emma focused on relaxing her body, exhaling as she asked for a canter. Shaking his head, the gelding leaped into his typical bouncy stride. She laughed off his antics and let him move out under her until he settled into a nice steady rhythm. He was one of those horses who required lots of "cantering down" exercise, which had been exhausting at first. Emma remembered feeling like she was going to fall off with exhaustion those first few days.

Riding Jimmy, let alone the other five she typically exercised, was enough to burn her out quickly since she was not used to riding this much on top of barn chores. Weeks later though, she was a stronger rider and more fit than she had ever been, and it was beginning to improve her rides on her own horse exponentially. Out of the corner of her eye, she saw Jenn approaching the outdoor arena's gate. Emma sat back in her saddle and asked Jimmy for a downward transition.

"How is our little superstar today?" Jenn said, patting his sweaty neck, his nostrils flaring.

"He was his usual self at first, but he normally isn't this tired after cantering for a few minutes; I think it's the humidity," she said. The sun was reflecting off his glistening neck, and he was breathing heavily, despite the short ride.

"He can be walked out and done. It looks like it's supposed to stay humid all day; let's just stick to a light hack for all the horses so no one gets dehydrated."

"Light hacks it is," Emma said, loosening her reins and patting him as she pointed the gelding towards the open pasture gate. She had made a habit of walking the horses out in a pasture behind the arena that had scattered oaks throughout, which provided a much cooler walk out for both horse and rider.

"Come find me when you're done riding the other horses; we have some things to go over before tomorrow!" Jenn called after her. Spinning around in the saddle, Emma called back, "will do," to Jenn and continued to walk towards the shaded pasture. Five horses and much more sweating later, Emma stood in the wash rack hosing off the black mare she had just ridden, sticking her head directly under the hose at the end. Emma wasn't sure which she wanted more in that moment: a tall glass of water or an ice-cold margarita. "Maybe both," she murmured to herself as she wrung her now sopping wet hair out.

The stall door connected with the latch with a bang as she shut the door, making no effort to let it shut quietly behind the little black mare who was already beelining for the pile of hay in the corner of her stall. Jenn was in the office and peeked her head out when she heard the stall door shut.

"Come on in, Em, the AC is on in here!"

Power walking until she reached the office door, she felt the cool air of the office hit her with welcomed relief. Emma slumped into the chair closest to the vent, wishing she could close her eyes and pass out right there. Jenn reached for the checklist that was laying across the desk.

"Ok so...," she said pausing to read the list. "You are scheduled to pick up the girls from the airport at 4:00 pm tomorrow, so we will have you leave around 3:00 pm. Prior to that, we will have to make sure everything at the farm looks nice, and I know we are supposed to get a storm that starts tonight, so I'm sure there will be some tree branches and things that will need picked up. We can have Michael and Mateo handle most of that and have you focus on making sure the barn and horses are clean and that everything is organized..."

Jenn rattled on about the other items on the checklist, and Emma spent the rest of her energy trying to keep her eyes open and focus on the tasks they were discussing. What was it about this heat and humidity? It had completely wiped her energy out.

"....so that's about it. If you have questions about anything, let me know, but I will leave this list in the office for you so you can reference it tomorrow."

Emma nodded. "I'll make sure everything looks good tomorrow, no problem." Excusing herself, she was eager to finish the rest of her tasks so she could head back to her house sooner than later; she had every intention of going to bed early.

A little over an hour later, Emma was sweeping the aisle when she heard Jenn shutting the barn office door behind her. "Hey, that storm looks like it might be worse than they originally anticipated; let's make sure all the windows on the stalls and the barn doors are latched well tonight, ok?"

Emma nodded, half-awake now, and murmured, "no problem," to Jenn, who might have told her goodnight, but she honestly wasn't paying much attention at this point. All she could think about was taking a cool shower and going to bed. A long sigh escaped her as she began checking the stall door latches, then the latches on the exterior windows, followed by the Dutch doors that led to the back side paddock and finishing with the barn doors as she closed the barn for the night.

Feet all but dragging across the sandy grass, she stumbled through her front door and peeled her dirty clothes off at the door before stepping into the shower turned on cool. Emma stood there a long while, letting the water wash away all the dried sweat and the grime that had been sticking to her for hours.

Ignoring the pile of clothes still lumped up near the front door, she grabbed the first pair of pajamas she could find and shut off the lights before crawling into bed, letting sleep overtake her almost immediately.

Emma sat straight up in bed, a strange sound pulling her up and out of a deep dreamless sleep. Half awake, she tried to place the sound as her mind caught up with her body.

After listening a moment, she identified the sound of screeching trees scraping against the side of the guest house. That may have been what woke her, but there were other sounds she was concerned about now. Pounding rain echoed off the roof, but in the distance was another alarming sound, the thud of a wood door slamming against the side of the barn. The blood drained from Emma's face as she matched the sound to the object making the sound in her mind.

For a moment, she sat in bed frozen at the thought of what this sound meant. Her body and mind caught up to one another in the same instant, launching herself out of bed and snatching her raincoat off its hanger in the closet. She shoved both feet into her tall rubber boots without taking the time to put socks on first. If she was right about that sound, she had time for nothing else.

Emma began opening the door, but a gust of wind pushed the door open the rest of the way for her, revealing heavy rain and wind. Tightening the drawstring around her head, she pushed through the raindrops threating to blind her as she sprinted towards the barn door. She tried to see through the rainy darkness, but the thud of wood in the distance was not visible. The barn door was still latched when she reached it; a slight calm washed over her rattled nerves momentarily knowing the barn doors were still intact. Sliding it out of her way with all the power she had left, she quickly stepped into the barn aisle and shut the door behind her.

Spinning around to scan the barn for the unknown sound, she saw something that stopped her heart for half a beat. Clutching her chest, a moment in panic, she stared at the empty stall and open Dutch door that led to the back paddock. "Jimmy John," she croaked.

Spinning back towards the barn door, she let herself out into the pouring rain and ran as fast as she could toward the paddock on the back side of the barn. Standing there speechless, the wind whipping into her face making it hard to breath as she stared at the empty paddock with the top rail broken on the side closest to Jimmy John's Dutch door. Time stood still for Emma as reality and raindrops slapped her in the face. She should have been formulating some sort of plan, but all she could hear was the sound of rain bouncing loudly off her raincoat.

A sudden thought crossed her mind; perhaps it was not the best plan, but it was the only one that her slow churning mind could come up with at this point. Valentine stared wide-eyed at her owner running full speed through the barn doors toward her. Emma grabbed a halter and lead rope and flung open the stall door, which bounced back off the wall with the force in which she had opened it.

She pulled the halter as quickly and gently as she could over her mare's ears and attached the lead rope clip to one side and tied a knot on the other side of the halter's hardware, looping the makeshift reins over her neck. With a few hops and some struggle to get her leg over the mare's back, she settled onto her bareback and clucked her out of the stall and down the barn aisle towards the open sliding barn door, just open enough to let them through.

Valentine slid to a stop when the hard rain began falling onto her back, throwing her head up and stepping sideways. Emma caught the whites of her eyes as her head flung back. She took a moment to pat the mare and relax her own body in hopes it would convey some calm to the mare. "Please trust me," she said over the pounding rain.

The mare's expression began to relax a little, and Emma asked her forward into the darkness. One ear was rolled back, one forward as they hesitantly trotted forward. They picked up a canter down the farm's fence lined perimeter as Valentine's hooves sucked in and out of the sloppy ground. Emma knew this path well now and felt grateful for all the times she took this route on she and Valentine's evening hacks. The porch light of Michael's trailer at the end of the property was like a lighthouse on the shore as she cantered half-blind down the fence lined path.

It was maybe two minutes or less before she reached his trailer.

"Michael! Help!" Emma screamed his name over and over, hoping she wasn't being drowned out by the screech of wind and rain. If she got off her horse now, she may never get back on. A few moments later, a light flickered on behind the curtained windows, and his front door flew open, catching the wind just as hers had.

"Thank God for thin trailer walls," she thought.

"Emma?" Alarm rang in his voice as he scanned the scene of the girl bareback on her horse, soaking wet now.

"I need your help!" She screamed over the rain. "The Dutch door came open somehow, I swear I checked the latch, but I was so tired and now I'm not sure if it was latched at all and…"

Michael held his hand up stopping her word vomit momentarily, one hand pulling a coat from the chair next to him. "Slow down…what's going on?"

"Jimmy John escaped and he's missing!" She blurted out. Michael paused as Emma had, taking that in. Slamming the door behind him, he approached the horse jigging under Emma, and placed one hand on the mare's neck.

"We need to find him; this internship… it's my only chance at a future career." Desperation was all over her face now, and her voice broke every few words as she held back tears and hysteria.

"Take the far-left side of the property, and I'll check right half. I'm getting on the four-wheeler; we check the entire property first before we panic."

"I'm already panicking," Emma thought but only nodded to Michael instead of voicing her inner monologue.

"Wait here, I'm getting flashlights," he said. Michael jogged to the trailer and disappeared inside momentarily before emerging back into the stormy night to hand Emma a flashlight.

Michael adjusted his ball cap down to shield the rain from his face and took off on Twin Oaks' four-wheeler that was parked on the far side of his trailer.

Emma made a kissing sound to Valentine and she trotted off; the mare's back was getting more slippery by the minute, and now she only had one hand to steer. If there was ever a moment she needed to put her absolute trust in this horse, it would have to be now. Rain continued to pelt their faces while Emma shifted her flashlight from side to side as they trotted back down the path they came from. Reaching the entrance of the farm, Emma doubled back and went through one of the paddock gates in hopes Jimmy John had decided to instinctively run toward his typical turn out spot.

Hearing the low roar of the four-wheeler slowing getting louder as it approached her, she prayed under her breath that Michael was headed her way with good news. Emma used her leg aids and a little rein on her mare's neck to spin her around the opposite way and they trotted towards the headlights of the four-wheeler. It slid to a stop a few feet from the horse, but Emma did not like the look on Michael's face.

"The top rail of one of the perimeter's fences that borders a neighbor's farm is cracked; I think he jumped it and ran off property."

That was not the news she was hoping for.

"How are we supposed to find him now?" She asked.

"Maybe we should let Jenn know what's going on..."

"No way, this is my responsibility. I'm putting a saddle on my horse and I'm going to look for him off property."

Michael stared at her, one eyebrow raised.

"He thinks I'm crazy...maybe I am," she thought. Giving him no time to respond, Emma spun Valentine around and headed back towards the barn.

"Wait."

She pulled up her mare and craned her head around to see Michael following slowly, still on the four-wheeler.

"I'll help you."

Nodding, she dismounted, and hand trotted the mare into the barn. Emma grabbed the essentials from the tack room, wasting no time, and mounted the mare again, ready to head back into the deluge.

Michael was parked in front of the barn entrance waiting for her.

"I'll trigger the automatic gate with the four-wheeler; follow behind me and I'll show you the side gate into the neighbor's property."

"Let's go!" Emma said, walking Valentine out into the night, ducking under the threshold of the barn. Michael slid the door shut behind her to avoid any more of the wind and rain getting in the barn.

The four-wheeler slung mud as he gunned it, getting ahead of Emma and opening the gate for them. Emma stayed on the grassy part that ran parallel to the road and picked up a steady canter as Michael sped down the concrete.

Leaves and debris flew around them, but the mare kept going forward as Emma encouraged her with her voice and the flashlight that lit the path in front of them. Ahead, she saw Michael turn off the road and on to what looked like a path between paddocks. Before she caught up, she saw him swing the gate open that led into the neighboring farm's property. He was already pulling into the pasture area when she reached the gate.

He was pointing towards the back side of the property as he yelled, "Check the back side! I can't get over there with the four-wheeler." Emma nodded, clucking her horse on. Before she reached the furthest fence line of the property, she heard a horse screaming in the distance. The rain was letting up a little now, but the wind was still whipping her sopping wet hair into her face.

Trotting up to the fence, she shined her light out into the distance. A thick forest of trees and foliage covered most of the area beyond the fence line. She still couldn't see him, but she could hear him. Emma doubled back towards the head lights of the four-wheeler.

"Michael!"

He cut the engine, waiting for her to approach.

"What's on the other side of this neighbor's fence? I can't see anything but pine trees and brush, but I hear Jimmy John."

Michael shook his head.

"There is a house tucked maybe two acres out from that fence; it's a very secluded property, mostly pines and brush all the way out there."

"How do we get in there?"

"We will have to go out of our neighbor's property and enter through the driveway of the other property, but it's going to be hard to find him with all that heavily wooded area..."

"So are you helping me find him or not?" She snapped. Michael glanced at the land in the distance, hearing the horse's call somewhere off in the distance. Emma took that as no.

"Good girl Val, let's go," she said with a gentle squeeze around the mare's barrel, steering her toward the property gate they came in through. She picked up a canter alongside the driveway towards the tree lining ahead without looking back to see if Michael was following her. Even if he was, she wasn't going to hear him over the wind in her ears and the sound of hooves suctioning in and out of the ground.

"Thank God you are barefoot," she said, leaning slightly over the mare's neck in a two-point position as her canter turned into a soft gallop along the half mile long driveway. Emma pulled up at the edge of the tree lining, bringing her horse to a halt. She closed her eyes, waiting for the horse to call out again. A minute passed until she heard the horse call out again.

"Gotcha," she said, walking her horse into the pine tree forest towards where Jimmy John had called out. Emma shined the flashlight on the ground directly in front of her horse, walking her cautiously around pine trees as she headed in what she hoped was the direction of the missing horse.

Jimmy John whinnied again, and this time Valentine replied, causing the two horses to call out back and forth for a few minutes as she continued to get closer to the gelding. Her flashlight caught the reflection of two horse eyes in the distance. She shined the light lower, examining him with it as she approached. She could see a small trickle of blood on the horse's front left leg, but nothing wrapped around it. He stood shaking under a tree that appeared to shelter him from most of the rain.

"Jimmy!" She called to the horse who nickered back, clearly happy to see a familiar face. The gelding walked towards the mare, his nostrils blowing wide open; he had obviously been on the run for some time before ending up here.

It was in that moment she realized she had no way to lead the horse back to the barn. She hoped he would follow her mare out of the wooded area...but then what? Lead him back down the spooky road where everything blew around? She didn't really have a choice now. Patting her leg and calling the gelding's name, making all the clucking and kissing horse sounds she could think of, she began a slow trek back towards the clearing. He followed the mare and Emma like a puppy. Once or twice, she considered the possibility she was going the wrong way. Every pine tree looked the same as the last.

"EMMA!"

A voice muffled by the wind and brush between them somehow made its way to her ears. Emma resisted the urge to call back for fear it would spook the already flighty Jimmy John. Following the direction of Michael's voice, she finally saw where the four-wheelers' headlights were shining through the trees. Still making her slow and steady way through the last of the wooded area, she placed one hand on her horse's back to steady her as she glanced behind her; Jimmy was still walking a few feet behind them.

Emma turned back around, taking her first steps onto the grassy area next to the driveway. She could see Michael now that the headlights weren't blinding her; in one hand he held a lead rope, which he gently looped around the gelding's neck, snapping one end to itself to secure it. Michael shook his head, a smile of disbelief crossing his face. "I can't believe you found him."

"Yeah, I had my doubts too," she said with a sarcastic laugh. Emma took what felt like her first real breath since she woke up over an hour ago.

Michael handed her the lead rope with Jimmy John on the other end. "He will probably do better walking beside your mare than he will walking beside my four-wheeler."

Emma nodded as she said, "Good call."

Walking her mare down the long neighboring driveway and then down the road with Michael trailing behind her slowly, they were finally headed towards Twin Oaks Farm. Jimmy remained calm enough as he walked close to her mare, who at this point, was immune to the whipping winds and now light rain that fell. Emma had never been happier to see the lit-up palm trees at the entrance of the farm as she was right now. Michael dismounted the four-wheeler and punched the code in the let them in. When they reached the barn, Emma slid off her mare. Her legs felt like they were made of Jell-O.

"Do you mind getting Valentine's cooler on her for me? I need to look at Jimmy's leg," she said, motioning to the cooler that hung on the bar on her mare's stall.

Michael nodded, touching his ball cap as he did, and led the mare to her stall, pulling off her tack. Emma inspected the gelding's leg which had a small, jagged cut where a stream of watered-down blood was very slowly leaking from the open wound. She wasn't sure what exactly had caused it, but she suspected it had something to do with the wooden rail he had taken out when he jumped out of the pasture.

Emma stood up, pushing her fingers into her forehead as she sighed. "I'm going to have to tell Jenn about this; he may need to see a vet."

Michael had just finished putting on her mare's cooler and turned to her with a worried look. "Look, I know you're worried about losing this internship; I've been here a lot longer, so if you want to leave...," he said, latching the stall behind him.

"She left me in charge of making sure everything was latched. This is my fault; we can tell her together." Emma replied. Michael shot her a sympathetic look and before pulling his phone from his jeans' pocket and dialing Jenn's number.

"Jenn? Sorry to wake you but you'd better come down to the barn. We have a little situation..."

Jenn was at the barn in five minutes flat and clearly had put on the first pair of sweatpants she could find, tossing her hair in a messy ponytail.

Emma stood in the aisleway with Jimmy John now wrapped in a cooler on the other end of the lead rope. The bleeding had stopped with the pressure Emma had applied to it with a piece of gauze, but it still did not look pretty.

"Jenn, I am so sorry."

"Emma what happened here?" Jenn was now close enough to the horse to see the jagged cut on his leg. Emma and Michael took turns filling her in on the events of the last couple hours. Jenn's gaze bounced between them until they stood speechless at the conclusion of their story. Michael shoved his hands in his back pockets and Emma looked down, unsure what the barn manager's reaction would be. She stared at them both a moment, only blinking, before turning to Emma.

"...And you are sure you checked the latches?"

Emma nodded solemnly. Jenn said nothing but headed towards Jimmy's stall where the Dutch door remained open, thudding lightly now against the side of the barn. Jenn examined the area carefully before turning to Emma. "It looks like part of the latch mechanism broke off, probably due to the high winds or Jimmy could have kicked it too, which could have contributed to it snapping. Jimmy has pretty bad storm anxiety, so it wouldn't surprise me if that was the case."

Emma stared at her, not sure whether she should be relieved or not. Did this mean she wasn't fired?

"However...," she continued.

"I should have been informed immediately when you discovered he was missing. Emma, I appreciate you taking responsibility for this and wanting to find him yourself, and it's honestly a miracle you did, but next time inform me right away if there is ever a problem with one of the horses. Understood?"

"Yes ma'am," Emma said remorsefully.

"Now it is three in the morning, and we have a lot going on tomorrow so let's wrap this up. Emma, it looks like the bleeding stopped so let's clean this out, apply some wound cream, and wrap it so he doesn't get shavings in it. I'll call the vet out first thing in the morning. Oh, and let's give both these horses some bute; I'm sure they will be sore once all that adrenaline wears off. Michael, please replace that latch and let's figure out a second form of reinforcement tomorrow so we don't have this issue again."

Jenn turned and walked toward the barn doors. "Oh, and Emma? That's a nice mare you have there. Most horses would have dumped you in the mud long before you found that gelding." Jenn said and winked at the her before she slid the barn door closed behind her.

Emma had not taken a moment to realize just how tired she was until now. As her own adrenaline began draining from her body, it left her with nothing but exhaustion and relief. Michael got to work on replacing the latch on Jimmy's stall as Emma cleaned out the horse's laceration and wrapped it with gauze and Vetrap. Once Michael had the stall secure, she put him back and gave his dark bay neck a pat. "You caused a lot of trouble tonight you know. It's a good thing you're so handsome," she said smiling at the horse who was taking long gulps of water. Emma glanced at Michael who stood near the doorway ready to shut the barn lights off.

She gave her mare a quick kiss on her damp nose and dumped some of the bute mixed in with a little grain that she had pre-prepped into the horses' respective feed bins before heading out of the barn. Michael shut the lights off and slid the door closed before turning to Emma.

"Well, we better go get some rest."

"Yeah, we probably should."

Michael turned, walking towards his trailer.

"Hey um...," Emma stammered. Michael turned back around toward her, and Emma took a few steps his way. "Thank you for helping me look for Jimmy tonight. I know I was probably a little demanding..."

"Just a little," he teased with a smile.

"But it meant a lot that you went after me and honestly, I wouldn't have been able to get him home without you."

Emma took two more steps toward him, closing the gap between them and wrapped her arms around him, pulling him into a hug whether he liked it or not. At first, he stood there, stiff with surprise, but slowly he lightly reciprocated her embrace. His jacket smelled like a mix of wet horses, dirt, and a little bit of lingering cologne. Already mentally blaming the lack of sleep, she inhaled deeper. There was something about Michael that felt safe. Even though tonight marked the first time they truly connected, she felt a security with him she couldn't explain.

Pulling away, she stepped back a few feet, a thankful smile on her face, before turning back towards her house as the now light rain she didn't notice anymore continued to fall.

ele

Morning came too soon for Emma as she silenced the alarm chirping in her ear on the nightstand.

In a way, it was a blessing in disguise that she had gone to bed early last night before her rude awakening; she needed every ounce of extra sleep she could get after running around in the pouring rain for hours looking for a missing horse. Sunlight beamed through the windows as if last night's storm had never even happened. Stepping out of the front door though, her eyes took in a different story. Branches, debris, puddles, and miscellaneous barn items were scattered across the entirety of the property.

"This should be fun," Emma murmured to herself, chugging the remainder of her coffee in one gulp before closing the door behind her.

Normally, Emma loved mornings on the farm; the morning sun, the horses nickering at her in anticipation of breakfast, the smell of the air in the morning that had a little extra salt-air moisture to it. She liked being the first one out here because it gave her a chance to ease into the day before seeing any of the other farm staff, Jenn, or the owners. But today, her stomach was in knots as she strode past the veterinarian's truck parked close to the barn's open doors.

Yes, today was a different day in many ways, and this made her uneasy. If Emma was honest with herself, she was a creature of habit. It's what made moving across the country and starting this job so hard for her at first. But she had come to love this internship, this farm, these horses; it made the weight of responsibility for everything that happened last night that much worse.

Mornings bring clarity, and in this morning's clarity she also felt some guilt for running Valentine all over God's green earth in the pouring rain. Of course, she had been sure to wrap her horse's legs, give her some much deserved pain relief, and throw a cooler over her, but she was no spring chicken; there a was a good chance her mare was feeling sore and tired just like she was. Emma paused at the front doors, wishing she could climb back into bed instead. Walking through the barn doors, she plastered a smile on her face that she hoped wouldn't come off as fake as it felt.

Jenn was standing in the aisle holding Jimmy John's lead rope, and the vet was kneeling beside the small gash on his front leg.

"How is he?" Emma's voice was soft and low. ameow

"Nothing antibiotics and time won't fix," the older vet said as he stood up. Emma watched as the vet headed back to his truck to begin preparing the horse's medication.

"I'm so sorry again Jenn, if there is anything I can do..."

Jenn held her hand up, surely seeing the desperation on Emma's face. "No more apologies; accidents happen, especially with horses. Just keep an eye on him and his wound. I checked on your mare this morning as well, and she appears to be doing ok. Just make sure you pull those standing wraps off her."

"Thank you, Jenn. I assume the horses need fed still?"

"They do, and after that we have a lot of post-storm cleanup."

"Saw that one coming," she thought.

"I'll make sure this place is spotless," Emma replied.

"I'll have Michael help and Mateo too after he finishes cleaning stalls. I had him start on those first thing this morning since we have a lot to do in a short amount of time."

Emma was so focused on what was happening with Jimmy John that she hadn't noticed the wheelbarrow sticking out of the furthest stall at the end of the barn. "Thanks Mateo!" She called to him before heading to the feed room to begin her morning routine. After all her regular chores were done, Emma went to the front of the property where she saw Michael and Mateo were already picking up branches. It appeared they had already grabbed most of the of the farm's items scattered about and had part of the front half of the farm cleaned up.

As she approached Michael, she wondered if he would act differently around her after last night's forced bonding. Before the storm, he had not spent more than a total of thirty minutes a day total in conversation with her, and it was always strictly work related. Michael was always polite to her, and honestly, she didn't know why he hardly spoke to her. He wasn't exactly a "chatty Cathy" with Mateo either, but at least he said more than a handful of words to him.

Emma had always chalked it up to her being the newbie and had considered that he just wasn't the type of person to make much small talk. Mateo, on the other hand, was always talking to her about his wife and kids, the weather, or asking what her life was like back home – pretty much whatever came to mind while they cleaned stalls or turned-out horses together.

Emma felt almost awkward as she closed the gap between them now. Should *she* act differently? Or wait for him to spark up conversation? Besides Mateo and the occasional dinner with Lily, she had no friends here, and it would be nice to have another person to talk to that was closer to her own age.

"Hey guys! How's it going out here?" She asked, hoping to sound more casual than she felt.

"Just cleaning up an endless pile of branches," Mateo said in sarcastic tone. Michael looked up at her, and for a moment she wasn't sure he was going to say anything to her.

"How tired are you today?" He said nonchalantly.

"There isn't enough coffee or ibuprofen in the world. I'm not sure if I'm more tired or sore," she replied, glad he decided to speak first.

Michael made a sound that sounded like a laugh and a grunt put together, and then looked back down at the branches he was picking up. Emma wasn't sure exactly what to say next, so instead she focused on the tasks at hand.

It took them almost two hours to get the farm back to pristine condition. If she thought she felt sore before, she was twice as sore now. Sitting down a moment to stretch her legs, Emma checked her watch which read 2:33 pm.

"I need to get to the airport," she thought. Emma walked quickly to her house and changed into clean clothes, taking a moment to refresh her tired looking appearance. She wasn't thrilled about the deep bags under her eyes, but there wasn't much she could do about that now. Heading back towards the barn, she saw Mateo and Michael were fixing the broken fence in the paddock Jimmy had jumped out of the night before.

Mateo waved as if he knew what she was headed their way to ask. "Keys are in the truck, Miss Emma!"

Michael glanced up, but only nodded at her. Emma brushed off Michael's less than enthusiastic greeting, yelling a "thank you" to Mateo. Letting the sun warm her aching muscles, she strode across the grass towards the Twin Oaks company truck. She let the excitement of getting off the farm wash over her as she fired up the diesel engine and put it in gear. This time of day route twenty-seven was breathtaking. The slow rolling hills dotted with horses and live oaks behind black wood fences laid before her as she drove a little slower than she needed to, taking in the view of some of the prettiest horse country she had ever witnessed, all shining in the late afternoon sun.

A little over an hour later, she was pulling into Orlando International Airport's passenger pickup area. Although Jenn had never disclosed the age of the owner/riders flying in, only their names, she had simply assumed they would be older than her. The thought hadn't crossed her mind that these would be young riders, but looking back on conversations with the trainer, she supposed it made sense. In her mind she imagined thirty-somethings with good jobs who could afford to send their horses to Florida for the winter and spend weekends down here periodically.

In reality, these high school students' parents were the ones with good jobs, and their teenage daughters were the lucky ones who got to spend long weekends at the horse shows.

Emma mentally brushed away the pang of jealousy that flared up at the thought; her teen years had been spent mucking stalls and working a part-time job so she could afford board and to attend local horse shows. However, she knew the caliber of horses and riders who came to Florida to show in the winter; it was the reason she wanted to come down here in the first place. She quickly promised herself not to hold the privilege these girls had against them.

A girl with long dark hair stood next to a girl with dirty blonde hair who waved excitedly when she saw the truck with the Twin Oaks emblem on it. Emma smiled and waved back to the girl as she rolled down the window. The two girls who appeared to be about sixteen threw their luggage into the back of the pickup and climbed in the back of the cab.

"Hi! You must be Emma; I'm Stephanie," said the girl with dirty blonde hair. Her bubbly greeting reminded her of Hailey.

"I'm Ashley," the brunette said softly.

"It's nice to meet you both! I hope you had a good flight."

Both girls said "we did" almost in unison, before picking up where their conversation must have left off while waiting for Emma.

"These girls seem nice enough," Emma thought, turning the radio back on quietly as Stephanie talked a mile a minute, letting Ashley chime in now and then. The girls mostly chatted amongst themselves until they were a few minutes passed the Ocala border. Both girls now had eyes glued to the rolling pastures Emma had been admiring on the way in.

"So, you're from Ohio, right?" Stephanie asked Emma.

"Yes, I am, and I hear you're from Chicago? I actually have some family there," Emma replied. For the next fifteen minutes, Emma and the girls got to know each other, and she began warming up to them.

"Maybe I could be like a big sister figure to them while they are here," she thought to herself.

Suddenly, Ashley caught her breath.

"Is that Post Time Farm?" She asked almost at a whisper as some of the arenas and racetrack came in to view for the first time.

"Yeah, it is! Can we please stop so I can show her the jumper ring? Just for a few minutes...please Emma?!" Stephanie begged.

Emma paused a moment; she had yet to check out the show grounds, and honestly, she wanted to get the lay of the land before the first day of competition. The horses didn't need fed for another hour anyway...

"Ok, but we need to make it fast," she finally answered. Both girls let out a high-pitched squeal as she turned the truck into the long entry road of the farm. One of the jumper rings, where some of the smaller height classes were held, was immediately to her left and trees lined the driveway and were scattered all over the property as far as she could see.

A flutter of excitement filled her at the thought of showing her own horse in that ring. Emma pulled further in the property and found a parking spot. Both girls were leaping out of the vehicle and on to the dusty gravel the moment the truck stopped moving. "Be back in fifteen minutes!" She called after the girls as they sprinted towards the other side of the show grounds.

Shaking her head with a smile at their teenage horse-loving enthusiasm, she turned toward the racetrack that lay in the front and center of the property. About twenty horses were scattered about the track going different paces. Emma walked over to the railing that lined the track and hung her arms over it. She was happy to just stand there and watch as the assortment of horses and riders passed by. The competition was not set to start for a few days, but many riders and horses were already setup on the horse show grounds, using these pre-show days to acclimate to the grounds and school their horses.

Some horses were walking out casually in pairs, their riders chatting about the upcoming show and how their schooling had gone that day. Others appeared to be hacking for fun, trotting or cantering around the outside. Occasionally, a rider who was clearly trying to canter or gallop their horse and would come flying by causing the other riders to briefly stare before resuming focus on their own rides again.

Emma peered around at the low-key activity in nearby barns, vendors starting their setup process or horses being hand grazed nearby. There was something about show grounds Emma loved, even when the competition had yet to start. It was almost like there was a kinetic energy in the air. A few other people were also hanging out on the rail watching the riders on the track, and Emma made sure to shoot a friendly smile to anyone she made eye contact with. It seemed like a good idea to be friendly to anyone she met at the show grounds.

"You never know what connections you can make that may help your future career, and I could stand to make a few more friends," she thought.

Thoughts of her friends back home echoed in her mind; she regretted how secluded she had become on and off after her breakup, and now here she was all but desperate for companionship in her home away from home. Emma pulled her phone from her back pocket; maybe a call to Lily would ease the wave of homesickness that had washed over her. "Emma! How's working student life?" Her friend's familiar voice said on the other end of the phone. Emma caught Lily up on the past few day's events, and with each minute that passed she began to feel better.

"Honestly, Lil, I know we don't get to see each other often but just knowing I have at least one friend nearby, well, sometimes it's the only thing keeping me from wanting to pack up and go back to everyone I miss at home."

"Trust me, Em, I'm in the same boat; I miss home too."

The girls sat there on the phone in silence a moment, thinking of all the things they left behind.

"Ok enough pity partying for us! Speaking of parties, I'm glad you called because I have been meaning to tell you about a huge party Ben David's farm is throwing as a season kick-off. Everyone he knows in the horse world down here is invited and he knows I have a friend interning from home and offered for me to invite you as my guest! I know you said your farm heads to Wellington mid-season, but this party is before you leave."

"Lily that's so cool! I would love to come. Text me the details; I'll be there."

The girls chatted a few more minutes longer, and then Lily excused herself to finish her work but promised to call her friend again soon.

Emma took a deep breath, letting the smell of the show grounds fill her lungs and enjoying this mini escape from her daily working student life.

"I didn't have many friends when I came down here my first year either."

Emma turned to her right where a lean, medium built, dark-haired guy sporting a five o'clock shadow stared at her a few feet away. He had a lead rope slung across his arm and was wearing a backpack. He didn't look like a rider but maybe a groom? She could only assume he was talking to her.

Emma must have had a look of confusion on her face because he quickly added, "Oh sorry, I overheard part of your phone conversation," as he walked a few feet closer.

"I'm Robert, but all my friends call me Bo," he said in a thick southern accent, hand outstretched.

Emma shook his hand and smiled his way. "Emma," she replied.

"Well, it's nice to meet you, darlin. So, I take it this is your first year working down here, huh?"

"Yes, I'm a working student at Twin Oaks."

"Oh yeah, the Williamses, they sure are well known around here. I'm a groom for Highpoint Stables. I'm pretty much always around the grounds, so if you need any pointers, I'm your guy," he said with a wink.

"Thanks, I could probably use all the help I can get."

The man who had been standing next to Bo walked over now, curiosity on his face. "Oh, hey man, sorry, I was just talking to this little lady who's new to the circuit this year. Emma, this is my buddy, Jerry. He works at Highpoint with me; it's actually his first year here as well."

Jerry said nothing but offered his hand to Emma and nodded as they shook.

"Jerry don't say much," he said, jabbing his buddy in the ribs. Jerry didn't defend himself against Bo's teasing but threw Bo a look of annoyance.

"So where are you guys from?"

"I'm from Clay County, Alabama, and Bo is from just outside Atlanta, Georgia."

"Well, it's nice to meet you both...," she began, but Emma was cut off by the sound of two teenage girls jogging toward her, calling her name.

"Sorry, I've got to go. But I'm sure I will see you around next week?"

"Nice meetin' you darlin," Bo said with a boyish smile. Emma stepped away from the two men who had turned their attention back toward the horses on the track.

"I made sure to show Ashley every show ring, and of course where all the vendors will be so we can go shopping in between classes," Stephanie said proudly, beaming at her friend.

"I'm glad you girls had fun but," she glanced at her watch, "we've really got to go."

Both girls frowned a little in disappointment, but obeyed Emma and hopped back into the truck. Emma pulled into Twin Oaks just in time to see Jenn stepping out of the barn. *"Hopefully she won't say anything about why it took us so long to get home,"* she thought. As Emma hopped out of the truck, she caught a glimpse of the back door of the main house opening in her peripherals. Liza and David stepped out, waving at the girls. Stephanie and Ashley waved back and hugged the couple when they reached them, already chatting excitedly about wanting to see their horses.

"Emma, will you please escort the girls to the barn?" Liza asked. "Girls, when you are finished head back up to the house and I'll show you where your rooms are. We are going to get a fire going in the fire pit here in a couple hours in honor of Stephanie and Ashley's arrival. Emma, Michael is still out doing a repair in the barn, but please let him know we would like you both to join us."

"No problem, Liza, thank you for the invitation," Emma replied.

Neither Stephanie nor Ashley waited for Emma as they sprinted towards the barn. Jenn tossed Emma a sympathetic look and mouthed a, "thank you," with a teasing smile as she headed up to the main house. Both girls had their horses haltered and were walking towards the cross ties as she stepped into the barn aisle. "Emma can you please set the fences for us? Maybe some lower ones and a few bigger jumps?"

Emma was almost glad to have a moment of peace from the non-stop chatter that seemed all but constant between the two excited girls.

"Sure, I'll be outside if you need me. Sun sets in about an hour, so don't take too long tacking up, okay?"

Emma smiled to herself, shutting the sliding barn door behind her as she stepped into the arena's deep sand and began adjusting the first jump she came to. *"Your horse and your friends, as horse crazy as you are, were the only things that mattered then,"* she thought, remembering being a horse crazy teenager, although, that seemed like another lifetime ago now.

"You want some help?"

Emma was surprised to hear Michael's voice a few feet behind her.

"Sure, if you aren't busy, thanks."

"Nah, I'm done for the day. I was about to head up to the trailer when I heard those girls ask you to reset the whole arena and figured I'd offer to help. They sure are loud aren't they," he said, chuckling a little.

"That's teenage girls alright. I can't judge them too harshly though; I was probably just like them once."

"I can't see you being *quite* like them," he said, chuckling again.

"I'll take that as a compliment," she said a little sarcastically. They worked in silence while setting up the next few jumps, and Emma began thinking about last night again. Before she had time to edit her inner monologue, Emma began speaking what she had been thinking.

"I hope we can be friends," she blurted out.

Michael's head spun around, a look of surprise on his face. He lowered his ball cap a little, trying the hide the flush of red that flashed in his cheeks. Emma saw it before he had lowered his head though and couldn't help but be surprised at his reaction. He typically showed little emotion and had proven to be less than chatty.

"I'm sorry, that came out wrong," she said, but it was too late to turn back now. She might as well just tell him how she'd been feeling.

"It's just, well, after last night, I hoped things can be different between us. I hope we can be friends because honestly, I don't have many people here that I can consider a friend, you know, besides Lily and she's busier than I am. Anyway, I'm not sure if you even want to be friends, and I know you aren't super talkative per say..."

Michael lifted his head after placing the last pole in the jump cup, and cut Emma's rambling off, laughing a little as he spoke.

"Listen, I get it. I was lonely when I moved down here too."

Emma stared at him a moment, realizing she didn't know any-thing about where he came from. "Where are you from?" She asked. What kind of friend was she? All this time she had been so focused on his aloofness that she hadn't realized she was half the problem. When was the last time she had asked him anything about himself? Before he had a chance to reply, she added, "Michael, I'm sorry. Here I am all but guilt tripping you about not being very chatty when I have made no effort to ask you anything about yourself."

Michael opened his mouth like he was about to answer but was interrupted by the sound of the sliding barn door and horse hooves on the concrete.

"The course looks great, thanks Emma!" Stephanie said.

"Thank you, Emma." Ashley said politely.

"You're welcome. I'm going to sit right over here so just let me know if you need anything," she said stepping out of the arena and onto the grass. Clearly, her conversation with Michael would have to wait. Michael stood up from where he had been making a last-minute adjustment on a jump's height and stepped out of the arena as well. Emma walked over to him.

"Hey, I almost forgot, we were invited up to the main house for a little fire pit celebration tonight. I probably won't go long, I'm still exhausted from yesterday, but I figured I should make an appearance. Liza mentioned you coming as well."

"Sure, I'll stop by. I'm going to change, but I'll meet you over there in a little bit."

"See you then," she said, turning her attention back on the girls who were now warming up and talking about the jump course.

A little over an hour later, the girls had finished riding and were putting their horses away.

"I'll close up the barn, girls, you can head up to the house."

"Thanks Emma!" They said almost in unison again as they jogged towards the light of the fire pit. It was almost completely dark now, with maybe only minutes left of the water-colored painted sky that lingered on the back side of the farm as Emma walked towards the fire pit after shutting the barn down.

Michael, Jenn, Liza, and David were already sitting around the fire, marshmallows hanging on the end of metal sticks as they chatted.

"Glad you could join us!" Liza said, and David smiled in her direction.

"How are the horses tonight?" Jenn asked.

"All tucked in, and I put a light sheet on everyone since the temperature is supposed to drop."

"Perfect, thank you, Emma. Grab a stick and feel free to make yourself a s'more!"

The Twin Oaks team spent about an hour talking and enjoying the fire. Emma enjoyed herself more than she'd expected; it reminded her a little of the times she spent at Lily and Hailey's apartment, but it also reminded her of Liam. She couldn't help but wonder how he was and if she had made a mistake pushing him away. However, the fact that she was here, and he was back home, despite what could have been, made it the right decision to not pursue anything with him.

Who knows? Maybe there hadn't been anything between them after all? It's not like he had gone out of his way to make any feelings known. She shook her head and the thoughts from her mind and told herself to enjoy the present. The last half an hour or so, Emma kept her promise to herself and enjoyed some much-needed bonding time with her co-workers and the young riders. She had to admit, they were growing on her.

"Have a good night, everyone," Liza said, as she and David stood up to go inside. Jenn, Stephanie, and Ashley followed suit.

"Goodnight!" Emma said. Where had the time gone? So much for going to bed early.

"I should probably get to bed soon too. Are you going to head back to your trailer?" She asked Michael. She was exhausted, but part of her still wanted to finish their conversation from earlier.

"I might sit here a few more minutes; I haven't sat around a fire in a while," he said, pushing his hands further into his hoodie pockets and resting his boots on the stone that surrounded the fire pit.

Emma decided it was now or never if she was going to get to know him better. "So, you said you aren't from Florida? Where are you from then?"

"Kentucky," he replied.

"Hey, look at that, we are from neighboring states," she said, with a playful smile. "I'm from Ohio. So, how did you end up here then?" she added.

Michael paused a moment, his forehead scrunching a bit in thought.

"I needed a fresh start," he said, squirming in his chair, clearly uncomfortable.

"Can I ask why?" She asked softly.

"Her name was Jane."

A few minutes of silence passed as they stared into the dying fire.

"She was my fiancé," he finally added. "She went to pick up take-out for us one evening, and she never came home. A drunk driver killed her on impact." Michael cleared his throat, shifting in his chair again. The air hung heavy, and Emma knew nothing she could say would be right. What do you say to someone when something so tragic has happened to them?

"Michael...I'm just so sorry."

"Thank you," he replied. Michael paused a moment before he continued again. "I couldn't stay in my hometown after that. I tried for almost a year, but in the end, I knew I needed to make a big change if I was going to move on. So, I started looking for out-of-state handyman type positions that had onsite live-in opportunities, and when I found this one, I packed up and never looked back."

"Is that what you did back home too? Handyman type work?"

"Sort of. My grandfather is a cattle rancher, and I worked for him on and off most of my life. He had horses too, and always needed something fixed; he taught me everything I know. Of course, I never chased down horses in the middle of a rainstorm until last night," he said chuckling a little.

"Too soon," she replied, laughing too.

"How did you end up deciding to come here? It seems like you miss home a lot. Why come all the way to Florida?" He asked. Emma sighed, making a whistling sound. "I lost my college grants and funding for my last semester of school and was forced to drop out. I was an Equine Business major, and this internship was sort of my Hail Mary for my future career. Most of the farms you want to work for that will give you the experience you need are out-of-state. So, I left home and came here."

Emma and Michael exchanged a glance, then sat in silence; the fire was almost out now. She mulled over their conversation in that silence. She had truly misjudged him, and it seemed they had a few things in common after all. One other thing was now apparent too, his aloofness was not as much a personality trait as it was a consequence of a horrible thing from the past that seemed to haunt him even years later.

Emma felt for him and everything he had been through that led him here and hoped maybe their friendship would pull him from that hard outer shell that he clearly used to protect himself. She'd created a similar emotional barrier for herself after her ex-boyfriend had left her; she understood why he was the way he was.

"We better get some sleep; I feel like I haven't slept in days," she said. Michael laughed a little at that.

"That's because you haven't."

They both stood up and began walking toward the far side of the fence line. Emma glanced at the sky one last time as they approached her guest house, which was crystal clear tonight: a glaring contrast from the night before.

"It was nice talking to you, and thanks for letting me in a little. I can't imagine it's easy to talk about."

"To be honest, I haven't talked about it since I left home. I think my past has made me stubborn when it comes to letting people in, and Mateo doesn't pry like you do," he said with a low chuckle.

"Sorry," she said with a little sarcasm.

"Eh, it's fine. It was nice to be able to say it out loud for the first time in a while. My old therapist would be proud."

"I'm glad I could help. Goodnight, Michael."

"Goodnight, Emma," he said, turning to walk back to his trailer.

Emma hit her pillow a few minutes later and fell into an instant, dreamless sleep.

Chapter Nine

The day prior to the first competition of the season had flown by in a whirlwind of pre-packing what they could into the trailer, bathing the horses, and, of course, all her regular chores.

Emma walked through the barn doors; a feeling of change was in the air. The last three and a half weeks on the farm had been in preparation for this day, and she was bound and determined to make sure everything went smoothly. Jenn was already in the barn, brushing down one of the horses who had managed to cover himself in shavings overnight.

"Good morning!" Jenn called down to her as she walked out of the feed room with the first round of grain for the horses.

"Good morning, Jenn! Is there anything special you need me to do after I feed?"

"Since you will be at the show grounds assisting us all day, don't worry about your regular chores; Mateo will handle things here while we are gone. We will be leaving in a couple hours with the four horses we bathed last night, so just focus on spot cleaning them for now."

Several hours later, Emma was shutting the door of the tack room attached to the packed up and ready horse trailer. The horses were loaded, and they headed to the show grounds located only a few minutes down the road. Emma hopped out of the truck and onto the dry dusty horse show grounds at Post Time Farm. Horses called out to one another from across the grounds as riders and grooms both on and off horses were walking past them; Emma felt an intensified version of that magical electric-in-the-air feeling she had the first day she visited the grounds.

After the horses were unloaded and tied to the trailer, they tacked up Stephanie's and Ashley's horses first as the girls slipped into hunt coats and put on their helmets.

"Alright girls, take a nice long scenic route to the warm-up area by your ring and let your horses check everything out. Emma and I will meet you there in the golf cart and claim a jump to get you warmed up."

Both girls walked towards the far side of the show grounds, chatting non-stop to one another. Jenn and Emma hopped into the golf cart and headed towards where the girls' first jumper class would be. Emma had not yet been this far into the grounds, and it was even prettier than she imagined.

Scattered oaks were everywhere; some were even in the riding rings themselves. The bustle of the horse show was already in full swing, and vendors lined the main dirt road leading to the other rings. White tented barns dotted the outskirts of the back side of the grounds and stretched further out than Emma could even see. Horses were flying over warm up fences as they pulled into the golf cart parking area in front of the warm-up ring. She could see the girls walking up in the distance and took this time to soak in everything going on around her.

"Go trot ladies!" Jenn called out to them as they approached the ring. Emma followed Jenn into the sandy warm-up ring and stood beside a jump until the trainer that was currently adjusting it had finished with her client.

"Stephanie, Ashley...take this cross rail!" She said, dropping one side of the pole and Emma followed suit. Emma and Jenn raised their respective jump cups up several times, and the girls took turns jumping until they had reached just past the height they would be showing.

"Let's walk. Look at the course pictures I sent to your phones; you're four riders out!" Jenn hollered out to the girls.

Emma followed Jenn to the ring's entrance gate so they could watch another rider or two on course. "Emma, can you please grab my boot rag from the golf cart?" Emma nodded and jogged off towards the golf cart. A wave from a few familiar faces caught her eye just before she reached the golf cart. "Emma!" Bo and Jerry stood next to two horses with sleepy expressions in the grassy area near the warm-up ring.

"Oh, hey guys!" She decided she probably had a minute before she needed to get the boot rag to Jenn; after all, there were still a few more rounds before the girls went in.

"How's your first day at the show going, darlin?" Bo asked when she was closer. Jerry nodded politely as she approached.

"So far, so good! Our riders are actually up in a few rounds, so I need to get something for the trainer out of the golf cart, but I wanted to say hi."

"Well, a bunch of grooms and some working students are popping open a cooler near the back side of the grounds near our stable tent if you want to join. It will be right after the show ends, so you'll probably still be here."

Emma had to admit, a chance to meet other people like her would be a good idea. "Sure, I'll stop by for a bit," she replied.

"See you later then, darlin'!" Bo said.

Emma jogged a little faster this time back to the golf cart to grab the boot rag before returning to Jenn. She made it just in time too, because both girls were walking up to the ring and were a round away from their turns.

"Thanks, Emma," Jenn said, wiping off the girls' boots with the rag.

Stephanie stepped in the ring first, looking confident. Her horse picked up a nice forward canter and made it around in the optimum time without knocking any rails down. Ashley stepped in next, and while her horse also picked up a nice on course canter and stayed consistent, he did take one rail due to a bad distance. Poor Ashley seemed nervous and came into a combination a little short.

"That was a great start to the season girls, well done! You have a couple hours before your next class so let's pull off the tack and you can hand graze your horses for a bit." Jenn said to them.

"Emma, if you could please tack up Jimmy John and take him to one of the rings out of the way, he will need some time to canter down a little before I hop on him to warm up over fences."

Emma was thrilled; she may not be showing today but riding around the show grounds was the next best thing.

"Sure thing!" She said, wasting no time as she headed back to the trailer. She had Jimmy tacked up in no time. Emma peeked at the small cut that appeared to be mostly healed now; thankfully it hadn't affected his ability to show.

Emma climbed aboard the tall dark bay and took the scenic route to one of the warm-up rings she had passed that was out of the way. Riders on foot and horseback passed her, and she let the excitement in the air wash over her again. This wasn't her horse, and it wasn't her day to show, but for a moment she pretended it was.

There were only three other riders in the warm-up ring, and it was quiet in this part of the show grounds. She took deep breaths of the still cool mid-morning air and asked Jimmy John to trot long and low to stretch his back and relax. His canter felt even floatier today in this unfamiliar arena, and before long he was offering a nice forward but controlled canter that she knew Jenn would be thrilled about.

After cantering for enough time that she felt he was well warmed up, she let him walk and took a different scenic route back. She knew she had more than enough time to do a little exploring on horseback while he walked out. Emma meandered under the large live oaks parallel to vendor row, stopping a minute to watch the bustling activity before heading to the far back side of the property where tent stabling stretched further out than her eye could see.

As much as she enjoyed the excitement of the show grounds, she couldn't help but be captivated by the quiet, rolling hills scattered with oaks and the stable tents that stretched for acres. Morning dew still clung to the grassy areas that were shaded, and a few people were silently hand grazing horses nearby. Jimmy's ears swiveled as he walked on a loose rein; he seemed to be enjoying this little field trip as much as Emma was. They looped around towards the end of the tent rows and made their way back where Jenn was sitting in a chair under a tree next to their trailer.

"How was he?" Jenn asked.

"Really good, he was really trying hard for me today. I took him on a nice long walk around the property too and he seemed to really enjoy that."

Jenn smiled and scratched the big bay's neck. "Good, I'm glad he got a chance to see everything. We have big plans for this one."

Emma patted the horse's neck before sliding off his side. An hour later, Jenn was mounted up on the gelding and headed to the largest ring at the show grounds, the same one where the Grand Prix and the other large classes were held.

Emma had her eyes glued to the horse as Jenn headed towards the large warm up fences in the warm-up arena, fences so high she couldn't even imagine jumping them. Emma made a mental goal right then and there as she watched Jimmy and Jenn flying over the first warm up jump; someday, she hoped that could be her.

Jenn brought Jimmy to a walk and exited the warm-up area after jumping a few more fences. Emma walked beside them and stood at the entry gate as they watched the last few rounds before their turn.

"Good luck," she told them as she patted the horse's neck before he stepped into the expansive arena. Grandstands lined the far side of the ring and a tented viewing area sat on a hill behind them. Flags flew in the wind silently on the far end of the ring, opposite of where the warm-up area was. The whole area oozed professionalism, and the jumps were brightly colored with sponsorship names on either side of most of them. She was a long way from the schooling shows she attended back home; this place was its own little world of pro riders and well-bred horses.

"Now in the ring is Freaky Fast, ridden by Jennifer Meyers, owned by the Twin Oaks Syndicate."

Jimmy cantered off the moment the buzzer sounded, needing almost no encouragement from Jenn. He had a focused look on his face that Emma had not seen at home or even in the warm-up ring. This horse knew his job, and he was here to do it. Jimmy cleared the first fence, a tall bright orange vertical, with room to spare, landing and turning on a dime towards fence number two. Jenn legged him up to a longer spot to the second fence, a wide oxer, which he soared over as well.

By the last fence Emma realized she had been holding her breath; Jimmy landed without touching a single rail, giving them a double clear round. They were certainly going to place with the time they had made cutting on the inside of two jumps; a move not many riders seemed to be attempting today. Emma beamed at Jenn as she walked out of the gate. "He looked amazing!" She said.

"He's a cool horse, isn't he?" Jenn replied, smiling at the dark bay whose nostrils flared as he jigged under his rider. It was as if he knew he had done a good job and was proud of himself.

"Will you please check on the girls and be sure they are tacking up and getting ready for their next class?" Jenn added.

"Of course!" Emma said, petting the sweaty gelding one last time before heading back to the trailer.

The rest of the afternoon went by quickly; both riders had great second rounds and Jenn took the last horse, a young mare in training, into one of the last classes of the day. The young mare, who was still very green, had a refusal at a scary looking fence, but managed to get over it the second time and finished strong.

Overall, Emma felt good about her role in what she considered a successful first day of the circuit. Emma took the young mare to be cold hosed, and the horses stood by the trailer eating out of hay bags as they dried.

"Emma lets go ahead and load up the horses; we are all done for today," Jenn said, untying Stephanie's horse from the trailer as she spoke when Emma arrived back with the young mare. Once everything was loaded up, Emma decided to approach Jenn about the get together.

"Hey Jenn...would you mind if I hung out here another hour or so? I was invited to a little get together with some of the other grooms and working students."

Jenn paused to think a moment

"Sure, that's fine; just be sure to be back within a couple hours to do night check on the horses before you head back to your house. I can throw feed to the horses for you tonight. Have a good time, and thanks for all your help today, Emma. You did a great job."

Emma felt her heart swell; it had been a long exhausting day, but she felt good knowing her hard work had paid off. The sun was just starting to set as she headed towards the tents that lined the back side of the show, parallel to the rings, where Bo had said his farm's stable tent was.

Emma heard laughter and loud chatter behind one of the tents and saw a small group of fifteen or so people chatting around an open cooler. The group was a mix of males and females of varying ages but most seemed to be early-twenties to mid-thirties if she had to guess. Bo spotted her heading their way and waved.

"Everyone, this is Emma, she's new this year and a working student at Twin Oaks."

"Hey Emma," a few said before resuming their conversations. A younger woman, maybe late twenties, that had been standing on the outskirts of the group approached her. "I'm Callie, it's nice to meet you." she said.

"Emma," she said, shaking her hand.

"This is my second year, but I remembered how it felt being the new kid on the block here," she said with a smile. "Where are you from?"

"Ohio," Emma said.

"Oh cool! I'm from Massachusetts. Being in Florida sure does beat being back home in the winter, doesn't it?"

"I can't say I miss not feeling my face this time of year," she laughed. The two young women talked for half an hour, sharing their background, and talking about horses: the easiest conversation in the world for Emma and for her new friend.

As Emma chatted with a few others in the group, one thing was becoming clear to her; the realization that almost everyone she met here was a lot like her. Most were far from home and came here to work with the love of horses as their focus. Emma sat on the grass, sipping the beer she had just pulled from the cooler and the day seemed to catch up with her all at once.

Bo saw her sitting in the grass alone and sat beside her. "Havin' fun?" He asked in is typical thick draw.

"I'm having a great time. Thanks again for inviting me."

"How did your first day on the grounds go?" He asked.

Emma spent the next twenty minutes talking about her day, and Bo sat closely, listening to her go on and on about the farm and the horses.

"So do you have a horse of your own too?" She asked.

"Nah, I didn't know much about horses until my cousin told me about being a groom. He worked for a local farm that also traveled to Florida in the winter and got me a job with them at first. A couple years ago I got hired on with Highpoint and then got my buddy Jerry a job too."

Emma was a little surprised by this; she couldn't imagine working with horses and not having an outside interest in them. Horses had always had a pull on her soul she couldn't explain; but it seemed not everyone who worked in the horse industry had the same feelings she did.

"Do you like your job though?" She asked out of curiosity.

"Yeah, horses are pretty cool I guess," he said with a shrug. "But the best part is meeting pretty ladies like yourself," he said, scooting a little closer.

Emma smiled, not sure how to respond to that. She quickly changed the subject and they talked about some of his favorite places to go in Ocala on his days off. Bo followed Emma's eyes down to the raised jagged scar that ran from the top part of his hand and down his wrist. She hadn't meant to, but she been staring at it on and off for the last few minutes of their conversation.

Emma blushed; she felt bad about subconsciously staring at it.

"I'm sorry," she said in a broken tone.

"It's aight. Old motorcycle accident from when I was a teenager," he said.

"That must have been terrible; I shouldn't have stared," she said.

"I had a rough childhood; I did dumb stuff back then thinking I was invincible."

"Can I ask why?" She asked quietly.

"When I was a little kid, I watched my momma die of cancer and it really screwed my dad up; me too I reckon. Turned him into a raging alcoholic so I had to raise myself, I guess. He only paid attention to me when he wanted somethin' from me."

Emma wished she had a better response than "sorry" again. But what else could she say? Before she could answer, Bo chimed back in with, "I'm getting another beer, want one?"

Emma checked her watch before answering, sensing it was getting late.

"Hey, actually, I better call an Uber or something. I need to get back for night check on the horses. It was nice talking to you though," she said brushing the grass off as she stood up.

"Our farm is just up the road; want me to take ya?" He asked.

"That would save me some time waiting for a ride, sure, thanks."

Bo motioned toward the back parking lot where many of the riders, trainers, and grooms not pulling trailers parked for the day. The show grounds had become almost eerily quiet, aside from the random horse calling out or snorting as they munched on hay.

"This is me," Bo said, unlocking the truck. He walked towards the passenger door of the truck and opened it for Emma to get in. Emma turned around to thank him but hadn't noticed how close he was to her and bumped into his shoulder lightly.

"Oh sorry...," she began, but before she had time to finish, he had wrapped one arm firmly around her waist, pulling her in tightly and was leaning in to kiss her. She firmly pushed him away, ducking under his arm to completely escape his grasp. Surprise was written all over her face as she backed away from him.

"Um, I'm sorry if I gave you the wrong impression, but...I'm not really trying to..." She was so thrown by his unexpected gesture that her words were coming out jumbled. Before he had time to speak, she spun around and started walking away quickly.

Had she given him the wrong impression? She replayed their conversation in her mind. Sure, she had been friendly, but she had not given him any signals that she was interested in anything but friendship. She wiped away angry tears as she was thinking about the fact that she may have just ruined any chance she had at making friends here; all the people she met tonight were friends with Bo and Jerry. It was embarrassing to say the least, but more than that, she felt violated. There was no going back from what he did.

Emma hadn't really planned out where she was walking to, and at this point she was in no mood to sit in a car with a perfect stranger. Pulling her phone from her pocket, she called a saved number.

"Michael? I need a favor..."

Michael's truck tires crunched to a stop on the gravel road of the show grounds less than fifteen minutes later. Emma pulled the door open and climbed inside, tossing him a thankful look, hoping the truck's dim interior light was hiding her red eyes.

"Emma, are you ok?"

"So, he did notice," she thought.

Like a dam breaking, Emma let the story of how the night had unfolded come pouring out. Michael's forehead scrunched as he looked out the windshield where the headlights shined on the gravel in front of them.

"He did what?" He asked, his voice low and gruff. Emma wasn't sure she had ever heard him sound this way.

"Michael, really, I'm fine. I'm still not sure how it happened, but maybe I somehow led him on? I don't know..." Emma bit her lip to keep it from trembling as she attempted to keep her emotions in check.

Michael shook his head, clearly in disagreement with her statement but pulled the truck away from the grounds toward the main road. Emma exhaled, glad that they were headed back to the farm; she just wanted to check the horses and go to bed.

"There is no excuse for his behavior," he finally said in a low voice as they pulled in the farm's entrance. Michael stopped short in front of the barn doors and turned toward Emma.

"You sure you're ok?"

"I'm ok. As soon as I pushed him off me, I walked away, and he didn't follow me. I honestly just want to forget it ever happened," she said, opening the passenger truck door. After her feet hit the ground, she turned back toward the truck's interior.

"Thank you for coming to get me. I really needed a friend tonight."

"Anytime," he said.

Emma shut the truck door as softly as she could, hoping not to wake anyone up, and slid through the sliding barn doors to check on the horses before heading back to her guest house.

—ℓℓ—

"Emma, can you stop in the office when you are finished with that stall?" Jenn's voice said, echoing down the barn aisle.

"Sure, I'm almost done!" She called back, sifting the last bit of shavings through her pitchfork from the pile in the corner she had be working on. After she had finished picking through the remainder of the stall, she dumped her wheelbarrow and headed to the barn office. Jenn was reviewing some paperwork when Emma knocked on the door, pushing it open the rest of the way.

"Come on in," she said, and Emma slid into the chair across from the desk, happy to have a moment in the air-conditioned room.

"So, I have a little field trip I need you and Michael to take this afternoon," Jenn said, pulling a piece of paper off the top of the stack she had been looking over when Emma came in the room. Jenn wrote an address on the back of the flyer. Handing Emma the paper, she saw a picture of one of Twin Oaks' young project horses, Ellie, on a for sale ad.

"A farm near Williston has agreed to take Ellie on a trial and potentially purchase her. I need Michael to haul her over, and I need you to make sure the horse gets off the trailer and settles in alright. They said they may want you to do a quick hack on her for them so they can watch her go around with someone she knows, so bring your tack and gear just in case. I also thought this may be a good opportunity for Michael to give you a crash course on driving the trailer once it's empty after she's dropped off. You two can get ready to head out now; they are expecting you in about an hour or so."

"I'll get Michael. I think he's still out back repairing one of the fence boards."

"Thank you, Emma, and let me know how it goes when you get back."

Emma all but skipped down the barn aisle on her way to the pasture where she had last seen Michael fixing a fence. Getting off the farm for a bit was always a nice change of pace; learning to drive the trailer and seeing another local farm was borderline exciting. She spotted him hammering a nail into a fence board as she approached.

"Hey you," she said beaming, still riding the high of their impending field trip. Michael smiled back but tilted his head sideways curiously.

"Why are you so excited?" He asked.

"Because you and I have been assigned to take Ellie to a farm near Williston. They are taking her on trial, and Jenn has also tasked you with showing me the ropes on driving the trailer on the way back," she said, each word dripping in enthusiasm.

"Is that so? Well, it's a good thing I'm an excellent teacher then, isn't it?" He teased, his green eyes sparkling as he spoke. Truth be told, the thought of spending some time alone with Michael was part of her enthusiasm for this trip. Things had certainly changed between them, and since they had, she was excited for this little break from the farm. Work had simply been too busy to allow for any deep conversation between them since the night of the incident with Bo. Not to mention, she had not quite been herself the first few days that followed that night.

However, the way Michael had now come to her rescue, twice, and the way he acted around her now made Emma sure he cared about her in some way. It made her want to know more about what made him tick.

"I'm supposed to bring tack in case they want to see her ridden, so I'll get her and the tack ready if you want to get the trailer hooked up?"

"Deal," he said already walking toward the Twin Oaks truck.

Twenty minutes later, Emma was loading Ellie and the tack into the trailer and she and Michael were driving out of the Twin Oaks gates.

It was a perfect day for driving, seventy something degrees and sunny. Emma had not been this direction on route 27 and spent most of the trip with her eyes glued to the scenery passing by with the rolled down window.

They arrived at the farm a short twelve minutes later, and a woman who appeared to be in her forties stepped out of the large grey barn moments after the truck tires hit the gravel driveway. Emma slid from the passenger seat and walked over to shake the woman's hand.

"You must be Emma. I'm Shirley, it's nice to meet you."

"Nice to meet you! I'll get Ellie off the trailer for you; were you wanting me to ride her for you?"

"Would you mind? My client is here too and would love to see her ridden by someone who knows the mare."

"Not at all, I'll get her tacked up and meet you at the arena. Does that work?"

"Perfect, thank you." Shirley said.

Emma pulled the dapple-grey mare off the trailer and tied her on the side of it so she could tack her up. After tacking up Ellie, she mounted and walked the mare through the already open gate of the spacious outdoor arena. Shirley and her clients were already hanging over the side of the fence, anxious to see the prospective horse go around. Michael followed behind Emma, closing the arena gate for her after she stepped through. He folded his arms and rested them on the top rail, his eyes following Emma and Ellie.

She hadn't expected to feel the small wave of nerves that came now that all eyes were on her and the young mare. Emma asked the mare into her floaty trot, sitting easily for a few extra beats hoping to showcase how comfortable it was to sit her trot. Ellie trotted along, her typical easygoing demeaner despite her age was apparent. Emma asked Ellie for her equally floaty canter, sitting it easily as well.

Glancing over briefly to where Michael stood, she noticed a look on his face she had not yet seen. Admiration, maybe? His eyes were wide and glued to her, or maybe to the horse? She couldn't be sure. Bringing Ellie back to a walk, Shirley came around the ring and entered the gate.

"She's lovely Emma, thank you for riding her for us. If you want to pull your tack, I think my client is going to hop on her while she's warmed up. Please thank Jenn again for us and let her know we'll be in touch."

Emma pulled her saddle off Ellie, and Michael handed Shirley the mare's halter. She gave the mare a quick pat while saying, "be good for your new owners," and headed back to the truck. Michael drove a few minutes down the road until he found a large empty parking lot and he and Emma swapped seats.

"Ok Em, just drive around the perimeter of the lot nice and slow, get a feel for how the trailer feels behind the truck. Remember, stop slower than you think; you need to get used to the feeling of the trailer pushing the truck when you stop."

Emma nodded, putting the truck in gear and circling the lot several times, getting the hang of it by the last lap.

"Good, now let's work on the hard part: backing up. Put your hand on the bottom of the steering wheel. If you want the back of the trailer to go to the left, turn your hand to the left. If you want the back of the trailer to go to the right, turn your hand to the right. If you want the trailer to move sharply, turn the steering wheel before you move the vehicle. Got it?"

"I think so," she said, putting the truck in reverse and her hand on the bottom of the steering wheel like he instructed. They practiced backing up for twenty minutes or so until Emma felt she had a firm grasp on it.

"Not too bad for your first time," he said, looking over at her as she put the truck in park.

"Well, I had a pretty good teacher," she said, grinning broadly his way.

"By the way Em, I'm not sure I realized what an incredible rider you are until today," he said, his eyes looking to the floor now. Emma caught his cheeks flushing a slight pink despite the ball cap that partially hid them.

"So, maybe that was some form of admiration I saw," she thought.

"You've seen me ride at Twin Oaks countless times...," she started.

"I know, but usually I'm in the middle of something. Today was different; I was able to *really* watch."

"Did you ride much? I mean, at your grandfather's ranch back home?"

"I wouldn't say I was all that good at it, but I rode a couple times a week growing up, in the summer mostly. My Grandpa Joe is the real rider and horseman; he truly loves his horses. They are his co-workers on the ranch in a sense, and he always made sure I understood the importance of caring for them and treating them the way they deserved. It's part of why I took this job; I may not be much of a rider per say, but I love being around the horses. They were one of the only things that gave me peace after Jane died."

It was then she realized they had even more in common then she already knew. Horses had always been her safe place, her happy place. The thing in which she found the most peace herself. Perhaps it was also part of why she felt naturally safe with him; they were quite like minded, she was discovering. And of course, the fact he had come to her rescue twice now helped with that feeling of safety when she was around him.

"That's how I've always felt about horses too," she said quietly.

He looked back over at her, holding her gaze a moment.

"When you first came to the farm, I know I wasn't the most welcoming. You should know, that wasn't your fault. It's because you remind me so much of her, of Jane, I mean. She was a lot like you; sweet but strong willed, funny, passionate...," he trailed off a moment, pausing before he spoke again. "The more time I spent with you, the more I realized it. I guess in a way I felt guilty for feeling drawn to you like I had been to Jane. So instead, I pushed you away and kept you at arm's length. Of course, like it or not, you took a sledgehammer to those walls I put up," he said, laughing lightly.

Emma remembered thinking that night with him by the fire pit that his aloofness was due to his grief over his fiancé. In hindsight, his rection to her those first few weeks at the farm ran much deeper than she could have imagined.

"I'm sorry, I had no idea I made you think about her like that...," she began.

"Don't be. Jane would have wanted me to have a friend like you."

"Do you still miss her?" She regretted asking the moment the words left her lips, but still, she wanted to know.

"Every day. But in a different way than I used to. Her memory doesn't make me sad anymore; it brings me peace. Truth be told, your friendship has helped with that. It's why I felt so guilty at first, but now, I'm thankful for it and I've made peace with moving forward."

"I'm glad we are friends too," she said, resting her hand on his shoulder a moment.

They locked eyes and held one another's gaze a moment before Michael finally spoke again.

"Alright Em, you ready to drive this rig home?" He asked, motioning towards the road just outside the parking lot.

"Ready!" She said, putting the truck into drive as she headed towards the road ahead of her.

This had been much more than the fun off-the-farm field trip she had anticipated.

Today had been the day she realized just how much Michael and his friendship meant to her. They were no longer simply friends because of proximity. And perhaps, he felt the same way too.

Emma stood next to Valentine as she brushed off the dirt that had managed to settle on her back on the short trailer ride over to the show grounds from the farm. Trying to shake the nerves off, Emma pulled her tack from the horse trailer tack room; today was the day she showed for the first time in Florida.

This was a moment she had waited for since the day she had accepted the internship, and she wasn't going to let anything get in the way of being the best rider she could be for her horse. Stephanie and Ashley stood nearby, both horses were pulling thick mouthfuls of grass from the ground while their freshly hosed coats glimmered in the late afternoon sun. Jenn was already at the ring watching a few rounds of Emma's class and told her she would be there to school her over a few jumps before it was her turn.

Another wave of nerves and nausea flooded her; this was certainly a far cry from the schooling show back home. Valentine had been doing so well schooling back at the farm since they arrived, and she had no reason to be this nervous, but she was.

Emma still remembered her very first horse show back home when she was just thirteen years old. She had been so nervous she almost threw up. Maggie had pulled her aside, sat her down and told her, "It's ok to be nervous; being nervous just means you are passionate about what you're doing. You wouldn't be nervous if you didn't care, but don't let those nerves affect your ride. Turn the nerves back into passion and give it your all."

Today, she would channel her nerves back into passion, just as she had when she was younger. Emma swung her leg over Valentine's back; the mare's ears were pricked and swiveling, taking in the atmosphere. Clucking to the mare, Valentine walked on at a steady pace but still looked around wide-eyed at the bustling activity around her.

Emma took her typical scenic route to the main jumper ring, taking this time to let her own mind, as well as her horse's, relax a little. She had spent the last few weeks at this horse show, and she felt like she knew this place inside and out already. It was strange to think a week from now she would have her world turned upside down once again when they made the trip to Wellington.

Walking along, she thought about the research she had done last night, partly to take her mind off today's competition, and partly because she wanted to get an idea of what it would be like. It turns out, Wellington is nothing like Ocala. It may be just under a four hour drive, but the fact that these two cities share a state and are both home to some major horse shows seemed to be the only thing they have in common. At least, according to her preliminary research.

Emma shook her head, clearing her mind; she could think about the move to Wellington later. Right now, she needed to focus on her horse.

The warm-up ring just outside of the ring where she'd be showing was packed. Emma turned to look at the same ring both Stephanie and Ashley had ridden in countless times now. A large oak tree sat in the dead center of the ring; she remembered thinking how cool it was. Now, all she could do was stare at the over three-foot-high fences of the winding course in front of them.

"Go trot, Emma!" Jenn called to her as she approached. Emma exhaled, willing her body to relax before asking for trot; her horse was a typical chestnut mare and fed off her every emotion. Valentine curled her neck and Emma felt the tension in her horse's body.

"You're still not relaxed," she thought to herself.

This time, Emma focused on every muscle in her body; the more she focused on her own position, she felt her mare respond by being lighter and more relaxed. Emma asked her horse to pick up her rocking-horse style canter, still focusing on keeping a light connection and focusing on her own body's position.

Valentine rolled out from underneath her with a soft floaty canter and some of that sick to her stomach feeling lessened with each passing stride. Jenn was standing next to a good-sized cross rail, waving her down.

"Come take this cross rail!" She shouted over the sound of the other trainers and pounding hooves all around her. Emma sat in a light three-point position and clucked lightly at the base of the fence; the spot she saw was a little deep.

"Come again!" Jenn shouted, as she put up both sides of the jump to create a vertical.

Emma sat down in her saddle, keeping her body tall and feeling each stride as she focused on the other side of the fence, counting down the strides in her mind.

"3...2...1..."

Valentine soared over the single vertical, shaking her head as she landed. Emma laughed at this; the mare loved the bigger jumps a little too much.

"Circle Emma!" She called out, setting the back rail up this time to make a ramped oxer. Jenn waved her back over, and Emma circled one more time to regulate her pace before approaching the intimidating oxer. Emma closed her leg and sat up tall. "3...2...1," she said, aloud this time.

Valentine took off from a long spot but powered over the oxer with ease and sped up a little this time after the fence, shaking her head harder than before. Emma smiled at the mare's antics; this horse loved to jump.

"That looked good! Let's walk to the gate," Jenn said.

Emma nodded in agreement; with this mare, as she had learned from experience, it was best to stick to a couple warm up fences and be done before she went into full on "dragon" mode. They watched the rounds before her turn, discussing what turns and paths the rider took and what the best path would be for them as well. Emma swallowed hard as the gate keeper smiled at her and said, "You can head on in."

"Next to go is Valentine ridden and owned by Emma Walker," the announcer stated through the loudspeaker.

Emma beamed despite the butterflies doing summersaults in her stomach. This was her horse that came from the back of some dusty round pen at an auction in Ohio, and she was now out here about to compete with the best of the best in her division at a horse show almost every rider would recognize by name. A sudden determination to prove what her horse could do came over her, replacing the butterflies.

Emma halted, petting her mare on the neck to calm her as they waited for the buzzer that chirped in her ear moments later.

Barely having to ask with her leg, her mare cantered off strongly towards the first fence which she took out of stride landing as she hunted down the next fence that was only a couple strides out.

She was halfway around the course before she knew it, flying down the long side of the ring through a six-stride line. Landing, she turned her body and stepped into her outside stirrup, asking the mare to turn on her haunches as they took the rollback fence. Another sharp turn led her to the second to last fence; Emma felt the horse take off too early and made sure not to catch her in the mouth over the jump. Valentine was soaring over everything with room to spare though and had no interest in touching the poles as usual.

Emma kept her focus, the last fence always felt like the hardest, last-fence-itus as she called it. Valentine had a blistering pace now and seemed to gain a little more sped after each fence. Emma closed her legs, and half halted as her horse locked on to the final fence.

Emma felt her horse leave the ground earlier than she anticipated and she stretched her arms towards the mare's ears, staying off her back and out of her mouth. She felt the mare's hind leg rub a rail but waited until they landed before looking back; it had stayed up.

"Good girl!" She all but yelled as she scratched the mare's neck, still cantering towards the in-gate, pulling her up at the last minute as the gate keeper rolled it open to let them out. Jenn smiled up at the pair and patted the mare's neck too as she took a rein to slow the jigging mare down as they moved out of the way of the next rider.

"She looked great out there Emma, and so did you. I'm sure that was a placing round; it looks like you made good time. Go walk her out; I'll see you back at the trailer."

A certain bliss that follows a good jumper round hung in the air around Emma as she walked towards the shaded path at the outskirts of the barns. Valentine needed to be reminded to walk instead of trotting several times; she was clearly proud of herself as well. Walking down the dirt path of the horse show grounds, Emma soaked in that, "it was all worth it," feeling. Nothing could shake this feeling today.

Nothing that is, until she saw Bo and Jerry leaning against the rail of the track where she was headed to finish walking her horse out. Both men stared at her as she approached.

Emma had made every effort to avoid Bo since that awkward night a few weeks back. She had been successful so far, only once had there been a close call. Last week, while hand walking one of the horses, she had rounded a corner to see Jerry facing her and Bo with his back turned to her. Emma had quickly made an about face, however, it was still possible Jerry saw her. Either way, she hadn't stuck around to find out.

The thought had briefly crossed her mind to hunt them down and clear the air, but as more time passed, she felt more awkward about approaching them. Especially after everything Bo had told her about his past; it wasn't that she was excusing what he did, but maybe in her mind she justified his actions because of it. But here she was, unable to pretend she didn't see them. She was either going to have to face Bo and have an adult conversation about what happened or steer her horse away and really make it awkward.

Emma exhaled silently. "*Adult conversation it is,*" she thought.

"Hey guys," she said, trying to sound casual but it came out sounding weak and breathy; she cleared her throat.

Jerry and Bo exchanged surprised looks. "Well look who it is," Bo teased "Where ya been, Emma?"

Emma felt her face flush red; she hoped it wasn't as obvious as it felt. "I've been pretty busy," she said, hoping her voice sounded more confident about what she was saying than she felt. "Um, Bo...," she stammered, not sure how to say what needed to be said. "...Listen, I'm not sure if I gave you the wrong impression, but I'm not...well I'm not interested in you that way and..."

This wasn't going well.

"Ah, it's aight little lady," Bo said cutting her off. She couldn't tell if he meant that or not, but at this point she was too distracted by the way Jerry was staring a hole through her. Honestly, he looked more thrown off at Emma's presence than Bo did. What had she done to Jerry? He wasn't even the one she rejected. Maybe it was some sort of bro code? She also didn't like how casual Bo was being about all this.

"Well, actually it's not alright. You shouldn't have done what you did. Either way, I leave for Wellington next week, so you won't be seeing me around, but I just wanted to clear the air once and for all."

She wished she hadn't said that part; she just wanted this conversation to be over, but she might have added fuel to a fire.

"Wellington?" Jerry asked, cocking his head. Emma was pretty sure this was the first time Jerry had spoken to her since the day they met.

"Yeah...my farm goes there for a bit to compete and then we come back here to finish out the season."

Why did she feel like she was being quizzed?

"Anyway, I've got to get this girl hosed down; I just finished walking her out," she said.

"Pretty horse," Bo said, looking the mare up and down.

"Thanks..."

"Haven't seen her compete here before," Bo interrupted.

"Oh well, she hasn't...she's mine actually."

Despite the awkwardness of the moment, Emma couldn't help but smile down at the mare momentarily but quickly remembered she was trying to end this conversation.

Before the conversation could go any further, she spun the mare around and began walking toward the trailer. She left no time for them to respond but heard a muffled, "see ya," behind her in between the sound of her horse's shod hooves clanking against the concrete.

You know that, "I'm being watched," feeling? Emma still felt it lingering even after some distance away from the men, so she spun around in her saddle. A cold chill ripped through her when she saw the way Jerry was still staring holes into her. She turned back around quickly, pushing the tense conversation with the two men from her mind. By the time she arrived at the trailer, her focus was now back on cooling her horse down.

After sliding her tack off, she led the mare to the closest wash bay and hosed her down. Valentine craned her neck and lipped at the water coming out of the hose, splashing Emma; she couldn't help but laugh at her quirky mare. Treating her horse to a nice long hand grazing session first, she walked the mare back to the trailer. Everyone else was already finished showing for the day, so Jenn and Emma loaded the horses back into the trailer and they headed back to the farm.

Michael and Mateo were in front of the barn chatting and clearly waiting for them when they arrived. *"Jenn must have sent them a text letting them know we were on our way back,"* she thought. Emma hopped down from the truck and the two men walked over, ready to help unload the trailer; it was the last day of the show for the weekend, so everything needed cleared and cleaned out. Michael met Emma at the back side of the trailer as she slid the latch out of the way, ready to pull the ramp down.

"How was Valentine?" He asked.

"Michael, she was amazing; honestly, she surprised me today. We placed fourth out of a competitive division; I think there were about twenty riders in our class."

"That's great, Em," he said, smiling at her.

She was thankful for the friendship that had formed between them. No thanks to the way the night had ended with Bo a few weeks back, she hadn't gained the group of friends at the show she had hoped for. The only person she managed to form a friendship with was Callie, who she had run into a few times on the grounds and got along with very well. Unfortunately, Callie was close friends with most of Bo's and Jerry's mutual friends, so that had been the extent of their friendship thus far.

Emma had since thrown herself into her work and training Valentine; perhaps the more time she spent here the less she cared about being lonely? Or maybe the few friendships she had in Michael and Lily plus calls back home were just enough now? Either way, the incident with Bo had squashed her need for additional friendships here in Florida.

After everything was unloaded, Mateo pulled a wheelbarrow around to clean the trailer while Michael helped Emma begin putting everything back where it belonged.

"You're never going to believe who I ran into," she said, as they cleaned bridles.

"Who?" Michael asked.

"Bo and Jerry."

Michael shot her a glance; he had already made his feelings known about those two.

"I know, I know...trust me, I wish I could have avoided that conversation," she said.

"What did he have to say for himself?" Michael asked, distain in his voice.

"Oddly enough, Bo seemed pretty whatever about it, not that the conversation lasted long. What was strange was how off-put Jerry was. He just...glared at me. Maybe he saw me last week when I thought he hadn't? Either way, I think I'll continue to avoid them when I'm at the show grounds. I'm almost relieved I'm going to Wellington next week; at least now I won't be peeking around every corner looking for them. Pretty much the only thing I'll miss around here is this farm, and you, of course," she said, lightly jabbing him in the side.

"Well, actually I have some news on that front. They asked me to join you guys in Wellington this year. They have more horses going than usual, and Mateo always stays behind in Ocala, of course, to hold the fort down. Since his family is here, I was the obvious choice apparently."

Emma beamed at her friend; this was good news for her.

"I'm sure you'll miss the seclusion of your trailer over a room at the rental house, but selfishly, I'm glad I won't be the only one trying to take care everything myself."

"Yeah, yeah, lucky you, there's a guest house on the property and of course they let you have it," he said jokingly.

"Sorry not sorry buddy!" She said, smiling still as she hung the last of the cleaned tack on the wall. "Seriously though, I'm glad you're coming with me," she said, shooting him a meaningful look.

"So am I," he replied, meeting her gaze.

Suddenly, this trip to Wellington seemed a lot more enticing.

Chapter Ten

Emma tried to smooth out the wrinkles of her sundress with her hands one last time before letting out a frustrated sigh.

She was going to have to iron the darn thing if she wanted to wear this particular dress to Ben David's party. Digging through the closet of her guest house, she finally found the iron she had remembered seeing when she was unpacking. As she pressed the wrinkles out of the light blue fabric, she thought about how quickly time had passed here in Ocala; she was only days away from heading to Wellington with the Twin Oaks team.

In a way, this party was like a farewell-for-now to Ocala, and of course, her friend Lily. After the show season started, neither of them seemed to have time to get together, until tonight. Emma shook the reminiscent thoughts from her mind. She was only going to be in Wellington part of the season, and then right back here for the rest of it. The rest of the Ocala winter show season was only a few weeks when they returned, and then her hard work the past few months would either pay off or it wouldn't.

"*It has to,*" she thought. Emma slid the now wrinkle free dress back on.

"Perfect," she said aloud to herself, watching it twirl in the mirror as she twisted from side to side. She hadn't worn a dress like this, er, any dress since she was back home in Ohio. Her life had been consumed by dirt and breeches for far too long, and it felt good to dress up a little for once.

Putting on a little lipstick and a pair of her favorite earrings, she stared at herself once more before grabbing her car keys off the kitchen table. Tonight was going to be a good night.

Ben David is one of the most well-known five-star eventers in Ocala, and pulling into the impressive entrance of his farm was like pulling into Disneyland for horse people. The light may have been a bit dim due to the setting sun, but the polished farm shined anyway. The entrance was, of course, gated, and every few feet of the driveway on each side had a lantern guiding the guests' way to the back side of the farm where the party was being held.

Emma's jaw dropped a little when the barns came into view: three bright white with hunter green shuttered barns and grand looking barn doors dotted a hill to the far left. Pastures with slow rolling hills to her far right continued behind the barns to the left and beyond what her eyes could see. Yes, this was paradise.

The long driveway curved to the right and tucked behind a cluster of trees was the main house. She tried to decide what was prettier; the mansion of a main house tucked in the trees or the rolling pastures and barns she had just passed; it was an impossible choice. Multi-colored lights pointed towards the sky behind the house, beaconing anyone who had a moment of doubt where the party was being held on the endless acres of the property. Emma saw a man in a green reflective vest pointing toward an area to her left where other cars had already parked.

Pulling into the parking spot, she wondered if she had underdressed. But these were horse people, right? How dressed up could they be? Emma quickly retracted her original thought as other guests passed in expensive looking short dresses or slacks and formal jackets.

"Too late to change now," she thought. The entrance to the party area just beyond the backyard of the main house had an archway of brightly colored balloons with several spotlights aimed at them.

As she entered, she tried to take in everything at once; string lights and spotlights on scattered palm trees, fire pits, several temporary bars made of wood, a dance floor and a DJ were some of the first things she saw. About a hundred people mingled and talked, or were dancing, and a few stood in line at the bars. Emma then spotted a table with more hors d'oeuvres than she had ever seen in one place stretched along the far side of the party set up. Feeling a little overwhelmed, she made it her mission to find where Lily was hiding in this massive party setting.

Passing through the crowd, she searched the faces for her friend and found many familiar ones she had met once or twice or seen around the horse show.

"Emma!"

Spinning around, she saw Lily making a beeline for her, fresh drink in hand. "Lil, this place is insane," Emma said, wrapping her arms around her friend.

"I know, right? This party is honestly even bigger than I expected."

Lightly punching her friend in the arm not holding a drink, she said, "You could have warned me there was some sort of unspoken dress code!"

"Hey, I'm not exactly wearing a top-of-the-line dress either! Seriously, this party way exceeded what Benny made it out to be; he is pretty humble despite all this," she said, gesturing at the breathtaking farm beyond the party. "But tell me, how has your internship been going? You leave soon for Wellington, don't you? I feel like we haven't talked in forever!" Lily said.

"It's going well, I just can't believe it's already time to head to Wellington in a few days."

"I know we hardly see each other, but Em, it's going to be tough without you in Ocala! Knowing you're around the corner, even if we don't see each other much..." Lily didn't need to finish her sentence; Emma had felt the same way since the first day she arrived.

"I know exactly what you mean."

Emma looped her arm through her friend's and took a sip of Lily's drink. They stood there on the outskirts of the party soaking in the action. It was moments like this when she slowed down and looked around that she almost couldn't believe how far she had come in just a few months. Her life had changed so much already and was going to change again in a few days, just as she was finding her groove here in Ocala.

"This must be your friend from back home," a voice behind them said. Both girls turned around in unison.

"Ben, this is Emma Walker."

"It's so nice to meet you, Emma. Lily has told me so much about you!" Ben said, offering for Emma to shake his hand.

"This must be what non-horse people feel like when they meet a celebrity," she thought. Emma could care less about meeting an actual celebrity. To her, meeting pro rider of this caliber was like meeting a movie star. Pausing awkwardly a moment, Emma finally managed to get the words, "Nice to meet you, this place is incredible," out of her mouth while shaking his hand.

"Enjoy the party ladies," Ben said with a smile as he turned to greet another guest.

"Come on, let's dance!" Lily said, pulling her friend onto the dance floor. And so they danced in a place that felt magical to her; it almost didn't feel real since it had been far too long since Emma, or Lily for that matter, had a chance to really let loose. It was the downfall of being a working student, little to no free time. But tonight, all of that felt like it was fading away as the two friends from far away danced beside well-lit palm trees until they couldn't stand another minute.

Emma and Lily laughed as they each slid into a reclining shaped chair at the edge of the party.

"My legs feel like Jell-O," Lily said, rubbing her calves.

For a while, the girls just sat and watched the action around them, chatting occasionally. Emma watched as one of the hired caterers dodged dancers, as he beelined directly towards her and Lily.

"Are you Emma?" He asked. Emma and Lily exchanged a quizzical look.

"Yes?"

"Someone handed me this note and pointed you out; they wanted you to have it right away."

The caterer turned to walk back to the table he had been manning, leaving Emma staring, confused, as he walked away.

"What was that?" Lily asked.

"I have absolutely no idea," Emma said, flipping the envelope over and pulling the barely sealed flap open, revealing a note card that was blank on the side facing her.

Lily leaned over, watching as her friend opened the unexpected envelope. Flipping the note card over, she saw the hand-written message on the other side that read, "You deserve everything you're getting." A small heart was drawn next to the last word of the message.

"That's...nice?" Lily stared at her friend, who was rereading the note. "...Isn't it?" She added.

"I mean...I think so?" Emma finally responded.

"Who could this be from?" Lily asked.

"I...I'm not sure," she said, peering back into the envelope to make sure she hadn't missed anything.

"Well, the heart was nice...maybe it's someone from the horse show?" Emma did see a lot of familiar faces tonight, people she had spent sometimes an hour chatting with while waiting at the rings for her riders to go in. Some even knew about how she ended up here, and about her and Valentine. She had just placed well in her decision with her mare; perhaps they heard about it? It was a small world at the show grounds.

"That's certainly possible," she said, sliding the note back into the envelope and stuffing it into her purse. "But I'll figure out who sent it another time; tonight, let's just enjoy this incredible party, ok?" She added.

"Good idea," Lily said. "So let's go get another margarita then!"

Pulling her friend from her chair, they headed back into the crowd. Passing through the dance floor, they were squeezing between people on a shortcut mission to the nearest bar. Emma scanned the faces as they wound through the small clusters of dancers. She couldn't help herself; she was curious about who sent that vague note. Why wouldn't they just leave their name? What was the point of leaving it anonymous anyway? It seemed like a nice gesture, so why hide it?

"Unless it wasn't a nice gesture?" Emma thought. She pushed the thought from her mind immediately after thinking it. Of course, it was a nice gesture; there was no need to dramatize this.

The girls headed back to their chairs, margaritas in hand, and Emma let the music and atmosphere capture her attention again. *"Nights like this don't happen very often,"* she told herself.

For the rest of the party, she immersed herself in the moment, enjoying the last chance she had to be with her friend in this horse-centered town she had called home for several months now.

—*ell*—

Emma was glad she had stayed until the end of the party.

Jenn had been nice enough to offer to cover night check on the horses for her before she left, so she figured she might as well take advantage of her night off.

When she got home, she shifted the car into park and opened the car door, stepping into the cool evening grass; the farm felt so quiet in comparison to the party she had just left. Walking towards the back pastures, she said her horse's name just loud enough so she could hear. Her mare's head flung up in response to her owner's voice and she sauntered casually over to where the girl now hung over the fence line.

Ducking and sliding under the middle part of the wood fence, she walked towards her horse. It felt almost like déjà vu, except this time a lot less was changing. Not so many months before she had come out to her mare's pasture at night back at Maggie's barn, wondering what to do about her future and how she was going to accomplish her dream of working with horses. Yet here she was, returning to this beautiful farm after the grandest party, hosted by a top-level eventing rider.

She had been working so hard since she arrived that she hadn't spent much time reflecting on what she had accomplished so far, despite her circumstances. Emma stroked her horse's neck, breathing in the warm air coming from her nose as she stood close to her.

Her future was still far from certain; after all, this position was a temporary one. Still, she had to give herself a little credit; she had come a long way from the person she was before her world came crashing down. Perhaps in a way, going through the motions in college had given her a crutch; one that gave her little reason to consider what she planned to do with her career and what she wanted out of life until after graduation. Only after the rug was pulled out from under her did she truly start to thrive.

It was in that moment she knew without a doubt she was exactly where she was supposed to be.

The last flake of hay in her wheelbarrow landed in front of her horse as Emma brushed her shirt off, attempting to detach the pieces that clung to her already sweaty tank top.

Emma gave her horse a quick pat before picking up a light jog back toward the barn doors. Sliding them open, she saw the sun must have risen while she was feeding. Power walking now, and hoping no one was watching, she headed back towards her guest house. The empty suitcase she meant to pack last night, but didn't, lay on her bed where she had tossed it this morning before heading to the barn.

"I really should have packed last night," she murmured under her breath as she began pulling open drawers to the dresser. A light knock came from the front door.

"Shoot," she swore under her breath. Emma swung the door open, wishing in that moment she had a peep hole.

"Morning Em, you ready to start packing up the trailer?" Michael asked, as he scanned the room. "Never mind," he said, muffling a chuckle at the sight of clothes everywhere, the empty suitcase answering his question for him.

"Listen, I had every intention of packing last night, really, I did, but I got a little distracted when my friend Mandy called, and we talked later than I expected. Long story short I'm panic packing now," she said, moving away from the door to stuff the pair of shorts she still had in her hand into the suitcase.

"Do you want me to help you?" He asked, still smirking.

"And let you rummage through all my undergarments? Pass." She said, grabbing more clothes from her drawer and shoving them any which way they fit into the suitcase. Michael laughed, raising his hands up in defeat. "Ok, ok, well I'll get started; just meet me in the barn when you're done."

"Ten minutes!" She called after him before he shut the door.

Exactly nine minutes later, she was leaning over her suitcase willing it to stay closed as she struggled to zip it shut. Pulling it behind her, she snagged her purse, rain jacket, and her phone before pausing in the doorway.

"It's strange to think I won't be sleeping here tonight," she thought.

Popping her trunk, she loaded her luggage into her car before heading back to the barn. As soon as she stepped through the threshold, she spotted Michael shoving hay into several hay bags. He checked his watch when he saw Emma enter the barn.

"Impressive," he said with a cheeky smile.

"Told you!" She teased, snatching a hay bag from him. The two pulled tack, blankets, food, and anything else they would need for their time in Wellington. It still seemed a little surreal to Emma though, as if they were just packing up to head to the horse show down the road like they had every weekend for so long now. If she had learned anything about herself since leaving home, it was that deep down she was certainly a creature of habit.

Emma heard the door of the trailer tack room shut behind her as she headed back to the barns. All that was left now was to load the horses and hit the road.

Jenn was haltering the first horse and leading him from the stall and Emma prepped Valentine to follow behind him. She led the mare out of the stall and hung to the side of the trailer to let the mare grab a few bites of grass while Jenn loaded the gelding. She took advantage of the moment to take in the farm's beauty one last time; she would never get tired of this view.

"Your turn, Em," Jenn called out from the trailer. Emma loaded her mare and the rest of the remaining horses. Jenn climbed into the driver's seat of the truck attached to the largest trailer Twin Oaks owned, followed by Liza and David Williams in the backseat.

Michael climbed into the other Twin Oaks truck, pulling behind the trailer caravan style.

"Wellington here we come," she thought, putting her car in drive as the trailer in front of her rolled towards the entrance of Twin Oaks Farm.

—*ele*—

Emma turned up the podcast she had been listening to for the past hour, shifting in her seat. This may be a shorter trip than the one she made coming down from Ohio, but that didn't mean almost four hours in the car wasn't a long time. According to her GPS, they were minutes from the Wellington border.

They had stopped at a rest area an hour ago, and somehow it seemed the air was already thicker with humidity than the first time they stopped. She had been warned; you could all but cut the humidity in south Florida with a knife.

"And I thought Ocala was humid," she thought. Rolling down the window, she could have sworn the air smelled different too, saltier and somehow wetter. It made sense of course, Wellington was only roughly thirty minutes from the coast of the Atlantic Ocean. Emma dreamed of laying on the beach on her day off a luxury she didn't have in Ocala since they were so far from shore.

"Welcome to the Village of Wellington," the sign read.

Pristine looking, Spanish inspired suburban houses dotted with palm trees passed her outside her driver's side window. Already, she was blown away by the night and day difference between Ocala's and Wellington's landscape. Canals and small pockets of water were everywhere, and it was much flatter than the slow rolling hills of Ocala's countryside.

As she drove deeper into this winter horse capital of the world, she saw street after street filled with prestigious looking farms, perfectly landscaped with tropical foliage, sandy arenas, and professional looking barns of various sizes. Some had monster sized houses and barns that were equivalent to boarding barn size, while others were smaller, and seemed to fit just a handful of the owner's personal horses. She wasn't sure what blew her away more, the extravagant homes or beautiful barns next to them.

Emma passed several gated communities, and from the glimpse of the farms behind those black iron gates, she saw farms even more impressive than the ones along the main roads.

While many had pastures, the amount of land each farm had here paled in comparison to the average acreage of the farms in Ocala. Momentarily, she felt a little out of her element; this place was like a whole other world of prestige and equestrians. Hedges and palm trees line the streets, and a minute later she saw the, "Welcome to Palm Beach International Equestrian Center," sign as the horse trailer in front of her turned into the entrance. Pictures had not done this place justice.

Palm trees were pretty much anywhere there was a green spot, and the rings she passed on the way back to their barn were a white-pink and powdery looking, almost reminding her of the beach, all of which were pristinely cared for. Perfectly groomed horses walked by with riders on them or wrapped in coolers led by grooms. Paths were perfectly landscaped with tropical foliage and flowers and white tents were everywhere – she wasn't even sure what they were all for, but she knew they weren't all stable tents or vendors like in Ocala.

They pulled into one of the front rows of a permanent barns that had hunter green wood stalls. It was almost directly across from the horse health and merchandise trailer across the street and steps from a food cart at the end of the row.

"This has to be one of the best stabling spots on the grounds," she thought.

Michael pulled ahead and parked in the parking lot located near the end of the barn and Emma followed suit. Emma heard the creak and thud of the horse trailer hitting the ground; Jenn was already pulling the first horse off the trailer when Emma and Michael rounded the corner of the barn. Pushing the last saddle onto the rack in the tack stall, Emma wiped the sweat threatening to trickle down her brow from her eye; it was certainly much hotter down here than it was just a few hours north.

Emma glanced over at Michael's shirt now almost soaked in sweat; it looked like they both could use a dip in that pool at the rental house right about now. She gave Valentine a quick rub on her forelock before tossing her and the other horses a flake of hay.

"Alright guys, I think that's enough work for one day," Jenn said, also covered in sweat. She handed Emma and Michael a piece of paper each.

"This is the address to the rental house; Emma, as you know, you get the guest house out back, and Michael you will be in the finished basement apartment. Feel free to enjoy what's left of the day, and I will see you both back here at 7:00 am tomorrow morning."

They turned to each other almost simultaneously and Emma beat him to the punch with a, "What are you going to do?"

Michael thought for a moment, and then said, "Dinner?"

"Only if there's margaritas and a gallon of water," she replied.

"Deal!"

They found a quint Mexican restaurant that met all of Emma's criteria. Scanning the menu, she downed the two glasses of water the waitress had brought them only moments ago.

"Maybe we should have told her to just leave the pitcher," Michael said, as the ice clanked against the sides of her empty cup.

"I could literally drink the ocean," she said, trying to suck out the drops of water still wedged between the ice cubes. The waitress came back with margaritas, chips, and guacamole the two ordered earlier.

"I still kind of can't believe we're here," she said. "Wellington is like a tropical paradise for horse people; it's hard to believe it's real. Have you been here before?"

"No, actually Ocala is the furthest south I have ever been," he replied.

"I've been to Miami, but to me, this place is way cooler. I mean horse farms and horse walking paths all over the place while still being a short drive to the coast? Count me in," she said taking another sip of her margarita.

Emma and Michael talked until their food arrived. They were both so hungry that shoveling food into their faces trumped conversation after that. Michael sat back in his chair after he set his fork down onto his now empty plate. Emma was picking at the bits of chicken leftover from the fajita skillet she ordered, trying to decide if she was done or not.

"Another round?" He asked her.

"Definitely," she said.

Emma caught Michael looking at her in a strange way. "What? Do I have something on my face?" She asked.

"No, sorry, I didn't mean to stare. I was just thinking about that night back at Twin Oaks when we first really talked by the fire pit."

Of course, she remembered; it was the night they had truly become friends.

"What about it?" She asked, curious now.

"I was just thinking about what you told me; about everything that happened that caused you to take this working student position. I guess I'm just wondering what you plan to do next, after the internship is over in a few months?"

Emma tilted her head, pausing a moment to look in his eyes while searching for the reason behind his question. Was he wondering if she was going to stay in Florida or go back to Ohio? Did he care if she did? She decided to see if she could figure out the meaning behind his question, if there even was one.

"Do you think I should stay in Florida?" She asked coyly.

"I mean...it does have a lot of opportunities for your career, or so you've said."

"But *do you* think *I* should stay?"

"Here's your drinks," the waitress said, interrupting as she placed fresh glasses in front of them.

"Thank you," Michael said politely. The waitress moved on to her next table, and Emma returned her gaze to Michael, one eyebrow raised, as she waited for his answer.

"I think you should stay," he said. "For your career," he added quickly.

Emma held his gaze. Until this moment there had never been anything but platonic friendship between them. If she was honest with herself, he had been her rock through most of her time in Florida. She couldn't imagine how much harder this whole experience would have been had they not become friends. Because of that, she never considered anything more with him;

the risk if losing the only friend she had on the farm, or creating a potentially awkward situation, was not worth it to her.

Not to mention that as their friendship deepened, she couldn't imagine losing him in general. A romantic relationship gone sideways was a guaranteed way for him to be out of her life for good.

Until recently, she hadn't thought a lot about what her plans were after the internship ended and had simply wanted to focus on her work and gaining the experience she so desperately needed. She knew the impression she made on the Williamses and Jenn would make or break it for her when looking for a permanent position, whether that was with Twin Oaks or elsewhere.

Truth be told, she had already made her decision about staying in Florida or going back home, but she had not planned on telling anyone yet for numerous reasons. Certainly, she had not expected Michael to put her on the spot and ask, but he had. She was going to have to either tell him or shut him down, which could put a strain on their friendship. Since they had become friends, there had been no secrets between them.

She had her reasons for not wanting to tell even Michael about the decision she made a few days ago, mostly so he didn't feel like he was lying to the Twin Oaks owners or Jenn by keeping her secret. But in addition to that, she felt like telling him out loud would solidify this choice she had made, making it harder if she changed her mind later for some reason. He was still staring at her, waiting for her to reply.

"What's more important? Michael's friendship or my secret?" She thought.

"Actually, I already made up my mind a few days ago. I'm staying in Florida permanently. If I can find a job, of course, but the odds of me finding a job in my field are much higher here than back home."

A smile broke out on Michael's face, and what appeared to be reflexively, he reached across the table and took her hand. Emma stared wide-eyed at the gesture but didn't pull away. Friends hold hands, right? In this moment, it seemed appropriate. After a couple seconds he pulled his hand away slowly.

"That's great, Em. I'm sure you'll find your dream job down here. My guess is you will end up in Ocala, right?"

Emma paused again; this was the part she hadn't decided on. Of course, Ocala was a viable choice and there would more than likely be job opportunities there. She loved Ocala; it was some of the prettiest countryside she had ever seen. But she had also decided not to rule out Wellington because it was the winter equestrian capital after all. She knew there were just as many opportunities here, perhaps even more so, than Ocala.

"I'm not sure, to be honest. I'm considering both Ocala and Wellington at this point."

A slight frown replaced his smile now.

"That doesn't mean we couldn't still be friends if I end up in Wellington," she added quickly, hoping she hadn't screwed things up between them. If he knew there was a chance she would be living four hours away, would that mean he wouldn't want to be as close as they are now? The thought of starting all over for a second time in a place where she didn't know anyone made her sick to her stomach. But, if the perfect opportunity presented itself and it happened to be in Wellington versus Ocala, was she really going to turn it down? She had worked too hard to throw it all away just because she was afraid of starting over again.

"I get it, you need to take the best opportunity you can," he said. It was like he had read her mind, which that only made her feel worse. She valued his friendship, and she had a gut feeling that choosing a job in Wellington would squash whatever was between them whether they meant for that to happen or not. In her experience, distance did not make the heart grow fonder; it was the thing that drove a wedge between relationships.

Emma had only been gone a few months and already felt like she had lost friends back home. Sure, she kept in contact a lot at first, but over time the calls and texts to her friends grew fewer and further apart. Now, the only people she really talked to from back home was Hailey and Maggie on occasion, her family, and Mandy. Lily too, of course, but that was easier since she was in Florida too.

Emma tried to think of something else to say, something that would revive the conversation from the downer it had turned into. The waitress appeared again, another margarita in her hand. Emma looked at her, confused. Had she forgot she ordered another drink? She was only halfway through her second glass; no way she was tipsy enough to order without remembering.

"Ma'am, a gentleman over at the bar bought you a drink," the waitress said.

The waitress slid the glass in front of Emma, who just stared at it, still a little confused. She was sitting across from a man who, for all they knew, was her boyfriend or husband. Was some guy really that brazen enough to be sending a drink to a woman sitting across from another man? The waitress was already walking away.

"Excuse me!" Emma called after her, and the waitress turned back toward her. "Can you please point out who it was?"

"Oh it's...," the waitress turned back toward the bar, but paused, scanning the bar up and down and then the nearby tables. "...Actually, it looks like he already left."

"Can you tell me what he looked like?"

"Dark hair, maybe late twenties, or early thirties? Little bit of a beard. Sorry, I wasn't really paying that much attention. He caught me on my way back to the kitchen; he wasn't my customer."

"It's ok, thanks anyway."

Emma and Michael exchanged puzzled glances; he was clearly thinking the same thing Emma was. Had she been sitting alone or with a group of girlfriends, the drink would have made more sense.

"Weird, right?" She asked. Michael seemed unsettled, looking around the restaurant.

"Michael, it's ok, really. Probably just some creep with nothing better to do than hit on girls sitting with other men," she said, forcing a laugh, hoping to lighten the mood. He didn't seem convinced, and his eyes wandered back to the bar occasionally for the next few minutes.

Emma downed what was left of her drink; it was probably better if they left. Snagging the waitress the next time she passed, she asked for the check. Shortly after, Emma and Michael walked out the front door of the restaurant and into the warm humid night. She still couldn't get over the level of humidity down here.

"Where did you park your car?" He asked. Emma pointed to a spot near the back of the parking lot; there had been a lot more cars when she had parked an hour ago.

"I'm walking you to your car," he stated, making it clear she didn't have a choice. She thought about protesting and telling him she was perfectly capable of walking across a parking lot to her own car but decided to let him have his way. The incident had been a little creepy anyway.

Pulling the keys out of her purse, she turned back around toward him. Normally they just said a casual goodbye and walked to their respective living quarters on the farm, but tonight felt different. Perhaps it was the conversation about her future, being in this new environment, or the off-putting drink incident. Either way, she felt some sort of change between them, and she couldn't put her finger on it. She was sure things would be back to normal by tomorrow.

"See you back at the rental house?" She asked.

"See you there," he stated.

She couldn't help but smile at his chivalry though; Michael was a good guy.

"Thanks," she said. Emma ducked into her car and started to punch the address to her new temporary home into her GPS. The circle of death on the screen continued to spin; clearly her phone's internet was in no hurry today.

A knock on her window made her jump, and she turned wide-eyed towards the sound.

A man who appeared to be in his thirties with a beard leaned in, staring at her through the window with a smile that was just a little too wide. Wide, and one hundred percent creepy. She rolled her window down a crack, just enough that she could tell him he wasn't interested in whatever it was he might be selling.

"Did you enjoy the drink I sent you?" He said, still smiling widely.

"The mystery drink creep?" She thought.

"Um, sorry, I have a boyfriend. Thanks anyway," she said firing up her car's engine, immediately putting it in drive and making it clear she was leaving whether or not he was still leaning against her car when he did. She glanced over, swearing under her breath when she realized Michael had already left the parking lot.

"Come on honey, don't be like tha...," he began, but was cut off by her foot on the gas and her tires squealing lightly against the blacktop as she sped away.

Emma hoped his disgruntled face in her rearview was the last she would ever see of that guy.

—*ell*—

The headlights of her car shined on a large stone house as she pulled in the driveway. The instructions on the paper Jenn had given her said her guest house was on the back right of the house, and to follow the driveway all the way back.

Emma took the fork in the driveway to the right and the guest house came into view moments later. It reminded her of a fancier version of the guest house she stayed in back in Ocala. Michael's headlights poured into the window of her hatchback, pulling next to the house, but still a little further down the driveway than he needed to be.

His truck door slammed before she had even opened her car door. She had already popped her trunk, and she saw Michael pulling a bag from the back as she slid out of her car.

"I can get my own luggage, Michael," she said trying to pull the handle to her suitcase from his grip; it didn't work. He moved the suitcase to the opposite side and began walking towards the front door of the guest house.

Emma rolled her eyes but smiled despite herself. She was a strong independent woman who rode thousand-pound animals without batting an eye; the last thing she needed was a man to carry her luggage for her. But she couldn't help but to enjoy the feeling that he was looking out for her; it was nice to have someone on her side. However, she had already decided not to tell Michael about the incident in the parking lot of the restaurant. Knowing him, he would only be mad at himself for not following her. It was over, and she was sure she would never see that creep ever again, so why bother upsetting him over nothing?

She used both hands and balanced her coat on her shoulder, grabbing the last of her things from the trunk so Michael couldn't. He had set her suitcase in the corner and was looking around when she drug the last of her bags inside.

Her original impression of this guest house was spot on, a fancier version of hers back in Ocala. It was a studio apartment layout, with flooring that was a grey and white marbled tile throughout; it didn't look like the fake kind either. The counter was a white quartz with a matching kitchen island and three bar stools with linen cushioning were on one side of the kitchen island. A large white plush rug sat under the bed. So far, everything about Wellington screamed prestigious, even their temporary living accommodations.

"This is nice," he said, stating the obvious.

"This place looks like the Taj Mahal compared to my guest house back at the farm," she said still taking in the room.

"I better go find my room before it gets too late. I don't want to wake the whole house up when I go in," he said.

"Thanks for helping me carry my luggage in," she said.

They both paused at the door. Normally they weren't the touchy-feely kind of friends. But this was a strange place and today was a strange day and there seemed to be this unspoken, "do we hug now or not," moment between them as he stepped out the door.

Before she could decide, Michael stepped into her personal bubble and wrapped his arms around her back, pulling her to his chest.

"Goodnight, Emma," he said in a soft voice, before turning and walking back toward the main house.

"Goodnight," she said in a hushed tone as he walked off. Emma shut the door behind her, leaning against it momentarily.

"That was weird, right?" she said aloud to herself.

But she wasn't sure that it was.

It wasn't even noon, and already the temperature was pushing eighty degrees. Back home in Ohio, the high temperature was expected to reach a whopping twenty-nine degrees. Sometimes, she forgot it was still winter, especially when the forecast showed a high temperature of eighty-two degrees for the day.

She figured after a week of being in south Florida she would have acclimated to the heat and humidity, but she was wrong. Sweat glistened on her forehead as she pulled up the buckle of the girth, letting the metal piece slide into the first hole of the billet as she tacked Jimmy John for Jenn.

"Meet me at the warm-up ring?" Jenn asked Emma.

"Be there in ten," she replied.

At least now she could find her way around the endless palm tree lined paths and numerous rings the show grounds had. She had gotten lost twice the first day she tried to lead Stephanie's horse to one of the arenas furthest from the barns. Stephanie had a rushed warm up on her horse and took a rail down in her class; Emma felt a little responsible and spent the following days memorizing every ring's location on the grounds.

This place had to be at least twice as big as the show in Ocala, and certainly had a much different vibe; the caliber of horse and rider here had a lot to do with that, and the well-polished appearance of the grounds echoed it. Despite feeling a little out of her element here, she had already made a few acquaintances with people who frequented the same rings as Jenn and the girls. So far, everyone she met was helpful and friendly; she had learned this early on when asking for directions every other hour on day one. Sliding the bit into the gelding's mouth, she then buckled the throatlatch and noseband. Clipping the lead rope to one side, she led him from the stall.

"I'm heading up to the Grand prix ring!" She called behind her to Michael, who was nearby cleaning some tack that had been used earlier in the day.

"See you in a bit!" He called back.

She clucked the horse forward and headed towards the horse path leading all the way to the Grand Prix ring that sat on the outskirts of the show grounds.

Emma was glad nothing seemed to have changed between the two of them since they arrived in Wellington. Perhaps, if anything, they were closer than they were before. They had not spoken about Emma's future job plans since that night at the restaurant, and it seemed they were going to avoid that subject until it was time to officially cross that bridge. Why discuss something that had yet to happen?

Emma closed her eyes and lifted her face to the warm sun. One of her favorite things had become this, leading the horses across this horsey tropical paradise. Now that she knew where she was going, of course. Emma felt a significant change in temperature as they entered the long part of the path that was heavily lined with palm trees. The shade was a welcomed relief form the mid-day sun.

"You better be a good boy today," she said, patting Jimmy John's neck as they walked. Today was Jimmy John's first competition in Wellington, and it was in the fanciest ring on the property.

Rounding the corner, she caught a glimpse of the back side bleachers in the tall, semi-enclosed arena. "Grand" was the word that had come to Emma's mind when she first saw it when she was trying to find her way around the grounds earlier in the week. She had later told Michael a joke, saying it put the "Grand" in "Grand Prix." She smiled to herself at the reminder of her own inside joke as they approached the warm-up ring.

Jenn took the reins from Emma and mounted up. Jimmy John looked slightly more sluggish than she was used to as they began warming up. Emma figured he was still adjusting to the temperature change; she sure was. Jenn must have assumed this would be the case too since she didn't have Emma canter him down today. Jenn legged on and clucked to him as they approached the first warm up fence. The gelding cleared it, but with a little less enthusiasm than usual. Circling, she began her approach to a large, ramped oxer. Jimmy took this one out of stride and landed with a head shake.

"*Ah, there he is,*" Emma thought, as the horse offered a tiny crow hop two strides later. Jenn patted the horse, bringing him down to a walk a couple warm up fences later and nodded to Emma as they headed towards the in-gate. They had spent enough time together now that words were hardly needed pre or post ride; she knew the drill.

Jimmy pranced as they entered the in-gate. This was the first time she was able to watch a round in this magnificent ring, and it was something she had been looking forward to for a while now. Tents lined the area that, during the real Grand Prix, held VIP guests directly behind the bleachers. Emma shifted out of the way of the busy in-gate and stood on the sidelines of the arena fencing.

Jimmy John powered towards the first fence, coming in a little strong but clearing it despite the long spot. He was a bit looky today, perhaps because of the endless distractions around the arena. Jenn had discussed with Emma the possibility of moving him up one level into the Grand Prix while they were in Wellington, which was a long-time goal of Twin Oaks for this horse. Jenn sat deep in the saddle, trying to focus the gelding as they came into the in and out. He took a much deeper spot this time and it set him up for an equally short, but good distance on the second fence. With each jump Emma felt her body relax for him; he was starting to jump much nicer than he had at the beginning.

The next fence was an oxer that was heavily dressed up, and it caught Jimmy John's eye, distracting him a stride out. He added a chip but jumped anyway and took a rail with his hind leg as a result. Clearing the remaining jumps, Jenn slowed the gelding to a walk, who breathed heavily and was covered in sweat. Walking him out of the arena, she heard Jenn praising the gelding.

"That was a big atmosphere for this guy," Jenn said, sliding off his side. "Hopefully next week he will do better."

Emma patted his neck but instantly regretted it as she wiped foamy sweat onto her light grey breeches.

"Will you please take him on a nice long walk? You can mount up if you'd like." Jenn asked.

"No problem, I'll hose him too once he's cooled off," Emma said, swinging her leg over the gelding's heaving sides. Jenn headed back toward the barns, and Emma turned to lap the outside of the arena. Maybe giving him time to take in all the action around the ring would help with his distraction next time. Passing a few pavilions and a carousel that sat near the entrance of the arena, she talked softly to the horse as he eyed the fake looking horses on sticks. After reaching a dead end she headed back the direction she came from, planning to find the shaded paths to finish their walk.

"Hey horse girl," a familiar voice said.

Emma pulled the gelding up, stunned. She knew that voice, but it didn't fit with the scene. She spun to her left, in the direction of the voice.

"Liam?!"

The same goofy grin she remembered from what felt like forever ago smiled up at her. She felt her heart skip a beat; she had forgotten how good looking he was.

"Surprised to see me?" He asked.

"That is the understatement of the year," she thought.

Emma slid off Jimmy John, fearing she might fall off in shock if she didn't; she could get back on in a minute.

"My Aunt Cathy is a partial owner in a couple of the horses that compete here. I usually come up at least a few weeks every winter."

That's right. She vaguely remembered him saying something about his aunt who owned horses. "I thought you didn't know anything about horses?" She pressed, remembering their past conversations.

"I don't," he laughed. "But my aunt does. She doesn't ride anymore, but she likes to do horse ownership syndication so she can still be part of this world," he said motioning to flawless looking grounds. Emma suddenly remembered Jimmy John standing next to her, still blowing a little.

"Hey, what are you doing right now?" Emma asked.

"Watching a bunch of expensive horses run around, why?" He asked in a joking tone.

"Walk with me? I have to get this horse cooled down."

"Sure," Liam replied. Emma headed towards the shaded path, still unable to wrap her head around the fact that he was standing beside her.

"I'm surprised you're even here; you made it pretty clear horses weren't your favorite when we first met."

"Yeah, I mean I come down because my aunt likes when I visit her. Plus, I've made some friends down here over the years, so mostly I just go out with them when I visit. Of course, my aunt always manages to drag me to the horse show at least a couple times."

"So, it sounds like you are close with your aunt then?" She couldn't help but think it was sweet that he obliged his aunt like this, even though he made it clear the horse shows weren't his cup of tea.

"Well...actually my Aunt Cathy raised me. My parents died in a car accident when I was six. I've lived with her ever since and she legally adopted me shortly after."

"Gee, Liam, I'm sorry..."

He waved his hand, cutting her off. "Seriously, it's ok. It was a long time ago, and my aunt raised me like her own."

They walked a few steps in silence. "So how is your internship going? Is it everything you thought it would be?"

"Where do I even start," she thought.

"Well, it's been a lot of work; probably more so than I anticipated, but I love it. I love being around the horses every day and I love Florida. Well, ok, so I don't love the humidity, but you've got to take the good with the bad I guess."

"Stop rambling," she told herself.

"Sounds like it's going well then," he said.

"It is." she replied, meeting his eyes this time.

"When is your internship over, and when are you coming home?"

Ah, there it was. Emma figured that question was bound to come up at some point; may as well get it out of the way now. Although, she was afraid that when she did answer him that it would promptly end whatever could have been before it began. She had let her mind wander about that what if so many times during those lonely days of her first couple weeks in Ocala. Maybe it was easier to do so then knowing there was no chance of seeing him again, which meant no chance to get her heart broken again.

"Actually, I'm not planning to come home. I'm going to look for jobs in Ocala and Wellington when my internship is over."

"That's cool, Ohio is boring anyway now that everyone I know is graduating. My aunt owns a house down here and spends more time in Wellington than back home now that she's getting older. I'm actually considering moving down here since I just graduated college. Also, don't tell her I called her 'older,' she'll have my head," he said with a wink.

Emma was surprised that not only was he not put off by her answer to live here, but that it sounded like he may wind up here himself. It had been a long time since she thought about Liam or toyed with what could have been based on their chemistry when they met back home. But now that he might move to Wellington...

They were almost back at the barns, and she stopped in her tracks, turning to face Liam again.

"Hey, I've got to hose this horse hosed down and get back to work. Maybe I'll see you around though?" she said.

"Come to my house tomorrow night? My aunt is throwing a cocktail party with a bunch of her girlfriends; you'd be saving me from an extremely boring night if you came."

Emma only needed a moment to consider this; it felt like some twist of fate running into Liam here. She had spent so much time pushing away the thought of opening herself up to a relationship again. But here was her chance, and it felt impossible to pass up.

"I would love to come."

"Here, put your number in my phone and I'll text you the address."

Emma took his phone briefly, handing it back when she was finished entering her number.

"Guess I'll be seeing you tomorrow then," he said with a wink as he turned to leave.

"See you then," she said, watching him walk away. Michael set down the pitchfork he had been using to clean a stall and walked over as Emma pulled the saddle from the gelding's back. He took it from her, handing her his halter.

"Who was that?" He asked, raising an eyebrow suspiciously. Emma's cheeks flushed; she hadn't considered Michael overhearing their conversation. Not that she should feel bad or embarrassed that he had; they were just friends after all. But still, she felt a twinge of guilt at what clearly sounded like Liam asking her on a date that involved meeting his Aunt Cathy. At least, she assumed it was a date.

"Someone I ran into by the Grand Prix arena. We actually went to college together back home and have some mutual friends," she said, hoping it made the situation sound better to Michael than perhaps it looked.

"So, he asked you out?"

Emma paused. She didn't know, honestly. There was a good chance this was simply two acquaintances from the same hometown getting together at his aunt's house with her friends.

"We're just catching up; his aunt is having a cocktail party."

That sounded casual enough, but the look on Michael's face said otherwise. "It's no big deal," Emma said, adding a shrug for emphasis as she replaced the horse's bridle with a halter.

"I'm going to cold hose him, I'll be right back," she said turning quickly away from what felt like an awkward conversation. She shook her head; why was she trying so hard to downplay whatever tomorrow's get together was anyway?

Emma sprayed the cold water on the horse's legs, moving up his neck and across his body. She was just going to see how tomorrow went before she made a big deal out of what could be nothing.

Chapter Eleven

As she pulled into the driveway of the rental house that evening, she had one thing on her mind: taking a shower.

Emma had never been so excited to take a shower until she came to south Florida. The only problem was within ten minutes post-shower, she already felt sticky again, especially if she so much as stepped outside. Perhaps after she showered, she would sit by the pool that was only steps away from her guest house behind the main house, after she showered off the dirt, sweat, and grime clinging to her skin, of course. Then, maybe, she would take a second shower after she got out of the pool; really, there was no such thing as too many showers down here.

Emma noticed a medium sized manilla envelope wedged in between the door and door frame. As she approached, she saw her name handwritten on the front. Popping open the top part of the envelope, she slid a stack of thick notecards paperclipped together. She read the handwritten note on the front notecard that said, *"Now I know where you are."*

She wasn't entirely sure what it meant, but it left her feeling a little scared. She pulled the top notecard away from the stack and gasped, clutching her chest as she scanned the image in front of her. The blood drained from Emma's face she continued flipping through the images. These weren't all notecards after all; they were pictures. Pictures of her in the guest house that she stood in front of right now. In the pictures, she was in her favorite pair of silk pajamas that she had worn several times since she had arrived in Wellington; they were so comfortable and light that she couldn't help but wear them more than once this week. These could have been taken on any one of those days.

Emma's hands shook as she shoved the images back into the envelope, picking up a full sprint towards the back door of the main house. The basement apartment Michael was staying in had a private entrance on the far side of the house, a fact he wished he had known the day they arrived, since he did in fact wake up Jenn and Liza Williams. Emma remembered him telling her the comical story about that night but she had not had a reason to go to this secluded side of the house until now. It was dark, only the dim lights beneath the water of the pool lit the way as she ran through the backyard.

She paused in the darkness when she reached the side of the house; what if the person who left the note was hiding back here? She pulled her phone from her pocket and shined the light into the space between the hedged fence and the side of the house. It was clear, and the dark door leading down to the basement was now apparent. Keeping her flashlight on, she knocked on the side door loudly.

Michael answered the door shirtless, but in a pair of basketball shorts. He stared at Emma in surprise, then turned to grab a shirt from the dresser nearby, flipping it over his head. He looked a little embarrassed, but Emma wasn't sure why; he certainly had nothing to be embarrassed about.

"Sorry... I was hot," he said apologizing for the partial nudity. He stared at Emma's face, still white as a sheet. "Em? What's wrong?"

Emma handed Michael the envelope, and he opened it examining the note and pictures it enclosed. She saw a mix of shock and anger cross his face as he flipped through the photographs.

"Who did this?!" He demanded, peering behind her as if the person could be standing nearby.

"I don't know," she said weakly. "I found it on my door when I got home."

"We should call the police and let the Williamses know," he said. Emma groaned, "Can we please not involve the Williams?" She pleaded. The last thing she wanted was to cause a scene or upset her employers.

"Em, they are going to know something is up when the police car is sitting in their driveway."

He wasn't wrong.

"Fine, let's call the police," she said, pulling out her phone.

"Do you want me to tell the Williamses?" He asked.

"Can you, please?" She answered.

"Sure, just...stay here. It's probably not a good idea to go back to the guest house until the police arrive."

She nodded, dialing 911.

—ℓℓ—

Flashing blue and red lights bounced off the trees and side of the house as the car rolled to a stop. Emma and Michael stood near the entrance of the guest house, watching as the officer stepped out of the cruiser. Prompted by the flashing lights, Liza and David stepped out of the house and shook the officer's hand.

"This is Emma," he said gesturing toward her.

"Officer Tom Paul," he said, hand outstretched for Emma to shake. He eyed the envelope Emma clutched in one hand. "May I?" He asked, pointing to it. She passed the envelope and handed the stack of pictures over to the officer. After he had gone through them, he had her give her statement once more and proceeded to inspect the door and exterior of her guest house.

About fifteen minutes later, he walked back over to where they still stood.

"Unfortunately, there does not appear to be anything we can use to identify the person who left this at your door, miss," he said. "Mr. Williams, is there a security camera on the premises?"

David pointed to where a camera was mounted to the top of the garage, facing the driveway. "The people we rent the house from gave us access to the footage, which is on this app on my phone," he said, opening the app and handing it to the officer.

"Ma'am, do you know approximately what day this could have been? What day you were wearing the clothes in the picture?"

Emma's face flushed hot and red; it felt like her worst nightmare. "Well, um...I wore them a couple times this week. Yesterday and maybe Wednesday?"

The officer excused himself and sat in his car reviewing the footage for the next few minutes before emerging again. He pushed play and turned the phone around so Emma and David could see it. A man walked from the street up the driveway in the middle of the day with a black mask covering his face. He had several rocks in his hand, throwing one then another until the camera lens shattered. From there, it was hard to make out much of anything as he got close enough to the camera to have any identifiable features.

The officer grunted, handing the phone back to David.

"Since he walked on to the premises, we do not have any license plates to track either. Do you know anyone who would want to do this to you?" The officer asked Emma, whose face was a pale white for the second time tonight.

"No, I just arrived in Wellington....," she began, but then the image of the man in the parking lot at the Mexican restaurant suddenly came to mind.

"Actually, there was this guy who followed me to my car recently...," she said, as she recalled the full story to the officer. He nodded as she spoke, jotting down notes.

"We will look into that," he said.

While the likely suspect was the stranger from the parking lot at the restaurant, she couldn't help but consider the fact that Liam had arrived at an extremely coincidental time. It didn't help that during her last interaction with him back home in Ohio, he said "Maybe I'll see you around, then." She had been thrown off by his comment even then. But could Liam really be responsible for something like *this?* Her attraction to him was definitely clouding her judgment, so she promised herself to keep Liam at arm's length until she knew if she could really trust him.

What did she truly know about him anyway? Certainly not enough to be sure it wasn't Liam leaving her notes, and probably not enough to make him a suspect with the police either. She decided to keep her suspicions about him to herself for now. David thanked the officer again and checked in with Emma once more before heading inside.

"That was mortifying!" Emma said to Michael now that they were alone.

"You know, you're probably not the first person to wear pajamas twice in the same week," he said, clearly trying not laugh given the circumstances.

"That doesn't mean it wasn't embarrassing telling my employer that in front of an officer of the law," she said rolling her eyes.

"When were you going to tell me about the guy in the parking lot?" He asked, one eyebrow raised.

"I didn't want you to feel guilty for not following me home. Besides, I didn't think something like this would happen."

Michael's forehead creased in concern, but he didn't reply. She took his silence as proof of her original theory. Glancing at her guest house, she realized she didn't really want to go inside and sit alone there with a stalker on the loose. However, she did want to put this envelope somewhere she didn't have to look at it or think about it for the rest of the night. Michael followed her gaze and saw the worry on her face.

"Listen, Em, if you don't want to stay in your house tonight, I have a couch in my basement apartment. Take my bed, and I'll sleep on the couch."

Emma's independent instincts told her to turn down his offer right away. But even she had to admit she was spooked, and she truly had no interest in sleeping in the guest house this evening after everything that happened.

"Ok, but I'll take the couch. I'm not going to kick you out of your own bed."

"Really, you can take my bed I don't mind..."

"I take the couch or no deal," she added quickly with a smirk.

"If you insist," he said, throwing his hands up in defeat.

"I insist, but first, I really need to take a shower."

Michael sat in the pool chair across from the guest house while he waited for her to take a quick shower and change. Emma had not protested this time when he had asked if she wanted him to wait outside for her; the thought of that creep roaming around outside her place while she showered made her sick to her stomach.

Fifteen minutes later, she emerged in a pair of soft fabric shorts and a loose-fitting t-shirt.

"No silk pajamas?" He teased.

"Too soon," she quipped, as they walked back towards the basement apartment. Michael pulled the extra blankets from the closet and Emma made a makeshift bed out of the leather couch.

"Leave the TV on or turn it off?" He asked, before climbing into his own bed.

"On, please." She could use the distraction from her thoughts. Emma laid down, but her mind still raced.

"I don't understand why that creep would go to such lengths...," she said, her voice breaking.

"You can't possibly try to understand the mindset of a psycho, Em," he said, trying to ease her mind. He was right, of course.

Eventually, the chatter of the sitcom on television lulled her to sleep.

_e_e_

Palm trees and well-lit mansions blurred by as she followed her GPS, turning onto a dead-end street.

"You have arrived at your destination," her GPS stated as she pulled into the driveway. In front of her was probably the biggest house she had ever been to. Well, the biggest she had been invited to that she wasn't merely driving past, that is.

"He's *loaded*," she whispered to herself, turning off her car.

She suddenly felt that out-of-my-element feeling wash over her. This was no casual cocktail party; this was the kind of party where people with money talk about things only other people with money talk about. How was she supposed to make a good impression under these circumstances?

"Just because they have money doesn't mean they are automatically snobs," she reprimanded herself, getting out of the car. She was glad in that moment she had worn one of the nicer dresses she had packed. She knew it was a nice house based on the address he had provided and some internet stalking, but Google maps certainly hadn't done it justice. Emma rang the backlit doorbell, exhaling audibly.

To her relief, Liam was the one who answered the door. He had on black slacks, a light blue button-down shirt that was unbuttoned a few holes at the top, and a black blazer. Until now, she had only seen him in casual clothes like t-shirt and shorts. "*He certainly cleans up well,*" she thought.

"Come on in," he said with a grin as he opened the door widely. The entryway was open and had a crystal chandelier that hung

above them, and it appeared there was marble floors throughout. The grand staircase with a dark stained wood railing wound
to the left, and she caught a peak of a grand looking dining room
to her right.

She quickly caught her jaw dropping and snapped it shut. Not
speaking yet, her eyes scanned the stunning home instead.

"The pool and courtyard are just back here," he said, gesturing
her ahead of him towards the back of the house. The large stone
patio had string lights hung in a zig zag pattern across the length
of the area, and she saw the lights inside the pool shining just
beyond that. The whole area gave her tropical secret garden
vibes; it made sense why he referred to it as a courtyard now.
Under the spacious pergola, she saw a small bar with a bartender pouring a middle-aged woman a glass of champagne.
She thanked the bartender and walked directly over to her and
Liam.

"So, this must be Emma," she said, taking Emma's hand and
kissing her on the cheek. Immediately, she couldn't help but like
her. The woman, who was clearly Liam's aunt, gave off an eccen-
tric-but-sweet vibe that felt welcoming despite the grandness of
her home and her obvious wealth.

"You must be Aunt Cathy. It is so nice to meet you; you have a
beautiful home."

Aunt Cathy immediately turned to her nephew before replying
to Emma.

"Liam, don't be rude, get the young lady a glass of champagne."

"Yes ma'am," he said, giving Emma a sympathetic look as he walked towards the bar, leaving Emma alone with his aunt. About five other ladies were mingling near the pergola, clearly on glass number two or three of champagne. It was obvious they were all of a similar caliber, and Emma hoped she didn't stick out like a sore thumb. Aunt Cathy turned toward her again, smiling as she looped her arm through Emma's and started walking towards the table set up on the far side with the hors d'oeuvres.

"I hear you own horses and ride as well?"

Emma flushed; she wasn't sure how her, 'I pulled a horse from an auction, dropped out of school, and am now a working student' story would fair with someone like her. But she promised herself she would be openminded, so she was going to be.

"Well, I own one horse, yes. I've been riding since I was twelve, but the rest is a bit of a long story."

Aunt Cathy glanced towards the bar; poor Liam had been snagged by one of his aunt's slightly intoxicated friends who was talking his ear off.

"I think we have time," she said, smiling genuinely at Emma. Emma spent the next five minutes telling Aunt Cathy a summarized version of her first horse, riding growing up, and how the last few months had changed everything for her.

"...And now here I am," she said, laughing nervously after concluding her life's story.

"I rode most of my life until this darn bad back of mine got the best of me. Do yourself a favor; don't get old. Now I enjoy my horses from the ground and let the young people ride them instead," she said with a wink. "But dear, I think what you've done, chasing your dreams like you have so far from home, is a very brave and dedicated thing. Clearly you love horses."

"I can't imagine doing anything else," she agreed softly. Liam approached them a moment later with two glasses of champagne, handing one to his aunt and one to Emma.

"My nephew knows me so well! Thank you dear," she said, lightly pinching his cheek.

"What did I miss?" He asked. Emma and Aunt Cathy exchanged a glance and burst out laughing.

"I like this one," she said, wrapping an arm around Emma's shoulders. "She's smart, she's beautiful, and she likes horses; what more could you want in a young lady, nephew?"

Liam shook his head, smiling at his aunt. "I had a feeling you two would get along."

"Come on Emma, I want you to meet my girlfriends," she said, linking arms with her again as they headed to the pergola area. Emma was surprised, despite her original judgment, how well she got along with Aunt Cathy and her friends. It was apparent they were all very wealthy, but because they all were involved with or owned horses themselves, the common interest made conversation much easier. She felt a little bit bad that Liam hardly had been able to get a word in, or that they had not spent much time talking.

However, talking to these ladies about her favorite thing in this world trumped the twinge of guilt that came and went as they talked for hours. Glancing at her phone for the first time in awhile, she realized just how late it had become.

"Liam, Cathy, I am so sorry, but I have to get going. I have to feed the horses early tomorrow, and it's getting pretty late."

"Oh, I am sorry you have to go, dear! Here, let me have your number so I can be sure to invite you to the Grand Prix party I'm throwing in a few weeks. I would love for you to join us."

Emma gave her number to Aunt Cathy, thanking her for a lovely evening.

"I'll walk you to your car," Liam said, placing his hand on her lower back as he walked her to the door. Emma breathed the slightly cool salty air in as she turned to face him when they reached her car.

"I'm sorry we didn't get a chance to talk much."

Liam laughed lightly. "Don't worry, I had a feeling my aunt and her friends might monopolize the conversations."

"Maybe we can go somewhere next time where we can get a chance to really talk?"

"I'd like that," he said.

Smiling at him, she pulled her car door open.

"Goodnight, Liam," she said.

"Goodnight, Emma," Liam said, kissing her on the cheek.

Her suspicions of his coincidental arrival on the same day as the stalker leaving her those pictures were quickly becoming but a distant memory now, even if in the back of her mind she knew that was naive. Perhaps his charm had ultimately pushed those thoughts from her mind, or maybe meeting his wonderful aunt had made it impossible to imagine him as a stalker despite the original warning signs.

Either way, Emma found herself smiling most of the way home; tonight had certainly gone better than she had expected.

ele

"Thanks for all your hard work today!" Jenn said as she headed towards the nearby parking lot.

"You're welcome!" Emma hollered back, setting down the saddle she had just cleaned and oiled to perfection. She looked up at the sun that hung low; she had about an hour before dark. Just enough time for an evening hack around the grounds with her mare.

Missing her evening hacks around the farm after work when she was in Ocala, she had revised her ritual to include a hack around the outskirts of the grounds. At least twice a week she made sure to school Valentine over fences in one of the warm-up rings; she wanted to keep her mare on her game for the next chance she had to show her. Typically, a quick light hack was all she had the energy for by the time the day was done.

"I'm headed back to the house, unless you need help with anything else?" Michael asked.

"No, I'm good, thanks. I'm just going to take Valentine on a hack around the grounds."

Michael nodded, knowingly.

"I'll probably just see you tomorrow then," he said as he turned to head towards the parking lot as well.

"See you!" She called after him. It had been three days since the cocktail party at Aunt Cathy's and Michael had only asked about it once. It went a little something like this:

"How did last night go?" Followed by her saying, "Better than expected actually," and a nonchalant, "Good," from Michael.

Emma got the impression he was asking to be polite and per-haps simple curiosity, but he hadn't seemed thrilled that it had gone so well. Since then, he hadn't acted strangely around her per say, but he seemed a little bit distant. They still talked at work during the day, and it certainly wasn't awkward, but something was just off. She couldn't say she was completely surprised; they were close friends and had become even closer since the incident with the pictures left at her door.

But until recently, she had not dated anyone and that seemed to be changing things between she and Michael. More impor-tantly though, she had not had anything strange happen since the night she found the envelope. Every night since, Michael checked out the exterior of the guest house for her so she didn't have to. She felt lucky to have a friend like him; she just hoped the fact that she was starting to see Liam wasn't going to affect her friendship with Michael.

Why should it? Neither of them had ever crossed that line of friendship.

Emma tightened the girth on her horse's belly and slipped the bit into her mouth, pulling the bridle over her ears. She hoped in time things wouldn't feel so awkward between them when it came to Liam. Maybe Michael and Liam could even become friends at some point. She thought back to the dinner she had shared with Liam just last night, a dinner she had not told Michael about. Why add insult to injury?

Swinging a leg over her mare at the mounting block located by the tack stall, she clucked her on heading to her favorite horse path on the far side of the property. It was the closest thing to a nature hack she had here, and the show grounds were quiet this time of day. The last few days had been busy. Stephanie and Ashley had been in town to show and Jenn and Jimmy John, as well as a few of the young horses Jenn brought along to school, had shown too. Everyone had placed well, and she felt good about her work. But a busy day meant she didn't have any time to daydream about how last night had gone.

Walking along the path in the low light as the heat from the day cooled off, she allowed her mind to wander back through the past few days. Her mind first drifted back to last night; a bottle of wine and three hours of talking and laughing at the restaurant that had all but kicked them out because they were there past closing time, solidified in her mind that he was in fact interested in her. Perhaps she could have come to that conclusion a while ago; after all, he did invite her to meet his aunt. But now, she was certain.

Tall trees planted only feet apart lined the path on either side as they picked up a working trot. Letting the reins drop from her hands to lay on her mare's neck, she stretched her arms out like an airplane, closing her eyes a moment as she let her horse move rhythmically under her. There was nothing like these evening hacks to help her decompress after a long weekend of working at the show grounds. She looped the grounds, enjoying the sunset as she headed back to the barns.

As she approached the barns, she saw that at end of the same row where their stalls were located, a small group of people were huddled around a stall. A young rider was in tears, another holding her as she cried. Emma dismounted and jogged over to the stall.

"Is there anything I can do to help? I'm Emma, I'm the working student for Twin Oaks; we are just a few stalls down," she asked the woman standing near the open stall door. Peering in the stall she saw a horse laying down, which is never a good sign.

A woman in her forties, presumably the horse's owner, turned to her looking surprised. "You wouldn't happen to be Emma Walker, would you?"

The fact that this stranger new her full name instantly made her feel nauseous; it couldn't be good.

"Yes...why?"

The woman pulled a crinkled notecard from her pocket and handed it to her, a scowl on her face. "This was on our horse's stall door. What did you do?!" Emma's eyes scanned the note quickly, re-reading it slower to make sure she had read it right the first time.

"You have Emma Walker to thank for this," the note said. For a moment, she was so lightheaded she thought she was going to pass out. "What...what's wrong with him?" Emma stammered, looking at the horse as a vet hovered over him, listening to his vitals.

"You should know! Your name is the one on the note!" Her voice was raised now. The vet stood up, holding his hands out as he approached. "Ok ladies, let's take a breath," he said, attempting to calm the woman before things escalated.

"I'll need to wait for the test results to be sure, but this horse appears to be pretty out of it. My guess is someone gave him a sedative," the vet added.

"Who did this?! My horse can't show for weeks with drugs like this in his system!" She took a step towards Emma, her face turning a bright red and tears were running down her face now. Emma stepped back, still holding the reins to her horse. She was connecting the dots; this notecard and that handwriting were the same as the note she had received at her guest house. Whoever sedated this horse was the same person who was stalking her. Who would do something like this to her? More importantly, who would hurt a horse to hurt her?

The vet took another step toward them, wedging himself between the two women, hands still held up in an attempt to keep the peace. The horse owner backed up, pulling her phone from her pocket. "I'm calling the police," she said.

Emma walked her horse back to her stall, numbly pulling off tack and brushing any sweat spots from her coat. She considered calling Liam and having him there when the police came. But as much as she would like Liam here with her, she found herself dialing Michael's number instead. It made sense since he already knew about the stalker.

Besides, she had just started seeing Liam and she had no interest in him seeing her like this just yet. And she didn't want him to witness the drama that this woman was more than likely going to cause the moment the police arrived. Three rings later, Michael picked up the phone.

"Michael? Can you come back to the horse show grounds? The stalker he...there was another note," her throat felt dry as she choked out the words. Michael didn't ask any further questions and told her he was on his way before hanging up the phone. She knew he would probably be here in ten minutes; the rental house was not far from the grounds.

Until then, she had every intention of hiding out in Valentine's stall.

ele

Michael opened the stall door, where Emma was slumped in the corner.

"Emma, what happened?!"

She lifted the note into the air, not bothering to get up. Michael took the note from her, eyes wide as he read each line.

"The horse at the end of the barn was drugged," she croaked. The police arrived shortly after. Emma hadn't cried yet and if she started, she didn't think she would be able to stop. She wanted to not sound like a blubbering idiot when the cops questioned her...again. Michael didn't have time to respond, and they were interrupted by an officer who knocked politely on the wood frame of the stall.

"Ma'am? We need to ask you a few questions," he said in calm tone. Michael handed the note back to Emma, a sympathetic look on his face. Emma nodded, pulling herself from the stall and brushing the shavings that clung to her breeches. As they walked back toward the stall where the sedated horse was, she saw officer Tom Paul from the other night and the horse's owner still scowling her way.

"Hello again, Miss Walker," Officer Tom said, tipping his hat. She was a little relieved to see him; at least he understood that this was not an isolated incident.

"May I see the note?"

Emma handed him the notecard, and the Officer Tom passed it to the officer next to him when he was finished.

"Does this appear to be the same handwriting as the one you received at your home?" He asked.

"Yes," she said weakly.

"Do you have any idea why someone would want to accuse you of something like this?" He asked. Before Emma could respond, the horse's owner interrupted, saying, "She must have done something wrong! This is her fault."

The other officer held his hands up, using his body to back her off while saying. "Let's step over here and let him do his job;

we will get to the bottom of this." The horse owner followed the officer willingly around the corner but sent death glares Emma's way until she was out of her line of vision.

"Miss, is there anything strange you can think of that happened since? Any other notes?"

"Nothing strange that I can think of. No other note...," she paused, as a memory of the waiter at Ben David's party handing her a notecard with the words, 'You deserve everything you're getting,' flashed through her mind. She hadn't even thought about the two incidents being connected until this moment. But this note was on the exact same type of notecard as the one left at her house, and the handwriting was identical.

Emma quickly briefed the officer on the incident at the party. As she did, a realization set in; someone had been stalking her much longer than just the couple of weeks she had been in Wellington. Whoever was following her had probably been doing so awhile, maybe even all the way from Ohio. Just because the notes started at the end of her time in Ocala didn't mean someone hadn't been watching her for much longer. Maybe she underestimated the parking lot creep; maybe he wasn't a random guy who tried to buy a drink for a girl sitting with another man. It would make sense why he didn't care who she was sitting with if he had been following her for much longer.

"Thank you, that information could be useful. We have not been able to track down the man you mentioned who followed you to your car at the restaurant since he paid in cash and doesn't appear to have returned since, but we will do everything we can to find this guy," Officer Tom Paul said, closing his notebook.

Emma watched him walk away, standing there numb. It was still at least seventy degrees outside, but a cold chill flooded her body. She walked back to Valentine's stall where Michael still stood, waiting for her.

"How did it go?" He asked. Emma shook her head, lip quivering. She managed to croak out the information she had relayed to Officer Tom.

Michael pulled her in, and Emma bit her lip hard. She was not going to give that horse owner the satisfaction of seeing her cry. She could still feel the woman's eyes burning holes in her back. How could she really think this was her fault? She would never do anything to put a horse in danger. Putting herself in the woman's shoes, she understood her anger; if anyone laid a hand on her mare there would be hell to pay.

"Are you ok to drive?" Michael asked.

"I'm ok," she said.

"I'll follow you back to the house."

Emma nodded, still fighting back tears. She walked bravely past the sick looking horse's stall and the woman who clearly hated her, making a point not to look their way as she marched towards the parking lot.

She wanted today to be over.

Emma took a Benadryl and a half before going to bed last night, and the fact that she had been out cold despite last night's drama meant it was worth the groggy feeling that lingered this morning.

"Nothing a couple cups of coffee won't fix," she thought, sipping the large cold brew she had just purchased. Today was what was considered an "off" day at the horse show. Since no competitions ran on Mondays, there wouldn't be the rushing and running around like on the weekends. Normally these days were a little boring, but after yesterday she could use a nice boring day at the show grounds.

She parked her car in the parking lot closest to the stalls as usual, but instead of taking the direct route to their stalls, which included passing the stall of the horse who had been sedated, she took the long way around. She had every intention of keeping her head down today. Those intentions lasted about thirty seconds.

Rounding the corner to their row of stalls, she saw the horse owner from last night talking to Jenn. Freezing in place, she wondered if they had seen her? Maybe she could take a walk and the woman would be gone when she got back.

"Emma?" Jenn had spotted her, and she had a very concerned look on her face. You know that feeling you get when you go over the first hill of a roller coaster and your stomach drops? In that moment, Emma's stomach was on an imaginary roller coaster. Last night's nauseous feeling followed quickly as she took a few steps towards Jenn and the woman, closing the gap between them.

"Emma, Linda here says you had something to do with her horse being drugged last night?" Linda had her hands on her hips and was glaring at Emma. Clearly, sleeping on it had not made this woman less angry with her.

"Um, Jenn? Can we please speak in private?"

There was no way this Linda lady was going to let her finish her side of the story without chiming in again.

"Of course. Linda, I'll catch up with you later if that's alright?" Linda nodded at Jenn but didn't appear happy to be left out of the conversation. She all but stomped back to her horse's stall. Emma watched the horse come to the front of the stall; he looked a little groggy but seemed a lot better than he had last night.

Emma felt some relief knowing he was ok. Of course, that didn't negate the fact that the sedative in his system meant he could not compete for some time because of the drug regulations and testing. Surely, this is what this woman was angriest about. Once she was sure she was out of earshot from Linda, she relayed the full story to Jenn.

"Emma, you really should have come to me about this last night. Linda is a dear friend of Liza's and David's; we have had a long-time working relationship with her, and she has purchased many young horses from us for her students in the past. It would be a pretty hard hit to Twin Oaks' business if that working relationship was jeopardized."

"Jenn, I am so sorry. I planned on telling you everything this morning. Really."

Truly, she had.

"I understand, but we just can't have this kind of tension between Twin Oaks and Linda's farm. I think its best you stay away from the show grounds for a few days. Let's give this time to blow over and I will talk to Liza, have her smooth things over."

This was not at all how she thought the conversation would go. Stay away from the show grounds? Away from her horse and the other horses she cared for? What if Liza couldn't smooth things over? The possibility of her internship being cut short and being sent home popped into her mind; that would ruin everything she had worked so hard for. Not to mention, it would look very poorly on her resume and would damper the glowing review she so desperately needed from Jenn and the Twin Oaks owners.

Emma couldn't believe this; her future career was hanging in the balance once again. There was no use arguing with Jenn since it was clear she had made up her mind about Emma staying away from the grounds.

"I'll head home," Emma said, her voice weak and defeated.

"I'm sorry Emma, I know this isn't directly your fault. I'll let you know when you can resume working."

Emma nodded and headed to the back side of the barns again; she still had no interest in passing the person who was single-handedly trying to ruin her life. Well, ok, technically Linda wasn't the one ruining her life; the stalker was.

Either way, her once bright future was muddled with uncertainty.

───*ℓℓ*───

The first call she had made when she got back to her car was to Liam. He was at his aunt's house and had a buddy over but had quickly brushed off his plans with his friend to meet Emma when she gushed the last few days' events. She felt a little bad being the girl who made the guy she was seeing break plans with his friend, but under the circumstances, she felt it was warranted.

Having no interest in sitting around and wallowing in her guest house all day, she headed in the opposite direction. Plus, she didn't feel all that safe there alone with everyone else at the show grounds. Liam had asked where she wanted to meet him, and at first, she didn't know what to tell him. After all, she had been driving aimlessly for the past fifteen minutes trying to clear her head. She took a moment to think about somewhere that would make her feel more relaxed, and then it hit her. "Meet me at Lake Worth Beach Park," she said.

If anything was going to make things better, it was the ocean. She kept driving until she ran out of land and took the A1A down until she reached the public beach entrance. Once again, she was glad it was a Monday; the beach was quiet today.

Emma kicked off her shoes, letting the warm sand wedge between her toes as she walked towards where the cool foamy water met the damp sand. Plopping down at the edge where the dry sand met the wet, she let the water wash over her legs as the tide rolled in and out. She closed her eyes, and for a moment she let herself forget about everything else in the world.

"What is it about the ocean? When your here you just drift; like the rest of the world doesn't exist. It's just you, the water, the sand beneath you and the sky above you," she thought, finally opening her eyes to stare at the waves again. Emma must have been sitting there longer than she realized, because the sound of Liam saying her name as he walked up behind her made her jump.

"Sorry, I didn't mean to scare you," he said, sitting down next to her, wrapping an arm around her shoulders. "I have a surprise for you," he added with a smile, pulling a bottle of white wine he had been hiding behind his back into view.

"You're an angel," she said, unscrewing the cap and taking a drink directly from the bottle; it wasn't like she had anything else to do today. Passing the bottle to Liam, he took a drink directly from the bottle as well. She exhaled slowly, letting the wine buzz hit her and the ocean carry away her worry. Within an hour, she was feeling a little better about her forced day off. If mindreading was real, she would have assumed that was the reason for what happened next.

Her phone vibrated in her pocket; she assumed it was Michael, who was probably worried about her. She hadn't said a word to anyone before leaving the show grounds, and she felt bad about not saying goodbye to him at least. He had been nothing but supportive through all of this. But it wasn't Michael. In fact, the number showed simply as, 'restricted.'

"Did you like your present yesterday?" It read.

She wasn't sad anymore; she was angry.

"Is everything ok?" Liam asked her. She hadn't noticed how tense and rigid her body position had become; her face was certainly giving away her emotions as well. She handed her phone to Liam, whose expression changed immediately.

"Is that *him?*" He asked. The look she shot him said it all. They stared back out at the water, not speaking for a few minutes. What could be said? Emma's mind turned over in those few minutes and before she had a chance to stop herself, she pulled her phone back out and began typing frantically before hitting send.

"What did you say back?" He asked, looking concerned.

"Liam, I can't keep living like this. He's trying to ruin everything I've worked so hard for and I'm not going to let him. The police don't have any leads, and who knows what stunt he will pull next."

Liam just stared at her; she still hadn't answered his question, but he didn't seem to like where she was going with this.

"I'm flushing him out," she stated finally.

Emma took another swig of wine as she continued to formulate a plan in her mind.

Chapter Twelve

A wave of anxiety washed over her as she pulled into the Mexican restaurant's parking lot.

If she was right about the creep from that night, she had hoped it would entice him to agree to meeting her here, in the place he had first approached her in person. Since he had agreed to meet her, she felt it was safe to assume she was either right or she just got lucky. Emma drove past the undercover detective's car, nodding to the person inside. After formulating her plan, she had called Officer Tom Paul, who agreed to help her by sending a detective to meet her at the restaurant. It was in a public place during a somewhat busy time of the day, so she felt safe enough between those two factors.

Now, all she had to do was walk in that door and execute her plan for real. She shut the car door behind her and mustered all her inner courage as she approached the restaurant door.

The hostess asked her if it was just her or if others would be joining her, and Emma asked if she could be sat in the middle of the room. She figured the more people around her, the less likely he would be to pull any funny business. She didn't turn around, but she heard the detective's voice behind her asking for a table as the hostess walked her to where she was being sat. After speaking to the detective on the phone several times, she felt at ease hearing his familiar voice not far from her. She pretended to read the menu, but she could not care less what she ordered. In fact, she probably wouldn't have the stomach to even eat; she was only here for one reason.

"Just a water and a side of guacamole, thanks," she told the waitress. She scanned the room quickly but did not recognize the man from that night. Not that she had exactly studied his face, but she was sure if she saw him again, she would recognize him. She spotted the detective, only four tables from her, just close enough to be able to reach her quickly if she needed him. Taking in a slow breath through her nose and out of her mouth, she was determined to get her life back, and, in her mind, this was the way she was going to do it.

Her cell phone sitting on the table vibrated, making her jump. It was only Michael asking her where she was. He was probably home from the show grounds by now and noticed her car was not parked by the guest house. She hadn't told him about this little plan of hers; he would only have tried to talk her out of it. Plus, the detective said the fewer people who knew about this the better the outcome. She flipped the phone over without replying; she didn't want to lie to him.

Unsure how long she had been here, she was now scraping the bottom of her almost empty bowl of guacamole with what was left of the chips. Looking at her watch for the first time in a while, she saw the time they had agreed upon had come and gone twenty minutes ago. A small surge of anxiety flooded her; she wasn't sure if she was more nervous about him actually showing up or not showing at all. She fought the urge to glance back at the detective; if her stalker was here, scoping things out before sitting at her table, the last thing she should be doing is giving away the fact that she was setting him up.

Emma looked back at the texts she had sent him that day on the beach.

"Can we meet? I want to apologize for what I did to you," she had said. The person on the other end had only replied, "yes," and she had spent a few minutes considering where to go before replying with today's date, location, and time. She had only received an, "ok," from him, but it was safe to assume that meant the meeting was on. Unless he had been playing *her* all along?

Another twenty minutes passed, and the waitress was asking for a second time, "if she needed anything else."

"I'll just take the check, thanks," she told the waitress. Glancing back at the detective, he replied to her disappointed gaze by shaking his head, and it was apparent her stalker was not coming.

Emma thanked the waitress when she brought the check, handing the credit card to her right away as she was eager to leave.

" she thought. But the wasted time was no comparison to the heavy feeling of realizing that nothing had changed; her stalker was still out there threatening her internship and her future and there was nothing else she could do about it. The detective

followed suit, and they walked out of the restaurant simultaneously; no use in pretending now.

"I don't understand why he didn't show," she said to him as he
walked her to her car.

"It's impossible to understand the mind of someone like this,
Emma. Keep your head up; we are doing everything we can to
find this guy."

Thanking the detective, she slid into her car and rested her head
against her steering wheel.

Today, he had won.

❧

Three more days passed in a blur of anxiety, frustration, and a
little bit of self-pity for Emma.

Her light at the end of the tunnel was that she had been giv-
en the ok to return to work today after a five-day hiatus. The
Williamses were also kind enough to install a temporary security system on the guest house which made staying at home feel
much safer than she had before. Although, it had hardly felt like
a vacation under the circumstances.

Liam had checked in with her daily, but she had only seen him
in person once for dinner. Michael had also checked in on her,
stopping by her guest house daily after work, and even brought
her take out from her favorite Wellington restaurant. She felt

bad about her anti-social behavior despite the people she cared about going out of their way to be there for her, but her fear had made her feel like isolation was her fortress.

The worry of balancing her friendship with Michael and new relationship with Liam seemed like a distance memory; she had bigger issues that out shadowed any thoughts of relationship conflict. It was as if some sort of survival mode had been internally switched and it consumed her. Driving through the familiar entrance of the show grounds, she had mixed emotions about going back to work today. She was glad Liza had been able to talk to Linda, the drugged horse's owner, and had assured her that Emma was not to blame for the incident.

Emma wasn't thrilled that Liza had told Linda about her stalker; she was sure it was being talked about all over the grounds by now. But Emma couldn't say she blamed Liza since it was probably the only way she was able to get through to Linda based on how angry she had been after her horse was drugged.

Emma decided there was only one way to handle this day despite her fears and anxiety – to face it head on. She took a deep breath and walked with as much confidence as she could muster past Linda's horses' stalls and over to Twin Oaks' set of stalls. Michael was already pulling a wheelbarrow towards the first stall but paused, a look of concern on his face as Emma approached. Jenn was coming out of the tack stall and offered a warm smile and a, "good morning," to her as she approached.

"Good morning, everyone," she said with more certainty than she felt.

"Fake it 'til you make it," she thought.

"Good morning," Michael also responded, clearly trying to sound casual. Emma knew him too well for that though; he was worried about how she was handling being back. That only fed her determination to prove to herself and everyone else that despite what had been going on, she could do her job and do it well.

"Emma, could you please tack up Jimmy John and hack him in one of the warm-up rings? We are moving him up to his first Grand Prix this weekend, and I want to make sure he is sharp throughout the week."

"Happy to," she said, and this time, she meant it. Nothing could help her shake last week's events like riding; today, she wanted to pretend like nothing had happened. It had been almost a full week since any strange notes had occurred and since her stalker hadn't showed up that day at the restaurant. She secretly hoped maybe he had given up. Maybe he knew about the detective and had decided to back off.

"Good riddance," she thought. Emma tacked up Jimmy John, enjoying every second of it, breathing in the familiar smells of humid, salty air and horses. She had missed this; it felt good to be back. Swinging her leg over his back at the mounting block, she felt him prance off a little after gently nudging him forward.

"You excited to have me back, bud?" She murmured to the horse. Truth be told he was probably just fresh from his day off, but she was going to take any win she could. She picked up a soft trot down the horse path as she headed to her favorite warm-up ring. It was set back a little from the other rings and was hardly ever busy.

Shortly after entering the ring, she let Jimmy John do his favorite thing, besides jumping, which was cantering. She knew this horse well now; it didn't take much to get him to transition upward. Sitting lightly in the saddle, she gave the softest kissing sound and he immediately picked up a lofty left lead canter that ate up the ground. By a couple laps, his dark coat was glistening with sweat, but she knew that meant nothing; this horse could canter for hours if she let him. She worked on his speed, asking him to lengthen his stride for 20 meters before asking for collection and repeated the pattern.

After thirty minutes in the saddle, he was being incredibly responsive. Sometimes, she couldn't believe how lucky she was to be riding a horse of this caliber and talent. "Let's end there, buddy! You were such a good boy today," she said, sitting deep and asking for the walk while reaching behind her to pat him on the haunches. Walking down her favorite palm tree lined path, she felt a sense of peace that she hadn't felt in over a week. This was where she belonged and in moments like this, she felt like no one could take that from her. She had been walking mindlessly for a while now, and almost didn't notice someone trying to wave in her direction while holding two coffees.

"Liam!" She said as she waved back.

He jogged now, trying not to spill the iced coffee still filled to the brim.

"I was pretty sure by the time I found you that this would be an ice-less coffee," he joked, flashing her that familiar goofy grin.

"This is so sweet, and so needed. Thank you," she said leaning over the gelding's shoulder to collect her half-melted iced coffee. She sucked down almost half of it in a few big gulps.

Compared to the climbing heat of the day, this half-melted coffee was like an oasis.

"Seriously, thanks," she said catching her breath after chugging a few more gulps.

"How has your first day back been?" He asked, walking beside her and the horse.

"Actually, it's been great. I'm glad to be back, and honestly, I needed to get out of isolation. It was probably making me feel crazier than I realized." she said.

"I'm pretty sure that's what I told you at dinner earlier this week," he teased.

"Yeah, ok well, don't get used to hearing this but you were right," she said with a playful smile.

"Does this mean I can convince you to come over tonight? I'm sure Aunt Cathy would be thrilled to see you."

"You know I love your Aunt Cathy, and I love the idea of a date night at your place but..."

"But?"

"...But can I take a rain check for tomorrow? I will probably be here late since I'm playing catch up, and I know I'm going to be exhausted. Rain check for tomorrow though?"

"It's a date." He walked beside her, and they chatted casually. She let herself live in this moment of perfection; it was as if nothing had gone wrong, as if she had never left this place and never would.

"Alright, I better cold hose this guy, he's more than walked out now. I'll call you after work," she said.

"Have a good day, Em," he said, squeezing her hand.

Emma smiled to herself as she walked back to the barns, letting herself be happy for the first time in a while.

The sun hung low in the Florida sky, warning those who glanced up that the sunset was only hours away.

Emma sat across from a saddle, dipping the tack sponge into the cool soapy water before rubbing it against the bar of saddle soap. There was something so relaxing about cleaning tack at the end of the day, especially this day. She had successfully made it through her first day back since last week's incident, and she felt good about how it had gone. Every horse she had ridden since Jimmy John felt productive, and despite her fears, she hadn't been met with awkward glances or people asking her a million questions about what had gone down.

"Are you heading back home anytime soon?" Michael said lightly as he pulled his truck keys from his pocket.

"I think I'm going to groom Valentine before I go. It's a nice night and I haven't seen her in a while," she said, glancing up at the sky that was beginning to show colors of pink and orange.

"Want me to hang out with you until you're done?" he said, tossing her a worried look. His concern for her was sweet, but she felt confident things with the stalker had died down. Besides, she needed some alone time just her and her horse after her hiatus.

"I think I'll be ok, thanks anyway though," she said, smiling his way.

"Ok, have a good night then," he replied before heading in the direction of his truck. She couldn't help but enjoy the feeling of normalcy that this day had brought her. Putting away the tack cleaning supplies, she pulled her grooming box out from the tack stall and grabbed her horse's lead rope and halter.

"How's my pretty girl?" She cooed to the mare, scratching her neck in her favorite place before slipping the halter over her head and tying the lead rope into a loose quick release knot on the bars of the stall.

Emma took her time, cleaning her mare's hooves out with care before applying hoof oil. She curried her well before beginning to brush her coat out with the soft brush. Her horse lipped at the pocket of her breeches, making her laugh. "Yes, I do have treats in there," she giggled like a little girl as she pulled one from her pocket, feeding it to her as she leaned against her shoulder.

It was only then she noticed someone standing far out, across from the stall, who appeared to be staring in at her. The setting sun blinded her and the person's distance away from her made it hard to make out who it was. She really hoped Linda wasn't about to give her a hard time again; there was hardly anyone at the show grounds this time of day, but Linda was usually here until after dark. Emma rolled her eyes and patted her mare's neck as she walked towards the front of the stall. Her mare was tied, so she left the stall door open; this conversation would not last long if she had anything to say about it.

"Linda? Listen I'm sorry..."

Emma stopped dead in her tracks only a few feet from the entrance of the stall door. The outline of a man with the hood of his sweatshirt pulled over his head stood in the distance. A slow, sinking feeling started at the top of her head and made its way to the soles of her feet, leaving her feeling suddenly cold and stiff. She couldn't make out the person's face in the lighting, but there was no need because her senses were already screaming one thing: *run.*

It was him; it was as if his whole being oozed anger and hatred. She could feel it in his stare, in his body language. She took one slow step backwards and as she did, he took one towards her. That was the only indication she needed to confirm her suspicion; her stalker was here, and he was coming after her. Emma fought the panic that welled in her chest and pushed it aside; she needed to think, and she needed to do it fast. She didn't turn around, seeing him coming at her would only cause her already clouded mind to become worthless.

She needed a plan; he was certainly faster and stronger than she was. He could overtake her in a second if he reached her. And Valentine was right here; what would he do to her if Emma simply ran? What if that was his plan all along? Destroy her by destroying what she loved most, her internship and her horse?

"There is only one way to keep us both safe," she thought, already pulling the lead rope on the stall bars and releasing the quick knot. There was no time to tie the lead rope to the other end of

her mare's halter like she wanted to. Emma used all her strength to jump as high as she could before grabbing the horse's mane to balance her as she pushed off the ground and swung her leg over her mare's back, thanking the Good Lord Valentine was not an exceptionally tall horse.

Half a hand higher, and she probably wouldn't have made it without the assistance of a mounting block; clearly, she didn't have time for that either.

Perhaps only fifteen seconds had passed since she had beelined for the stall, but it felt like an eternity. In those fifteen seconds her stalker had almost reached the entrance of the stall door since he had not been walking very quickly. In his defense, he probably had not expected the events that followed. Emma would later think back at this moment and wonder what went through his mind. Surely, he expected to trap her in here; what he would have done after she never let herself predict.

She made a kissing sound to the mare in the same split second that she finally looked at the stall entrance, realizing just how close he had come to trapping her. The mare hesitated only half a second in surprise but sprung forward into a canter obediently. This horse had always been sensitive to her riding aids and emotion, and in this moment, it was her saving grace.

With one hand on the lead rope and the other clasping a piece of mane, her mare barreled awkwardly out of the stall door taking a hard left as she barely missed plowing the man over, who jumped out of the way just in time. The mare's back end slid as she tried to gain traction on the concrete, almost taking out the man a second time as he recoiled from dodging the horse. Emma only briefly wished her mare had trampled him, although, the risk that her horse would have been injured in doing so pushed it from her mind quickly.

As she cantered towards the horse path, she heard the roar of a motorcycle engine starting up behind them. Her heart skipped a beat; she had assumed he was on foot and that his car was parked nearby. How on earth was she going to outrun a motorcycle bareback with basically no reins?

She could still hear the engine humming behind her as she cantered down the horse path, heading to the outskirts of the show grounds. She was going to run out of path in less than a minute, and from there she would have only her body and voice and half a rein. She trusted her horse, but certainly never expected their trust to be tested in such an extreme way.

Emma saw where the path ended, leaving her two options; try and cut back through the show grounds or exit the grounds and try to lose him off property. Option one was risky; there was a lot of places to become trapped on the grounds. Option two was not ideal either; dealing with cars and being on the roadside presented its own dangers but she had a good chance of losing him if she could cut through people's yards. She made the panicked decision to exit the grounds and ask forgiveness for any trespassing that was about to occur. She knew this area well now; she had a good shot of getting away.

Emma said a low, "whoa," to the mare and used her seat to slow the mare's gait down to a trot briefly so she could turn. Using her leg aids and her one rein, she managed to communicate what she wanted from her horse as she headed towards the road.

Thankfully, the road next to the show grounds was slower this time of the evening. Emma asked her mare to slow down again as she quickly glanced at the road for oncoming traffic. The roar of the motorcycle behind her was getting closer. One car was coming towards them but if she crossed now, she should make it. She didn't really have a choice anyway and asked the mare forward at a working trot, trying to make sure her horse didn't slide this time. Looking over her shoulder, she saw the crotch rocket style motorcycle cut the car off, who blared their horn. Ignoring the car, the motorcycle tore down the road almost parallel to them already.

"No!" Emma thought, asking her horse to canter again. This part of the road for at least another couple miles was walled off on one side by fence lining and tall tropical brush but had a path horses could use to get from the local neighborhood farms to the show grounds. Legging her mare on, they were now hand-galloping parallel to the road on the thin path that separated the road from the houses. The motorcycle held his position, keeping pace with her horse easily.

Emma kept her internal panic at bay, thinking of where the road and path would dead end ahead. At this point, she was headed towards an area that was heavily residential. One direction also had a neighborhood, but she knew it was gated and it was far too high to jump over at any point. The other was a neighborhood that wasn't gated, but that meant most of the houses would be surrounded by fencing or tall privacy shrubbery.

If she could find a point where the fence was low enough to jump, that may be her only way to get away. Otherwise, there was no way her horse was going to outrun a motorcycle, not to mention riding bareback full gallop was draining her strength as each second passed. Using what few aids she had, she asked the mare to slow again so she could veer to the left towards the entrance of the neighborhood. Valentine responded to her owner and slowed to a trot, turning off Emma's leg pressure.

The motorcyclist didn't miss a beat, turning on a dime onto the neighborhood street. Emma saw the winding street ahead of her; this was not going to be easy in their current one-reined state. Kissing her mare back to a canter, she hugged the out-skirts of the lawns where there was grass, searching for any areas she could quickly access a backyard, or get off the road. The motorcycle began pulling closer to the horse, causing Valentine to suck back. Emma couldn't blame her; she had been such a good girl despite the insane things she had asked of her.

A wave of déjà vu flooded her; she realized this was not the first time she had asked her horse to carry her bareback through strange places in unsettling situations. Not so many months ago, she was cantering through the pouring rain looking for an escaped Jimmy John.

"Good girl," she whispered as they cantered on, still looking ahead for any way off this death road. If she had any lingering doubt of this mare's heart, this situation had certainly quelled it.

Emma gasped, sitting back and yelling a loud, "whoa," as she pulled back on her one rein, supporting her mare with leg on the other side so she stayed straight. She had almost missed it, but there on the side of one of the large equestrian style estates was a metal gate that sat a little lower than the rest of the fencing. She swallowed hard; they were both exhausted and that gate had to be just over four feet. To date, she had only been training her mare up to a little over three foot three inches. Her mare had always shown incredible bravery over any jump she pointed her to...but this? She wasn't even sure if the mare would lock on to a gate.

The motorcyclist began doubling back after stopping just ahead; she had maybe ten seconds. She could still turn around...but then what?

"Let's go!" She called, more to herself than her mare. She sat back, lifted her hands, and used every ounce of body control she had left to rock the mare back on her hind end. Emma clucked, wrapping her legs around the mare's barrel. She counted the strides aloud; four...three...two...

Ears pricked, the mare pushed off the ground a stride too early. Emma grabbed a lock of mane, balancing herself the best she could, releasing her one rein as she reached her bascule position in the air. Valentine's hind leg rubbed the gate as they began landing. As all four feet touched the ground, she looked over her shoulder, catching the motorcyclist tearing down the road, surely hoping to catch them somewhere on the other side.

They cantered on across the property's open pasture, where she approached the pasture's fence line and another gate. Sitting back again, she got the mare underneath herself and soared over it, galloping towards an area on the property that had a cluster of trees, a pocket of foliage, and a thick wall of foliage behind the fence line. Emma slowed her horse to a walk and wedged her mare in the densest part of the foliage. They both stood there, breathing heavily.

Emma wished more than anything she could walk her out, and she would kill for a cold hose right now. The property was secluded other than the entry point she had jumped in through. Between heaving breaths, she could hear the motorcycle whirring up and down the neighborhood streets. Emma patted her pockets down, no cell phone. *"Darn, I think I set it on the tack box back at the barn,"* she thought. Not that it mattered much; no way her phone would have survived that ride even if it had been in her pocket.

Leaning over the mare's neck, she petted her even though it was drenched in sweat. "You are my good girl," she murmured, as the motorcycle continued to purr in the distance. She wasn't sure how much time had passed, but if she had to guess it had been about thirty minutes since they had wedged themselves in this little pocket of foliage. Every few minutes or so, she had the mare step forward a couple steps so she could peer out into the field to make sure he wasn't searching for them on foot.

At some point about ten minutes ago, she had stopped hearing the motorcycle's engine, and she felt more unsettled now that she couldn't keep tabs on his location. Valentine had started grazing lazily like nothing happened, only stopping to move forward and back when Emma asked. It was almost completely dark now; if she was going to leave the foliage to try and get help from the owner of this farm, she probably should have done it a while ago. Her fear kept her in their hiding place as the last of the light faded.

"Looks like we are staying here tonight," she said as the mare continued to graze. Sure, she could hop off and hand walk her way back through a couple acres of pastures to the house at the outskirts of the property, but what if he was sitting there waiting for her, knowing she was more than likely still hiding nearby? She couldn't exactly go leaping four foot fences in the dark and she was a sitting duck if she hand-walked her anywhere. It felt a little bit crazy, she realized that, but her mind was already made up.

The best way to protect her and her horse was to stay right where they were until morning. Surely by then he would have to give up and leave. At least then she had the light of day on her side if she needed to flee again. She slid off her mare's back, her legs buckling under her as she landed.

"Ouch," she said aloud, trying to stretch her sore stiff muscles. It was no use; she was going be next to crippled by tomorrow. Emma loosely tied the mare to a tree, allowing her to graze if she wanted. She sat on the cool grass, letting her body flop back in exhaustion.

She wondered if Michael knew she never came home. Not that he really had a reason to check on her anymore, and he typically went to bed pretty early. Liam had probably tried calling her and was certainly a little worried by now given everything that had happened in the past. But worried enough to call the police and report her missing? Probably not, since she had mentioned being at the barn late and odds were he would assume she fell asleep shortly after arriving at home.

It was almost dead quiet where they were; just the sounds of evening bugs and frogs in the background as if they were singing her to sleep.

Emma didn't even remember falling asleep; it was if one minute she was listening to the sound of her horse munching on grass and the next thing she knew the morning sun was leaking through her eyelids.

She sat straight up, first looking at her horse who was resting with one leg cocked, her lower lip loose and hanging a little. Emma couldn't help but smile at the mare.

"Hey Val," she said, standing up and taking one step toward her before stopping to stretch; the hard ground had done her already sore muscles zero favors. Walking gingerly now, she scratched Valentine's neck and pulled the lead rope free. Her mare sniffed her pockets, and then started pulling tufts of grass from the ground after realizing there were no treats hiding in there for her.

"I'm hungry too, kid," she said, feeling almost nauseous now she was so hungry.

She peered around the foliage; the morning sun shined on the still dewy grass that stretched for several acres in front of her. After scanning the fields another moment, she clucked to the mare and started walking across the open pasture cautiously as she continued to scan the perimeter for any sign of movement.

When they reached the edge of the pastures, she peered around the corner of the foliage wall before proceeding towards the barn that sat behind the estate. She could see a groom hosing off a horse in the wash area just ahead.

"Excuse me!" She yelled, jogging towards him with her horse in tow.

The groom whipped his head around in surprise, a look of shock on his face as he scanned the ragged looking young woman and the horse covered in dried sweat approaching him. It certainly was not the kind of thing he expected to see on private property in Wellington.

"Are you ok?" He asked as she reached him.

"It's a long story, and I'm sorry for trespassing but I need a phone; it's an emergency."

The groom pulled his phone from his pocket, handing it to Emma while looking her horse up and down. She could only wonder what must be going through his mind.

"Michael, it's Emma. Listen before you say anything, I need you to ask Jenn for the trailer. It's an emergency."

—ell—

Michael had tried pressing for details before hanging up the phone, but Emma assured him once she and Valentine were safely in the truck and trailer that she would tell him everything. The groom had offered her the address of the farm, and then had gone to get the barn manager.

Luckily, the manager was pretty understanding about the whole trespassing and hiding in their pasture situation once she heard Emma's story. The police pulled in shortly before Michael pulled in through the farm's barn entrance. If Emma didn't have to speak to another police officer ever again, it would be too soon.

She gave her statement to the officer while Michael loaded the still wet horse on the trailer; the groom had been kind enough to offer to cold hose her mare while she spoke to the police. Michael had thrown a hay bag together and her mare was already happily munching in the back of the trailer. She was so grateful Valentine was getting some relief from last night's epic ride.

There wasn't a lot of information to pass on to the police; she hadn't seen the guy's face and she didn't exactly have time to memorize his license plate the few times she glanced back at him as he chased her down. The only helpful information she had was a loose description of the motorcycle, which she couldn't imagine was extremely helpful since it was all black and she was no motorcycle expert.

The officer gave her the all too familiar, "Thank you, we will be in touch," before heading back to their cruisers.

Climbing in the truck her first words to Michael were, "Take me to a drive-thru; I'm starving."

He did not protest, and put the truck in gear as he headed towards the nearest fast-food establishment.

Chapter Thirteen

Emma tore through four breakfast burritos in a matter of minutes before coming up for air.

Michael tried not to stare, but she could tell he was dying to know what had happened. Sucking down a few more sips of iced coffee, she drew a breath before running through every detail about the events of last night. He stared at her, only blinking at first.

"So what now?" he asked. She had been thinking the same thing all morning. "I think I need to get out of Wellington until they catch him," she said gravely. As the words came out, she knew it could mean only one thing; she would have to quit her internship.

"What about your internship? You only have another month or so left; you can't throw everything away now."

He was right, of course, leaving the internship early would mean she would have nowhere to go. Odds were, she wouldn't find a job back in Ocala or elsewhere fast enough; not to mention, she suspected her stalker would simply follow her back to Ocala and that he may have been following her since then at the very least.

At this moment her only option appeared to go home, back to Ohio. It was really the last thing she wanted to do; she had already made the decision to stay in Florida and find a full-time job. She shook her head, tears welling in her eyes as the realization hit her; this stalker had officially ruined her future.

"Can we swing by the show grounds? I think I left my phone on the tack box."

They drove the five minutes it took to reach the show grounds, and Emma hopped out of the truck when they reached the end of the row of their stalls. Jenn was already there, tacking up a horse.

"Emma, are you ok? Michael told me he needed the trailer for an emergency."

Recalling her story to Jenn as she walked to the tack room to grab her phone, she felt bad that once again she was in the middle of a crisis and not working. Jenn shook her head. "It's probably safe during show hours for your horse to be here, but after hours..."

"I know," she said, afraid Jenn would say out loud what she was already thinking. "Jenn, I'm just so sorry for this whole mess. I should be working right now, but here I am again..." Her voice broke as she fought the lump welling up in her throat. Emma glanced at her phone for the first time since last night. She had twenty-three missed calls.

"Can you excuse me for just a minute?" She said, stepping away and pressing call back on one of Liam's many missed calls.

"Emma," his voice rang with worry on the other end of the phone.

"Liam, I'm ok...ish. It's a long story..."

Emma was getting sick of saying that. She was also getting sick of recalling last night's events over and over, but he deserved to know why she had ghosted him.

"Where are you now?" Liam asked.

"Well, I left my phone at the grounds and Michael picked Valentine and I up in the trailer. I honestly don't know what to do next though. The grounds are no longer safe for my horse after hours and I'm not sure my guest house is safe either since he clearly knows where I'm staying. Liam, I don't know if I have any other choice but to go home...like *home* home, to Ohio."

"But Em, you've worked so hard..."

There it was again, another person about to remind her of everything she was about to lose.

"I know. Trust me, I'm heartbroken over this, but what choice do I have? I can't keep living like this, putting myself or my horse in danger, not to mention the people I intern with are probably getting sick of me constantly having life-threatening emergencies that prevent me from doing my job."

He was silent a moment, and she figured he was probably coming to the same realization she had.

"I think I have an idea. Grab some of your horse's feed and meet me at my place."

"With the horse in the trailer?"

"Yes. Don't worry, I have a plan."

"Ok, well, I guess I will see you soon then."

"See you soon," he said before hanging up.

"Whatever his plan is, it has to be better than mine," she thought.

Michael pulled the truck and trailer into the long driveway of Aunt Cathy's estate.

"Are you sure about this?" He asked her as they climbed out of the truck.

"No, but what do I have to lose?"

Michael nodded as they walked in silence towards the front door. Liam and his Aunt Cathy opened the door before they had a chance to ring the doorbell.

"Oh dear, you look awful!" Aunt Cathy said, attempting to smooth Emma's wild looking hair.

"Yeah, riding for your life, bareback, and sleeping on the grass has that effect," she said, blushing.

"So, Emma says you have a plan?" Michael said, turning to Liam.

"When my nephew called me and told me what was going on, I called up a couple friends who owe me a favor," she said with a wink to Emma, cutting Liam off before he had a chance to speak.

"My aunt has a friend with a farm near West Palm Beach, about forty minutes from here. The farm is gated, and the entire property is surrounded by tall metal fencing...," Liam chimed in.

"...They even have a security guard. It pays to have wealthy friends sometimes," Aunt Cathy said cutting Liam off again and wrapping an arm around Emma's shoulders before she continued. "They offered to let you and your horse stay there until this creep is put behind bars where he belongs. You will be safe there, dear, I promise."

"Cathy, I can't begin to thank you for this. Are you sure they don't mind us crashing there? I mean this guy has proven to be good at covering his tracks..."

"Nonsense dear. They have so many acres and horses they will hardly know you are there! They have a pool house and two guest houses on property, and they offered you the one above the barn. I'm sure you would prefer to be close to your horse?"

"When do we leave?" She replied, a smile breaking out on her face for the first time in over twenty-four hours.

"They are expecting you within the hour," Cathy said.

"...And I will be following you in my car," Liam added.

"I can bring your things up from the guest house and some of Valentine's tack later today after I drop you off. That way, we can get you guys to safety right away," Michael said. Emma hugged Aunt Cathy and then Liam, thanking them again before hoping back into the truck.

"Thank you, Michael; you've been my rock through all of this." She wrapped her arms around his neck a moment before buckling her seatbelt.

They pulled away from the estate and headed toward the outskirts of Wellington. She wondered as they drove down the palm tree lined streets when she would be back. Twenty minutes later, Michael was turning onto the A1A, the road that runs parallel to the Atlantic Ocean.

"I guess the only issue we have left now is my internship," she said to Michael, keeping her eyes glued to the ocean water glistening in the sunshine outside of her window.

"I know it's not around the corner from the show grounds, but you could commute. Obviously, you'd have to leave before dark or when the show grounds are quiet; I can't imagine he would try to pull anything during the day when everyone is there. I won't let anything happen to you while you're there; I promise," he said, glancing her way, trying to assure her with his eyes.

Emma knew he meant that, and maybe commuting was a possibility. She felt anxious to call Jenn already and hash out the details. They only had a couple weeks left in Wellington though. What about when they went back to Ocala? Twin Oaks Farm wasn't exactly Fort Knox; the gate would stop any vehicles from coming in but anyone on foot could still hop a fence with ease.

They would pretty much be sitting ducks once they got back there.

Emma massaged her temples, feeling a stress headache coming on.

"One thing at a time," she told herself. Her thoughts were promptly interrupted by a sound that had haunted last night's dreams. It was muffled by the sound of the truck and trailer, but there was that familiar whirring sound of a motorcycle. Emma's face turned white, and for a moment she was frozen, only listening to the sound coming from somewhere behind them.

"There are other motorcycles on the road; this is Florida, right? Perfect motorcycle weather," she told herself.

After several more minutes passed, she began to relax. *"See, just a random motor..."*

Brakes squealed behind them, and on her peripherals she saw Michael whip his head to investigate his side view mirror.

"I think Liam's been hit," Michael said, voice choking.

"WHAT?"

Michael's only answer was in the form of punching the accelerator before switching lanes. Emma pressed her face to the glass, trying to get a better look from her side view mirror. Clutching her chest, she saw Liam's car now sitting half a mile behind them, spun halfway around and facing the opposite direction. She could hear the motorcycle louder now, but where was it? As if answering her unspoken question, she saw the front tire of a very familiar looking motorcycle.

"Michael!" She screamed, like there was something else he could do about it. They were running out of room between the car in front of them.

"Hold on," he said, putting his turn signal on as he started getting over again.

"Michael is trying to run him off the road," she realized. The motorcyclist hit the gas as the truck and trailer began merging into the lane he still occupied. The truck and trailer were halfway into the next lane now, inches from the bike as it continued to pull forward. With almost no room to spare as they finished merging into the next lane, the motorcycle pulled ahead of the truck.

"Why is he so far ahead of us now?!" She said, panic dripping with every word.

"What is he doing?!" She thought. The motorcyclist had continued speeding ahead, at least three car lengths ahead of them now, and was gaining more ground with each passing second.

Suddenly the brake lights of the motorcycle glowed red. The bike hit the brakes hard as the gap between the two vehicles began to quickly close.

Michael stomped on his brakes in response, and the moment he did the motorcycle veered quickly into the next lane. It was too late though; Michael had started to swerve and was losing control as the trailer pushed back on the truck despite his efforts. The tires lost traction as they hit the gravel on the outskirts of the road and the front end of the truck nose-dived into the trench next to the road. The trailer fishtailed behind them, landing so that it was tilted slightly before coming to a complete stop.

Emma's mind had stopped processing logic the moment the truck began sliding off the road. She was already opening the truck door and sliding out of the seat, letting herself fall into the water-filled trench below. She shot a glance over at Michael, who was fighting with his seatbelt, which appeared to be locked due to the accident. There wasn't time to wait for him; her horse needed her.

Scrambling to get out of the mud and water, Emma all but clawed her way out of the trench as she sprinted, now soaking wet, toward the back side of the trailer. She pulled the pin out and fumbled with the latch on the trailer, hands shaking. The doors swung open, catching the wind of cars passing by in a blur. She laid her eyes on the chestnut mare dancing in the corner of the trailer, who was unharmed but understandably distressed. There was no time for relief though; she could hear the low rumble of the motorcycle that had presumably turned around up ahead and was doubling back. *"Sitting ducks,"* she murmured to herself as she thrust the divider of the trailer open.

Pulling the quick release knot, she freed her horse from the trailer she had been tied to. She gave her mare a quick pat, looked her in the eyes, hoping to convey the importance of the situation.

"Here we go again," she thought as she tossed the lead rope over the horse's neck and tied it to the other side of the halter this time. Logic and reason still out the window, she once again pushed herself off the ground, swinging her leg over the mare's back. The rumble was getting closer; it was now or never.

She put one hand on the divider so it wouldn't swing and hit her horse as they exited the trailer. She gave a gentle squeeze, and her horse moved forward, hesitating slightly at the ramp, wide-eyed as cars continued to fly past them. She clucked louder now, wrapping her legs around the horse's barrel while saying, "It's ok; I know Val, it's ok."

The mare leaped out of the trailer, barely using the ramp, and Emma grabbed mane, making a desperate effort to catch her balance at the horse's unexpected launch. She heard the rumbling coming from next to the trailer as they descended; he had to be right next to them.

Feeling all four hooves hit the ground, she took half a second to look over her shoulder behind her, before asking her horse to gallop off. First, she quickly looked to where the truck was still sitting in the trench, hoping Michael was on his way to help protect her and Valentine, but he was nowhere to be seen. Emma then looked over at the man who was standing next to his motorcycle, staring in surprise at the young woman bareback on the horse once again, on the side of the busy road. His hands were was on his helmet as if he was ready to take it off; she shuttered at the thought of why. Would he have knocked her out with it? Or taken her horse out?

She should be asking her horse to go forward right this second, but something caught her eye that had her frozen, eyes glued. A long scar that started on his hand and appeared to continue to run down his wrist was partially covered by his leather jacket; something about it pulled at her memory. She spun back around, kissing to her mare as they cantered down the side of the road, hearing the motorcycle engine rev up and take off behind her.

Far away, she could hear police sirens in the distance; she would just need to keep him at bay long enough for them to arrive.

"Maybe Michael was able to reach his phone and called the police," she thought, simultaneously cueing her mare with her leg to gallop from a stand still, letting out a loud kissing sound as she did. Valentine responded quickly, launching into a gallop from a halt obediently. But, despite galloping full speed with the ocean on one side and the busy road on the other, there was something about that scar that lingered in the forefront of her mind.

"It looks familiar," she thought as the pounding hooves below her rattled her head.

He was just about caught up with them now, and she was already looking for a break in the wall of foliage or fencing that ran up the coast. If she could just get onto the beach, she could lose him.

Cop car sirens whined in the distance, still too far out. They were likely headed towards the site of the crash, which meant they would be delayed by the time Michael could explain that they had both taken off down the road. Ahead she saw what appeared to be a gap in the foliage, sand spilling out onto the grass in front of the path giving it away. She cantered on, knowing from some tricky rollbacks on the jump course that this horse could turn on a dime.

Four strides out she sat back, letting out a loud, "whoa," before adding her leg and rein turning aids. The mare was taken a little by surprise, but spun on her haunches, just making the turn as the brushed through the foliage and clamored to get all the way on the path.

Tires squealed behind her briefly before taking off again. He saw the same thing she had as soon as she had a clear look at what lay ahead of them. A short wooden bridge with about four or five steps lay at the end of the sandy path. Her mare had a collected canter now and she sat back, preparing for what she knew would feel like a down bank. Emma had not done much in the way of cross-country type jumping over the years since she had always stuck with show jumping.

What she did remember from the handful of times Maggie had taken them all cross-country schooling was this, taking a down bank felt much different than landing off a normal jump. In fact, her first down bank had almost completely unseated her. Valentine was soaring through the air now, her front feet pointed towards the beach below. Emma wrapped her legs around the horse, recalling the words of her trainer telling her to sit quietly and let the horse fall out from under her. Her hips opened and then closed allowing the horse's movement below her as they landed.

Emma pulled the mare up as she looked down the beach and listened for the sound of the rumbling engine. The sound of the waves was all she heard as she trotted down the beach back towards the direction they came.

"I think we did it," she thought, a smirk crossing her face briefly. Her gloating was promptly interrupted by the much louder sound of a motorcycle's tires kicking up sand maybe a mile down the beach.

"How did he...," she began to think, asking her mare to canter again. Odds were he found somewhere with easier access further down the beach. He was catching up quickly again. Emma

sat up, moving her body into a half seat position as she encouraged her horse into a full out gallop.

Her horse tore down the beach, eating up ground. Had she not been riding for her life, she would have thought that, under normal circumstances, this would have been a wonderful, exhilarating ride. Unfortunately for her, this was no joy ride. The wind rushed past her ears making it hard to hear anything else. The cop cars must be on the road above them because despite the whooshing sound of the wind flying by, she could still faintly hear them.

Despite her horse giving her every ounce of speed she had, he was not far behind them now. Glancing over at the water, she didn't know if her horse would slow and spook at the waves if she got too close, which would put them right in the stalker's path. Emma couldn't imagine a motorcycle would do well if the tide came in hard enough; she needed to get just close enough to the water.

Galloping on, she used her leg and outside rein to ask her horse to shift over towards the dark sand where the tide continued to roll in and out. Continuing to ask her horse to move over further as the ocean sucked the water back, and she could hear the motorcycle following closely as it crossed over a little into the dark wet sand. The tide was coming in now strong now and water rushed under her horse's legs as she galloped on, barely slowing as the waves splashed against her.

"Good girl!" Emma called out, asking her to gallop on. She looked under her arm; the motorcyclist saw the tide coming at him at a rapid pace and started to swerve away from it.

It was too late though; the foamy waves were already swirling around him as water began filling the space between his tires and the dark sand. He swerved hard, hitting the gas, hoping to pull away from the ocean's grasp. She caught her breath, turning around now as she asked her horse to slow down, and watched the events unfold before her.

The motorcycle spun out as the tide crashed into it, flipping over onto its side as it slid for what felt like forever before turning over several more times. The driver was ejected from the bike, turning in the air before he hit the ground. It came to a stop, and the driver lay motionless as the tide pulled the water away from them.

Halted now, she was staring at the lifeless looking man lying near the overturned motorcycle. She had almost forgotten about the sirens and police above them until now. Looking towards the direction of the road, she now watched as numerous police officers shuffled down to the beach, coming from several points on the coast near the crash site.

Guns drawn, they surrounded the driver still laying in the sand. Officers were running toward her too, but she hardly noticed. Her eyes were glued to the man slowly peeling himself from the sand right before another wave threatened to overtake him. His hands began to slowly raise above his head, and he pulled his helmet off as he followed the officers' commands as they circled around him. It was right then that the pieces began falling together.

"That scar," she whispered to herself; she *had* seen it before.

Her mind flashed back to that night in Ocala when she and Bo had been talking; she had stared at the scar on his hand prompting him to explain where it had come from. "I got it in a motorcycle accident as a teenager," he had said.

"Bo? Could he really be responsible for all of this?"

Of course, at one point he had briefly crossed her mind as a possible suspect, but she had quickly dismissed it, especially considering the incident with the other man in the restaurant parking lot. Why would Bo go to such lengths to follow and torment her like this? He would have had to quit his job, give up everything just to do so. Had she really made him so angry he would throw his life away to stalk her all the way in Wellington?

"Ma'am?"

Someone said loudly next to her. It sounded like he had said it to her more than once based on his tone. Looking down, a familiar face stared back at her with his forehead creased in concern.

"Officer Tom," she said as she exhaled heavily; she had apparently been subconsciously holding her breath.

"Are you ok, miss?" He repeated, although she hadn't heard him the first time.

"I know him," she said pointing in the direction of the man facing away from her, now being cuffed by an officer.

"You do?" Officer Tom said, lifting an eyebrow.

"I met him in Ocala; his name is Bo, er, Robert. He works for a farm called High Point. I don't know his last name, I'm sorry."

He wrote down the information she provided him before asking her if she was alright once more, then joined the other officers.

The team of police were now escorting the man to the cop cars. She caught a glimpse of his face as he turned to her before climbing a set of wooden stairs leading back to the road.

"So, it really was him," she thought.

It wasn't until he was completely out of sight that she snapped back to reality. She hadn't noticed, but she had been in a daze since she watched his bike crash, nothing else around her seemed to register. As the fear and adrenaline started to leave her body, the image of Liam's car spun out and Michael still in that wrecked truck flooded her mind. She looked down at her horse, breathing heavily. She clucked to her; she needed to walk this mare out first and foremost.

After all, this horse had saved her life twice in the past twenty-four hours. She promised the mare some pain medication and extra treats tonight when they were back safely at the show grounds. At minimum, the truck and trailer were still trapped in that trench, so who knew when they would be picked up.

Looking out across the ocean as they casually strolled along, it almost didn't seem real. It was though, and it was finally all over. Looping back after going half a mile down the beach, she saw someone jogging toward her. "Emma!" She heard him say. She couldn't exactly see who it was yet; he was still too far away. Waving back, the man picked up his pace.

"Michael!" She called back after he was close enough to identify. She slid off her mare, who was now breathing normally and fully cooled down.

"Are you ok?" Emma asked.

"I'm fine Em, my seatbelt was locked but I was able to reach my phone and call the cops. Are *you* ok? You're the one who just got chased down by a psychopath on a motorcycle for the second time," he said, still trying to catch his breath. He must have been trying to get her attention for a while now, but the waves and wind coming off the ocean next to her were so loud she wouldn't have heard him that far down the beach.

"I'm fine; Valentine had my back," she said with a smile, patting the mare's neck. "Liam? Is he ok?"

"He's ok. His airbag went off so he's probably going to be a little bruised and sore, but he walked away from the car on his own. He's worried about you, of course. I told him I would make sure you were alright; the cops drove me out here."

"Where is he?" She said, concern in her voice.

"His aunt insisted he go to the hospital to get checked out," he replied. This didn't surprise her; his Aunt Cathy was probably freaking out right now.

"What about the truck and trailer?" She asked. Michael shook his head side to side; his face said it all before he did.

"It's not good Em; the truck is probably totaled. The trailer is going to need some repairs, but it should be salvageable."

Emma's mind wandered to the reaction the Williamses and Jenn would have when they found out about the Twin Oaks-owned truck and trailer's condition. How angry would they be?

"I'll tell them what happened...," he chimed in, reading her mind.

"I'll go with you; this isn't your fault," she said cutting him off.

"It's not yours either," he said, holding her gaze for a moment.

"Any idea how we are getting this girl home?" She said, putting a hand on her horse's back.

"Actually, Cathy has that covered. She called a horse shipping company to pick your horse up. They should be here any minute actually."

"I guess we should head back to the road then," she said, giving the lead rope a gentle tug and her mare walked obediently behind her.

They walked along in silence, other than the sound of the crashing waves beside them. Both were lost in their own thoughts, processing the events that led them to the present. They found a small sand path that was easy for her to hand walk her horse up as they made their way back to the road.

Emma glanced over her shoulder at the ocean and the now invisible crater down the beach that marked the crash site. Turning back towards the road, she saw the trailer waiting for them about a mile down the road. She looked over at her horse, then Michael, appreciating the fact that they were safe and by her side.

Today could have been much worse.

Instead, today was the day she got her life back.

Chapter Fourteen

The announcer's voice echoed nearby as he called out the name and number of the next horse entering the ring.

Emma laid a hand on Jimmy John's neck as he chewed the bit nervously next to her. Jenn's eyes were glued to the current horse on course, watching their striding as they landed off the first fence of a combination.

"Yep, looks like a short five stride," Jenn murmured to herself, eyes still following the other rider. Being here for this horse that was now near and dear to her heart as he made his Grand Prix debut was something that, less than a week ago, seemed like an impossibility. But here Emma was, watching the last rider finish their course before the dark bay gelding entered the ring himself.

"Good luck," she said, smiling at Jenn and giving Jimmy a quick scratch before he began making his way into the ring as the rider on course landed off their final fence. "That's a clear round for

Molly Jobin and Voyage. Next on course is Jennifer Meyers riding Freaky Fast, owned by Twin Oaks Farm out of Ocala, Florida."

Emma let out a loud, "woo," as she made her way to the first row of bleachers where Cathy, Liam, and Michael were already seated with an empty seat on the end saved for her.

"I don't know who is more nervous right now, me or Jenn," she said, never taking her eyes off the gelding as he jigged in place waiting for the buzzer. Liam put one arm around her shoulders, and she wrapped one around his waist, giving him a gentle squeeze. He winced when she did, prompting a, "Sorry Liam, I forgot you're still sore," from the still-distracted Emma.

"It's ok, I'm sure you're thinking of nothing else but that horse right now," he said with a laugh and a teasing tone in his voice.

"You know it," she said, right before the buzzer sounded. She inhaled and knew she probably wouldn't breathe again until the horse had landed off the final jump. Jimmy cantered off with power and a forward pace as Jenn locked him onto the first fence. Clearing it with what seemed like minimal effort, Jenn sat back, collecting him for the turn ahead as they sailed over fences two and three.

"Halfway there," Emma said as she watched him land off the fourth fence, gripping the rail in front of her until her knuckles turned white.

Jimmy John was still jumping clear, and the pair had only a few fences left of the course. A daunting oxer that came off a sharp rollback lay only strides ahead. Jimmy didn't bat an eye as he pushed off the ground and sailed over it, causing Emma mild heart palpitations when he grazed the back rail with his hoof but still managed to not knock the pole down.

The second to last fence came seven strides later, a vertical decorated in a sponsor banner that most riders were slicing at an angle to set themselves up to the last fence. Still managing to keep a clear round, Jimmy John powered down the outside rail towards the final fence; another oxer positioned quite close to the bleachers. Pushing off the ground a stride early despite Jenn's efforts to bring him back, his front foot missed clipping the top rail by millimeters.

Emma was already on her feet, making a beeline for the exit gate; the pride she felt for this gelding was second only to her own horse. Jimmy danced as he exited the arena, as if he knew he had done well. Jenn beamed down at him, patting the gelding's neck, now a shade darker with sweat.

"How did you manage to pull off a clean round on his first Grand Prix?" Emma asked excitedly, mostly talking to the horse still.

"He's a special guy, but we already knew that didn't we?" She replied, looking down at Emma. "I couldn't have done it without your help this week, Em. After you're done cooling him down and tossing hay to the other horses, be sure to celebrate all your hard work."

With a grin no one could wipe from her face, Emma switched places with Jenn in the saddle, honored to simply walk out a horse like him. She noticed Liam, Michael, and Cathy headed her way before she walked the horse off.

"Em! Don't forget Aunt Cathy is having the after-party at the house. Do you think you'll be long?" Liam called out as he approached.

"I could probably be there in a little over hour or so," she answered.

"See you then!" Cathy said before the group headed towards the parking lot to their respective cars.

Emma clucked the gelding on, heading towards her favorite palm tree lined path to walk him out. She soaked it all in, knowing they were a week from leaving this slice of equestrian heaven. The last five days since Bo had been taken into custody had been strangely normal, as if she hadn't been fearing for her or her horse's life just days before.

Since then, her focus had been making sure her horse was comfortable after the traumatic incidents and prepping Jimmy for his first Grand Prix. Thinking of things like her future or the outcome of Bo's motives to do the things he had hardly crossed her mind. But walking down this familiar path with no other pressing matters had her considering everything she hadn't earlier that week. It still seemed strange to think that the future beyond her internship's end was her biggest problem in the not-so-distant past. Perspective has a way of changing the way you see things, and for Emma, that was exactly what had happened.

Sliding off the horse's side after he was cooled down, she began considering what exactly it was she wanted now.

—*ele*—

Emma walked through Liam's and Cathy's grand estate a little over an hour later wearing the same little black dress she had worn to Mandy's birthday party back home what felt like another lifetime ago.

Heading towards the sound of group chatter coming from the open sliding door that led to the backside of the house, she glanced around at the stunning architecture and décor of the home. No matter how many times she had been here, it always took her breath away a little.

Scanning the courtyard, she saw so many familiar faces of people she had come to call friends since arriving in Florida. Michael, Jenn, Liza, and David Williams were talking while waiting on drinks, while Liam and his Aunt Cathy were laughing as they chatted with several of the friends Emma had met her first night at the estate. Feeling lucky to even be here, she walked through the entrance of the courtyard to greet the hosts.

An hour passed quickly, and Emma ordered her second glass of champagne from the bartender before walking over to a couple of the other riders she recognized from the show grounds. Before she made it to the group, an unexpected face approached her.

"Officer Tom? I didn't expect to see you here," she said, curiosity ringing in her voice. He was dressed in khakis and a polo, and for a moment she almost didn't recognize him out of uniform.

"Hello again, Miss Emma. It's nice to see you under better circumstances."

"I didn't know you would be here this evening," she said.

"Well, Miss Cathy gave me a call earlier this week and invited me. She mentioned you may want some answers and bribed me here with the promise of good food and drinks," he said with a chuckle.

"That sounds like Cathy," she thought. Emma couldn't help but feel thankful for Cathy's meddling though, and she was right after all. Emma did want answers and had been putting it off all week. Sure, she had been focused on Jimmy and wrapping up their time in Wellington, but deep down, she had wanted nothing more than to forget any of it had ever happened. At least, until now; the answers were right in front of her in the form of Officer Tom. How could she not find out why Bo had done what he did?

"So, did he confess why he was stalking me in the first place?"

Emma had been called into the station shortly after Valentine was safely back at the barns the day he was arrested and had given her statement, however unhelpful it had felt at the time.

"The thing you have to understand, miss, is the workings of the human mind are something that still have even professionals guessing at times. We did a psychiatric evaluation shortly after bringing him into custody and based on the information you gave us, the information we could dig up about his past, and get out of Robert himself, we discovered he had a pretty rough childhood. His father was a raging alcohol and his mom, as you know, died when he was young. We discovered his father passed away from liver disease due to alcoholism a couple months ago. Seems the timing is close with the timeline of when you started receiving the notes. Right now, psychologists are tentatively diagnosing dissociative identity disorder based on his behavior and symptoms. You should know, Bo experienced periods of blackouts or amnesia during the times he was chasing you and likely when he was leaving you those threating notes."

"He seemed so normal when I met him though. I just don't understand how he could be capable of what he did to me," she said, shaking her head in disbelief.

"Well now, that's not entirely surprising since he was essentially switching to an alternate identity in his mind when he was stalking you. He did mention feeling mentally fixated on you when you met and had strong feelings of anger after you pushed him away. Mentally, he was a different person after being triggered. You can't blame yourself though; these kinds of things can be triggered at any point, and it's likely the root of his disorder was caused by the trauma he was exposed to as a child paired with his father's recent passing. This disease acts almost as a coping mechanism in the person's mind, when exposed to the trauma he has faced."

Emma stared at Officer Tom, her emotions ranging from one end of the scale to another. It was as if she didn't know whether to be angry or feel pity for the person she thought she once knew.

"Is he ok? I mean, his motorcycle crashed pretty badly."

"Couple fractures, some pretty significant bruises, but nothing that won't heal in time."

"What about the creep from the restaurant we assumed was stalking me? Was he ever found?" Emma asked.

"No, unfortunately he is still in the wind; we never did find him."

Emma only nodded, still processing the information she had just received. She jumped a little when Liam came up behind her, wrapping his arms around her waist. Letting go at her reaction, he scanned the emotions written all over her face.

"Sorry Em, everything ok here?"

Before replying she turned around to kiss his cheek and took his hand in hers.

"Yes actually, Officer Tom was just explaining the outcome of Bo, er, the stalker's physiological evaluation."

Liam raised an eyebrow, curious now.

"Do you mind?" She asked Officer Tom. Repeating the information he had just given Emma, she watched the shock and confusion cross Liam's face as well.

"Is he going to be released anytime soon? I don't want her in any danger in the future."

"No, certainly not anytime soon. Try not to worry, he won't be coming after her again," he assured Liam. His body language relaxed at this news, and so did hers. She hadn't even noticed how rigid and tense she was until now.

"Thank you, officer. I won't keep you any longer from this incredible food; Liam's Aunt Cathy always hires the best caterers."

"Of course, and if you have any future questions, you know how to reach me."

As Officer Tom walked toward the table of food, she turned and headed to the seating area at the edge of the courtyard. Liam started to follow her, but she turned to him before they reached the tables.

"Go socialize. I'm fine, really. I think I just need a minute to process."

"You sure?"

"Positive," she assured him.

Squeezing her hand once more, he headed back to where his aunt was still conversing with friends. Sitting down with her still full glass of champagne, she took a long drink and then closed her eyes. It was certainly not the answer she expected. The thing she returned to was the fact that Bo wouldn't be coming after her ever again.

Not quite ready to rejoin the celebration, she continued sipping her champagne while she processed the officer's information.

It was then a memory of a day in her Psychology class came rushing back: "...a person with DID has multiple and distinct personalities that can sometimes manifest in some patients as believing they are different people at times," the professor had said. "Some symptoms of DID are memory loss, delusions, and identity confusion, and this mental disease is usually caused by trauma, more commonly, childhood trauma."

There it had been, the reasoning behind the madness in the back of her mind all along.

Perhaps now she could finally gain some closure on what felt like an endless stretch of life-altering events.

—ℓℓ—

The familiar entrance of Twin Oaks Farms came into view as the trailer in front of her pulled through the gates. It wasn't her home per say, but pulling into the driveway and seeing her guest house and the barn through her windshield gave her that same homecoming feeling.

It wasn't that she hadn't loved Wellington, or that she wouldn't miss it, but she had so missed the rolling Ocala hills and the acres of land that seemed to stretch for miles in every direction. Although, she had to admit, the events that had occurred in Wellington probably made coming back to Ocala feel like a breath of fresh air in comparison.

Ocala and Wellington were both filled with beautiful horse farms, and, of course, the warm Florida sun, but they were also total opposites in so many ways. Emma hadn't written Wellington off her list of places she would be interviewing, but it was nice to get some distance for at least the next couple weeks considering everything that had happened there. Saying goodbye to Cathy, who had become like family to her, and Liam, of course, was still the hardest part of coming back to Ocala.

She sent a quick text to Liam, as promised, letting him know she had made it safe to the farm. Liam and his aunt were planning to drive up for the Million Dollar Grand Prix next week to visit and watch it with her. It was an event that would be a bittersweet, as it marked the end of her internship. Her plan was to take her recently updated resume and spend this week applying to full-time jobs in both Ocala and Wellington. It still was hard to even think about where she wanted to end up. Perhaps the perfect job opportunity would make that decision for her.

The part she did not want to consider was the fact that no matter which city she ended up living in, she would be far from one of the people she cared most about: Liam and Michael.

Getting out of her car and stepping onto the spongy grass while taking a deep breath, she took in the familiar scent of warm country air. She still thought it was funny how different the air was here even though Wellington was only a couple hours south.

"Mateo!" She called out, jogging over to her long-lost co-worker, hugging him before they pulled the trailer doors open.

"How was Wellington?" He asked. Emma and Michael exchanged solemn glances.

"Mateo, we are going to need to have a couple drinks before we talk about Wellington," she said, laughing a little as she did.

"Yeah, it's a long story," Michael added, leading the first horse off the trailer. They unloaded the tack after the horses were put away and thrown flakes of hay, and Emma couldn't help but enjoy being back at the Ocala farm. Out here, on this beautiful piece of land, she felt the slow-paced vibe wash over her once again. Even though she knew she would likely be leaving soon, she promised herself never to take for granted the feeling of life being just this – normal.

After unloading all her personal belongings, she met Michael and Mateo at the fire pit at dusk as planned. Michael stood up when he saw her approaching, walking toward the back side of the cooler. He pulled a pitcher filled with ice and a lime green liquid and a cup from its hiding place before returning to the fire pit.

"Cheers, Em! I figured you could use a pitcher of homemade margaritas after, well, everything."

Emma cocked her head to the right, unable to find the words for his thoughtful gesture.

"Michael you're the best; this is exactly what I needed."

Pouring the mixture into her glass, she sat across from the guys as she rested her feet against the stone that surrounded the fire.

"I'm almost afraid to ask again, but what happened in Wellington?"

"What didn't happen in Wellington," she said before taking another sip.

"Emma was stalked by a psychopath for starters."

"What!?" Mateo was on the edge of his seat now.

Emma and Michael took turns recalling parts of the story from their time in Wellington to Mateo. She had expected the story of what happened to trigger some sort of PTSD, but instead, she found the storytelling had the opposite effect. It felt good to talk about it, especially here so far from where it happened.

In a way, it felt like the final pieces of closure were falling into place as they laughed and cried into the night.

Time passes strangely sometimes.

One day can feel like an eternity while the next flies by before you know it. For Emma, the last week of her internship felt like someone hit the fast forward button on her life. A blur of phone and in-person interviews, her regular work, and helping to prepare for the annual Twin Oaks end-of-season farm party after the Million Dollar Grand Prix made it feel like she didn't know where the time went. But here she was, picking out a last-minute outfit for the evening's festivities.

Just last night, the Williamses had offered for her to remain on the farm until she accepted a full-time position elsewhere. But to her surprise, they had also informed her of a full-time job offer themselves. "We don't have a lot that goes on during the off season, but we still train our horses and client horses year-round, and, of course, we always have sale project horses that need worked," Liza had said.

While she had promised to consider the offer, it had been unexpected given the events of the past few months. Sure, they had mentioned this was a possibility when originally offering her the internship, but she had simply assumed they wouldn't want to keep her around after all that drama.

It wasn't that she didn't love Twin Oaks; this place felt like home to her. It was just that she had always had such big dreams about the next step in her career, and as much as she loved it here, she knew it was probably time to move on. Not that she planned to let Liam or Michael in on any of that; she had been keeping tight lipped about anything involving job opportunities since she started interviewing. Almost breaking her own rule more than once, she knew it was the only way she was going to make a decision that was best for her future and not what anyone else wanted.

Setting her outfit of choice for the evening on the ironing board, she went back to the mirror to finish getting ready. It seemed strange putting something on that wasn't breeches and boots before heading to the show grounds. But today, she and the other Twin Oaks Farm staff were simply spectators. Emma finished putting in the last earring moments before hearing a knock on her door.

"I'm ready!" She said as she swung the door open, grabbing her phone and a light sweater before returning to the door. Michael said nothing, only tossing her a, "sure you are," look.

"See? Ready," she said as she closed the door behind her.

"We should probably mark this day down on the calendar as the first time you've been on time for an event ever," he said, giving her a teasing nudge.

"Very funny," she said, although she had to admit, he knew her all too well.

Climbing into the truck, she greeted Jenn who was already in the front seat, and Mateo, who was on the other side of the back seat. Shutting the door behind her, she realized this is probably the last outing she would ever take with the Twin Oaks team like this. It made this night even more bittersweet and special.

"Are Liam and Cathy meeting us at the show grounds?" Michael asked.

"Yes, actually he called me a little bit ago, they are on their way from the hotel now."

"Good, tell him to save us a seat," Michael said.

Emma smiled to herself; it was nice that two of the most important people in her life got along now. The tension between them felt like a thing of the past. Surely the life-or-death situation had something to do with their forced bonding. Although, who knew how long that would last once she decided which city she would be living in.

"No need to think about that now," she told herself. This was a special night after all, and she wasn't about to ruining it by worrying.

A couple minutes later, the truck tires were rumbling across the gravel driveway of the show grounds as they headed towards the parking lot closest to the Grand Prix arena. Cars were parked everywhere; she had never seen it so busy here before.

As they walked toward the bright flood lights of the arena, Emma took in the atmosphere. People funneled in from all directions headed to the bleachers, grassy areas, or anywhere else they could find a seat. Feeling her phone vibrating in her pocket, she pulled it seeing Liam's name on her screen. "Hey, where are you?" He asked.

"Almost to the arena…"

"Come to the top of the hill, in front of the VIP tent. Bring the rest of the team too," he said before hanging up. At the top of the hill, Cathy waved enthusiastically to her, and Liam kissed her cheek as the rest of group exchanged greetings.

"You know we don't have VIP tickets, right?" Emma said to Liam.

"Well, it's a good thing I bought a table for all of us then isn't it," Cathy said, winking her direction.

"*Leave it to Cathy,*" she thought.

"Cathy you shouldn't have; those are not cheap," Emma said, knowing the cost of tables in the VIP tent were astronomical.

"Nonsense, you just enjoy the night, dear. Consider it an internship graduation gift," she said wrapping an arm around Emma's shoulders. The group was escorted to their table which overlooked the arena. The first horse was already on course, and despite the chatter at her table, it took several rounds for her to peel her eyes away from the ring. No matter how many times she watched a Grand Prix, she couldn't help but be impressed. These horses and their riders were nothing short of spectacular athletes.

"Emma dear, would you like to join me at the bar?" Cathy asked. Looking down at her still half full glass of wine, she began protesting but was cut off quickly. "Come along, dear," Cathy said getting up. Aunt Cathy was not someone you could say no to; she had learned that by now. After being handed two fresh glasses of wine, Cathy turned to her with a strange expression on her face that Emma couldn't quite read.

"Emma, I have a proposition for you," she said, gently pulling her off to the side.

"I want you to work for me. Now before you say anything, let me explain."

Emma nodded silently, letting the woman continue without interruption.

"As you know, I own a couple of syndicate horses in Wellington, and I like to stay involved with horses that way. Since the day I met you, I've been impressed with you. You're a special girl, and to be honest, you remind me of myself when I was younger. I've been considering this for some time now, and I figured it was time I get back to my roots. You don't know this about me, but I was an upper-level eventer as a young adult."

"You were? That's amazing," Emma couldn't help but chime in.

"Yes, there is nothing like the rush of galloping your horse cross country. Most of my connections in the horse world here were involved in show jumping, and because I live in Wellington, that's just primarily what we have out there as you know. Now, I know eventing isn't your comfort zone, but I think you would be excellent at it with some professional training, and you will already have the stadium phase down."

Emma opened her mouth, attempting chime in again but was firmly cut off.

"Now just hold on, I promise I'm getting somewhere here. Emma, you showed incredible bravery in the face of many tough situations. You're also trustworthy and you can ride anything. I want to purchase a farm in Ocala that focuses on my first love, eventing.

"I will provide you with training at a top-notch farm in the meantime, and, of course, your horse will be welcome to stay there as well. I know you will want to compete your own horse too, and I will certainly help you do so as an added bonus. Eventually, once I find the farm property I'm looking for, I want you to run the place. You will be the barn manager and oversee the farm for me. We will hire a full-time trainer, along with the other necessary staff, with experience to bring along young sale prospects. I see big things ahead for you Emma, and I would like to help you get there."

Wondering if she had entered the twilight zone, Emma stared, jaw dropped, slightly at Cathy. Was she serious?

"Cathy, I'm honored and I'm....well, I'm speechless. But I don't know that I am experienced enough to manage an entire farm..."

"Nonsense. You know what you're doing and like I said, you will have a full staff at your disposal to help you. It will take me some time to find the right property, and until then, you will be training and learning from professionals in the business. I still have a few friends in the eventing world I plan to reach out to as soon as you accept. At the end of the day, dear, I need someone I trust to run my farm, and that person is you."

"This is an incredible offer. Can I think about it?"

"Of course, dear. Liam doesn't know anything about this yet, so take some time and call me when you are ready. Let's head back to our table, shall we?" She said, looping one arm through Emma's.

Emma's mind raced as they walked back in silence. The night's event had barely started, and she had already broken her own rule not to worry about her future tonight. But how could she not?

"This changes everything," she thought.

Emma eventually forced herself to focus on the event and the excitement of the evening. The Million Dollar Grand Prix had been everything she had hoped for and then some, in more ways than she originally anticipated.

They had arrived back at the farm half an hour ago and were quickly setting up the tables and coolers for the party. Cars were already rolling in, and both familiar and unfamiliar faces were gathering in the grassy area behind the main house where they had lit a fire and strung lights around the spacious stone patio. Letting herself get lost in the excitement of the party, the thoughts of Cathy's offer left her mind. This was her last chance to enjoy this chapter of her life before it was gone for good, and that was what she intended to do.

"Hey Em, Aunt Cathy's ready to head back to the hotel for the night. I'll see you tomorrow for breakfast though?" Liam said to Emma.

"Definitely," she said giving him a quick kiss and Cathy a long hug.

"We'll talk soon, dear," she said, kissing Emma on the cheek as they headed back to Liam's car.

Emma made her rounds, making sure she talked to everyone she knew she may not see for a while. Lily had stopped by briefly before attending her own farm's party, and it was all she could do not to gush Cathy's offer to her the moment she arrived. This was her decision to make though and telling Lily would only make that harder right now. People slowly started to leave the party and a little after one in the morning it was just the Twin Oaks team huddled around the fire pit. It reminded her of how it all began; in a way, it was the perfect way to end the night.

"Goodnight, everyone!" Liza and David called as they headed back to the main house, shortly followed by Jenn. Mateo had left an hour earlier, leaving just Michael and Emma by the fire.

"Feels a little like déjà vu, huh?" She asked, standing up and stretching.

"Yeah, I guess it is," Michael said thoughtfully, also remembering the night they had truly become friends.

"I am beat. I think I'm going to head to bed too," she said.

"I'll walk you there. I should probably turn in too."

They walked side by side, and Emma looked at the cloudless night sky above them.

"Ocala certainly has its perks," she thought as they walked along.

"I can't remember the last time I had this much to drink; I blame Cathy's open bar," Emma said with a laugh. She had to admit though, it felt good to let loose a little.

"Same. We can definitely blame Cathy for getting the party started earlier," he said, laughing too.

"Goodnight, Em," he said, pulling her in for a hug when they arrived at her guest house door, holding her a little longer than normal.

"Goodnight, Mich...," she started to say as she pulled away but was interrupted by his lips briefly on hers.

She stared wide-eyed at him.

"Where did that come from?" She thought.

"Gee, Em, I'm sorry...I shouldn't have done that. Let's just blame the drinks and forget I did that, ok?"

"Ok," she said, still stunned.

He gave her shoulder a gentle squeeze, looking in her eyes a moment before he walked back towards his trailer. Emma stood there watching him walk away, unsure what to think. Instead of walking into her guest house, she found herself walking through the sliding barn door in the dark as she headed for her horse's stall. Slipping under the stall guard, she heard a low nicker as she approached her mare.

Standing in front of her and wrapping her arms around her horse's neck, she stayed there a moment, processing everything that had happened that night.

"I have a lot of decisions to make, Val," she murmured to the horse.

"But no matter what, I'm glad I have you by my side."

Pulling away, she cradled the horse's head in her hands, kissing her on the nose and running her hand up her forelock.

"You know what, though? We can do anything together, you and I," she whispered to the mare.

And in many ways, they already had.

Horses had taught her that she could do so much more than she believed she could, and that this was only the beginning of her story.

The End.

(To be continued in *Impulsion*, Book Two of the *Impelled Series*)

Thank you to the readers who took a chance and read
my debut novel. I hope you enjoyed reading it as much as I loved
writing it!

If you enjoyed it, please be sure to leave a review so others have
a chance to find it as well.

Reviews help me tremendously as an independently published
author and it also helps other readers!

Sincerely,

Sarah Welk Baynum

Subscribe to my newsletter (sign up form on my website home page) to be the first to know about the release date for the next book in the *Impelled* series!

https://sarahwelkbaynumauthor.com/

About the Author

Sarah Welk Baynum has an extensive equestrian background which became the inspiration behind her debut novel "Impelled."

While writing her novels, Sarah draws from previous experience as a working student, show groom, barn manager, working for FarmVet and other various other jobs in the horse industry over the years both in her hometown and in Wellington & Ocala, Florida. Sarah also attended Otterbein University and majored in Equine Business and Facility Management.

Sarah still owns horses and actively competes in show jumping and three-day eventing, and horses have been a big part of her life since the age of twelve. Her first horse may have been a gelding, but she has a bias towards mares and has primarily owned mares throughout the years.

Besides writing equestrian novels, Sarah also writes articles for Sidelines Magazine.

When she isn't writing or riding, Sarah also enjoys competing in local and national singing competitions, and mainly sings country music.

Today, Sarah lives in her hometown just outside of Columbus, Ohio, with her family which includes her husband, her two dogs, two cats and her two mares Tilly (a warmblood) and Letty (an off the track thoroughbred).

Printed in Great Britain
by Amazon

11786499R00180